Mona,

Remember to Buy low & Sell High.

Ji Paccolo

THE CHARTREUSE ENVELOPE

THE CHARTREUSE ENVELOPE

MURDER IN MEMPHIS

by

JAMES C. PAAVOLA

J & M Book Publishers. Memphis, Tennessee

ISBN: 978-0-578-05490-2

Published by J & M Book Publishers
Memphis, Tennessee

Printed in the United States of America

CONTENTS

Acknowledgements..9
Dedication 11
Introduction..13

Chapter 1: The Chartreuse Envelope................................15
Chapter 2: Waiting For The Other Shoe 25
Chapter 3: Eyes Peeled 37
Chapter 4: Families: Surviving, But Not Unscathed 43
Chapter 5: From Out of Left Field 49
Chapter 6: Families: When They Struggle Together...........53
Chapter 7: Help wears Gucci..57
Chapter 8: Let's Hear It For the Éclairs and Gucci............65
Chapter 9: Number Two, Or Is It Number One? 73
Chapter 10: The Opening Bell: The Prelude 79
Chapter 11: The Opening Bell: *Her* Addiction................87
Chapter 12: Families: When the Legacy of Violence Continues........91
Chapter 13: The FBI...97
Chapter 14: The Smile 103
Chapter 15: The New York – Memphis Connection 105
Chapter 16: FBI: Take Two 109
Chapter 17: Families: A Second Chance..........................113
Chapter 18: Working Through It: A Beginning...............117
Chapter 19: The Bloody Fingerprint 121
Chapter 20: The Device 125
Chapter 21: The Crime Board..129
Chapter 22: The Patent 133
Chapter 23: The Carpet 135

Chapter 24: Emotional Support 141
Chapter 25: The MPD Meets the FBI 151
Chapter 26: Dorothy..155
Chapter 27: The New York-Memphis Connections........161
Chapter 28: Logic Takes a Holiday.................................167
Chapter 29: The *Get Smart* Shoe 173
Chapter 30: A Blast from the Past 177
Chapter 31: The Hit Man Strikes Again.........................181
Chapter 32: The Hug Ball...191
Chapter 33: Redstone's Message 195
Chapter 34: Bret Thornton 199
Chapter 35: Limericks..203
Chapter 36: Scrambling in the Big Apple 209
Chapter 37: The Shot 211
Chapter 38: After Shocks 215
Chapter 39: Introspection 225
Chapter 40: In the Light of Day......................................227
Chapter 41: Do Blondes Really Have More Fun? 231
Chapter 42: The Mini Debriefing 233
Chapter 43: Hedging Her Bets..239
Chapter 44: All That Training Pays Off...........................241
Chapter 45: And That Makes Three 245
Chapter 46: Is Anybody Home? 255
Chapter 47: Regrouping...257
Chapter 48: The Website..261
Chapter 49: And Yet Another One 269
Chapter 50: Recovery: First Steps 275
Chapter 51: Fresh Air...281
Chapter 52: The Plan Comes Together.............................289
Chapter 53: All the Queen's Horses and All the Queen's Men 291
Chapter 54: The Healing Process 295
Chapter 55: Say What?...299
Chapter 56: The Extended Family....................................303

CHARTREUSE

SHAR-TROOZ , -TROOS , -TROEZ

The color chartreuse is named after the yellow-green colored French liqueur named *Chartreuse*, first developed in 1605 by the Carthusian Monks of La Grande Chartreuse, near Grenoble, France.

Today the color chartreuse includes a range of blends of yellow and green, and is often used to alert people to danger. For example,

Chartreuse colored **Mr. Yuk**™ stickers were developed in Pittsburg in the early 1970's as a replacement for the traditional skull and cross bones, to warn children about the dangers of poisons and cleaning products kept in most homes. See the Pittsburgh Poison Center, Children's Hospital of Pittsburg of UPMC.

Chartreuse coloring can be found on emergency vehicles, and safety vests worn by individuals who work in streets or highways.

Coming Soon

Look for the return of Lieutenant Julia Todd in

They Gotta Sleep Sometime:
Murder In Memphis

ACKNOWLEDGEMENTS

I'VE never been much of planner. Any goals I've had would more accurately be classified as short-term objectives. Thus, I approached the writing of this book in a nearsighted fashion. At first, I just wanted to see if I could do it. The actual writing was fun. The next step, allowing others to read it, not so much. It is here I want to express my sincere thanks to my wife, Marilyn, who never waivered in her support and encouragement of my writing. I also want to thank our adult children who offered their feedback and encouragement, especially Shannon, who also created the cover design. My brother Lee, who began writing fiction at a similarly late time in life, was inspirational. Then there are my friends who have been so positive about the fact that I wrote a novel, without ever having read it. That's what friends do.

At some point, my short-term objective evolved from *Can I do it?* to *Does my family think it's OK?* to *What do the professionals think?* It was at this point I discovered Bradley Harris. Brad likes to think of himself as a teacher-editor, or is it editor-teacher? All the *red ink* of his first edit gave me flashbacks. It took three weeks before I could actually look at his detailed comments and suggestions. We moved forward from there. And finally, it's always tough when a friend is placed in a position of reviewing one's work. But Margie Rhem, a retired university English professor and award winning short story writer, offered to read my manuscript. She provided key suggestions and encouragement. To all of you—Thanks.

DEDICATION

This book is dedicated to my wife Marilyn,
and our four adult children, Shannon, Joel, Nicole, and Nina.

INTRODUCTION

MY name is Dr. Forrest W. James. I'm a psychologist. Retired. In my private practice I consulted with law enforcement regarding crimes of violence and homicide. Since my retirement, I've been writing about the more complex murder investigations I was involved in—using court records, media accounts, and personal interviews.

Although it's impossible to reconstruct every detail of a case, I'm confident the core aspects are correct, and the supporting story is presented faithfully. Each story highlights the role of key psychological influences. *The Chartreuse Envelope: Murder In Memphis* is a story of trauma, resilience, and family.

Trauma experienced in violent homes is comparable to trauma experienced in war. Victims of domestic violence and soldiers in combat often share the experience of suffering life-threatening injury, witnessing the pain or death of others, and living with pervasive anxiety. Post-Traumatic Stress Disorder (PTSD) can be found in both populations, as well as the continuation of the cycle of violence towards others.

Yet horrific experiences do not always result in long-lasting negative outcomes. Some people are more resilient, better able to cope, adjust, and bounce back in times of distress and trauma. Resilience depends on such things as one's genetic make-up, perception of life events, sense of hope, available interpersonal support, and spirituality.

This analysis is not intended to justify any violent act. Rather, it is meant to give the reader insight into why people do what they do, and to show how different people who experience similar horrible events can be affected in different ways.

CHAPTER 1

THE CHARTREUSE ENVELOPE

MARCH *2008 … The Short-lived Celebration.* Michael Tibett smiled as he hung up the phone, the final call of a long week. He had secured a shipment of highly prized surgical screws that would guarantee the success of what was certain to become the industry's most advanced artificial hip joint. BL Technologies was on the verge of initiating full production of its latest development. The final phases of its lengthy research trials were wrapping up, and the results thus far exceeded expectations. As the lead buyer in the purchasing department, he had identified and purchased all the advanced materials for the new device. And, as icing on the cake, he locked in the prices for the next five years.

Tibett just sat, taking it all in, tired but happy. The team leaders, biomedical engineers Dr. Sturgeon and Dr. Huong, would be arriving shortly. He opened the lower right drawer of his desk and pulled out three small glasses, and the packaging cylinder containing a bottle of 20-year aged Balvenie single malt scotch. He kept it for special occasions only, just two drinks from this bottle. The first was when his son was born. The second when his grandson was born.

The two men entered expectantly.

"Well?" asked Sturgeon.

"I did it," Tibett said. His voice was quiet and controlled, but his eyes were dancing with excitement. None could hold back big smiles.

He ceremoniously removed the bottle from its container, removed the cork, poured each man two fingers. Handing both colleagues a glass, he raised his.

"After years of dedication and hard work ... To our success," he said.

"To our success," the two men repeated.

They could not know they would never see the final results. Within two months, everything would change.

***

May 18 ... And Then There Were None. Mac studied printouts of emails. "Damn, he's been talking to the SEC," he muttered. He pulled up the Tornadic Growth Investments website, and clicked on the screen showing the running list of email addresses that have opened the site. There's one hit ... there's two, he thought. That guy's been reading about my hedge fund, just like his boss did. Maybe he's even been reading about me. This ain't good. He grabbed his iPhone and punched in a set of numbers.

"Sneak, it's me," said Mac. "I've got a job for you." ... "No, I don't want you using that broken down little popgun you always carry." ... "I'm telling you, your damned rusty Smith & Wesson ain't no good. It's gonna misfire, like it did the last time. Get yourself a new one." ... "Well, find yourself another gun that's *lucky*." ... "I need the job done by next week. And I don't want anyone finding the body, period. Parsons will work with you on this." ... "Yeah, he'll take care of the guards and the security cameras." ... "And Sneak—you lisnin? Don't mess this one up!"

***

May 24 ... The Proctor Family. Josh Proctor had enlisted the help of his father, Brandon, to install a garbage disposal. The two men lay on the kitchen floor, their heads under the sink. Fifteen year-old Daniel was plugged into his iPod as he chomped on an apple, his hair in a customary state of nonchalance. Nine year-old Ollie paced the hallway, animatedly engaged with her cell phone. Josh's wife Tonya brought in the mail and dropped it on the kitchen table with a thud. The two men looked up. One piece caught their eye. Oversized, it was an iridescent chartreuse color. Josh stood, set his wrench on the counter, and pulled an envelope from the stack. As he did, red blotches jumped out from the chartreuse background.

"Hey! This kinda looks like blood," he said. Tonya moved closer.

"Feels a little creepy," she said, opening a kitchen drawer and fishing out a pair of yellow rubber gloves. She spread out a section of the paper to lay the envelope on.

"I see you've taken your HIV training to heart," said Josh, tongue-in-cheek.

"I've dealt with a lot of bloody noses and cut fingers at the clinic, but this is my first bloody envelope," she said. "Better safe than sorry."

Tonya grabbed the envelope, forcing her gloved index finger under the flap. Initially, it was difficult, but the glue gave way and she was able to free up the entire flap in one continuous motion. Everyone was watching.

"Is it really blood?" said Daniel. "Awe, sweet!"

"What is it, Mommy?" asked Ollie, concerned.

"Let's find out," said Tonya. Her gloved hands fumbled with the task. Seconds later she grasped a single sheet of paper and pulled.

More red, on crumpled paper.

"Oh, God. What *is* this?" Tonya said, laying it beside the envelope.

"It's a print of a left hand—thumb, part of the palm and the first three fingers," said Josh as he traced the outline inches above the paper. "Looks like someone laid a bloody hand on a piece of typing paper, and squeezed."

Focusing on the red, Josh had missed the black. A hand-lettered **JOSH** showed through the red fingers.

"What the ..." said Josh.

"Hey, Daddy. That's your name," said Ollie.

"Yah, sweetie, it is," he said, focused on the envelope. "Is there anything on the other side?"

Tonya turned it over—blank.

"I wasn't looking," he said. "Who's it addressed to?"

"Joshua Proctor," said Tonya. "But there's no address, no return address, and no stamps. Couldn't have been delivered by the mail carrier. This is either a really sick joke, or we need to call the police."

She turned, her gloves still on, and walked to the mailbox at the curb. There were no signs of blood. She looked up and down the street as if hoping to see someone waiving at her with a red paintbrush. No one. Tonya tried to remember whether or not the chartreuse envelope had been on top or under the other letters and magazines. The middle, she decided. That's why she hadn't seen it. She became aware of the rest of the family gathered around her.

"Looks like someone put it in our box after the mail was delivered," Tonya said. "Mail usually comes around one on Saturdays. That would mean it must have been put in the box within the last thirty, forty minutes. Were either of you outside then?" Both children shook their heads.

"Okay. What do we do now?" asked Tonya as they returned to the kitchen. "Should we call the police? Or, since it was in our mailbox, maybe the postal authorities?"

"I can't imagine either of them would consider this worth investigating," said Josh. "Unless this isn't the first bloody envelope that's been delivered in the city."

"Hey. We can take pictures like they do on TV. I'll get my camera," Daniel said as he raced from the room.

"Good idea, Daniel," Tonya said after him. "And we can store the envelope and paper in a plastic bag, at least for a while."

Ollie went to the pantry for a plastic grocery bag. Josh brought a lamp for better detail, adjusting the shade. Tonya flattened the wrinkled paper. Daniel returned with his camera, pulled up a chair to stand on, and began taking pictures. Ollie voiced her opinion as to how everything should be done, and who should be doing it. Tonya turned over both the envelope and the paper, and Daniel clicked more pictures.

Ollie handed Josh the plastic grocery baggie. "Here, Daddy," she said. "Here's the bag. Put 'em in, Mommy." Josh and Tonya complied.

Tonya rolled her eyes. "I feel like I'm in the middle of Hannah Montana meets CSI."

At Josh's request, Ollie retrieved a stapler, and, after folding the top of the baggie, stapled it closed. Daniel pulled the memory card from the camera, dropped from the chair, and moved to the family PC. Everyone followed, Tonya still in her yellow gloves.

The pictures were quite good. The colors jumped off the screen. The shot of the red handprint on the paper was exceptionally crisp. The fingerprints were clearly visible. There were individual shots of the envelope and of the paper, and there were side by side shots. The newspaper background helped to establish their size and the date. *Oohs* and *aahs* replaced the noisy activity level of the kitchen, as Daniel zoomed in and out on each photo.

Tonya and Josh returned to the kitchen to collect the newspaper and carefully clean the counter top. Tonya rinsed her rubber gloves in the bucket of water and bleach, and set them to dry. She and Josh made eye contact.

"You worried, Josh?" Tonya said. "That thing has your name on it."

"It's a little unnerving, I admit. But I really don't know what to make of it. And I don't even want to consider the possibility this isn't a joke."

"Any of your old fraternity brothers in town?" asked Tonya, knitting her eyebrows.

"Not that I know of, but it is a pretty adolescent stunt," said Josh. "How about you? I know your therapy clients love you. Any of them jealous of me?"

"Well, I do have a few with histories of aggressive acting-out behavior. But, I can't picture any of them doing something like this," Tonya said.

Josh was already in problem-solving mode. "I'm thinking we need to do a couple of things. First, let's send Daniel and Ollie to the neighbors to ask if they'd seen anyone around our mailbox within the last hour. Then, let's send an email to the local police precinct with copies of Daniel's pictures. That way we'll have kept them in the loop in case they're working on any similar complaint."

"That's my engineer," said Tonya. "Sounds like a logical, detailed plan. And, I agree. Taking specific actions should give us a sense of empowerment, reducing the anxiety and helplessness we're feeling, certainly the anxiety and helplessness I'm feeling. I'll get Ollie and Daniel. We'll decide what to say, so we don't generate any undo rumors or panic among the neighbors. In the meantime, think about your strange fraternity brothers."

The kids left to check with the neighbors. Tonya began an email for the police. As a clinical psychologist, she had been volunteering for several years with Memphis-area law enforcement. One of the police officers she'd worked with closely was Julia Todd. Julia would tell her straight up what she thought. Wanting to include any information from the neighbors, she waited to hear from Ollie and Daniel before sending the email.

Josh and Brandon returned to the garbage disposal. Concentrating on their task was more difficult, and the pipes refused to align correctly for Brandon. Josh said, "Here, let me try, Dad. Like you used to tell me, sometimes you just have to talk nicely to them." The pipes came together in seconds. Brandon didn't know whether to feel embarrassed, grateful, or just resigned to losing another skill to old age. He decided to feel grateful. After all, he was retired.

"Thanks, son," he said.

His joints creaked and a groan issued from somewhere deep inside as he managed to gain a standing position. Brandon chose to be grateful again. He walked to the front of the house to stretch his legs. Glancing out the window he was surprised to see at least eight noisy children of various ages in the front yard. "What in the world …" Then he realized whatever Ollie and Daniel had told the neighbors, it wasn't deterring rumors or curiosity. The children were inspecting the mailbox, the lawn and street nearby.

Ollie and Daniel reported that two of the neighbors were out, and none of the others had seen anyone around the mailbox. Tonya added this information to her email and clicked **SEND**.

***

Lieutenant Julia Todd was in her mid-thirties, and stood about five-eight. Her hair was light brown, cropped closely on the sides, spilling over from the top with a cute kind of mop look. She wore just a touch of make-up, no jewelry. She was trim, in good physical condition. The athleticism and obvious self-confidence with which she carried herself enhanced her attractiveness.

Todd's career in law enforcement began as a Police Service Technician, handling basic fender benders and directing traffic. After finishing her BA in Criminology, she graduated at the top of her class at the Memphis Police Training Academy, academically, physically, and on the shooting range. She worked undercover in her first months on the job, gathering evidence on a male dentist alleged to have molested female patients he'd placed under the effect of a gas anesthetic. She didn't remember any of it. But a revealing video tape and court testimony let her and everyone else know what she'd been through. Her fellow officers acknowledged her courage in volunteering to have this joker drill on her teeth, as well as placing herself in such a sexually vulnerable situation. They became very protective of her, and she never endured the usual hazing and harassment experienced by rookies and by female cops.

Todd served in the tough neighborhoods in the Community Policing program, rode in patrol cars, and worked in the Memphis City Schools. She transferred to homicide, and after three years, was promoted to Lieutenant. Last year, she was invited to be a member of the police department's Critical Incident Stress Debriefing Team, a program designed to reduce the long term effects of distress officers typically experienced during their more horrific or life-threatening calls. That's where she met Dr. Tonya Proctor, the psychologist who coordinated the program.

Todd was at the west precinct station on Union Avenue, reading through unsolved homicide case files. She left her office to get coffee. When she returned she checked her computer. Hey, an email from Tonya. Something must have gone down I didn't hear about, she thought.

"Huh? What's this?" She clicked on the attached photos. "Holy shit! Hey, Teresa! Come in here."

Teresa Johnson worked the clerical shift on weekends as part of her flex-time schedule. She was from one of the best known African American families of police officers and firefighters. She dreamed of following in the Johnson tradition, but a serious auto accident resulted in her loosing the full use of her right leg. Working with the police as a secretary allowed her to be involved in the action vicariously. Teresa had dark brown skin and full-tooth smiles. She was slightly overweight, and her clothes and shoes were what one might call *comfortable*.

"Whacha got?" said Teresa as she made her way over to Julia's desk, limping slightly. She bent forward to get a better look at the pictures on the monitor. "Hooyah! This is great."

"You ever seen anything like this, Terry?"

"New one on me, Lieutenant. Looks like something kids would do on Halloween. You think it's a prank?" asked Teresa. "But, hey, wait a minute. I do remember something about a chartreuse-color envelope. What *was* that? I can't put my finger on it. Give me some time. I'll track it down."

"Thanks, Terry. And this didn't come from some crackpot. It's from Dr. Proctor. She wouldn't be making up anything like this. The fact that she took these pictures means she's concerned. I'll give her a call. Heck, she doesn't live far. I'll just drive over to her house."

Todd pulled out of the Union Avenue police station and turned left on East Parkway. The median of East Parkway was well maintained. Massive trees shaded newly planted ones, and a large "M" comprised of hundreds of petunias burst colorfully from the face of a steep rise. She loved this drive through grand old Memphis homes. On her left was Overton Park, while the revamped access to I-40 was on her right. At the park's northern edge she turned left and made a quick right on the Proctors' street.

"Julia. I didn't expect you to come here. I wasn't even sure you'd be at the station today," said Tonya, inviting her inside. "I just thought you'd know what we should do about this envelope." She turned to her husband. "You remember Josh?"

"I remember all the attractive men I meet," said Julia, winking. "Good to see you again, Josh."

"Good to see you, too," said Josh. "Tonya's always telling me how much she enjoys working with you, and how much she's learned from you."

"Feeling's mutual," said Julia.

"And this is my father-in-law, Brandon Proctor. He's a retired attorney who specialized in education law, working with the city schools." said Tonya.

"Yes, indeed. I do remember all the attractive men I meet," said Julia, with a smile. "I met you when I was assigned to the Memphis City Schools. We worked together on an assault involving a student who had a special-ed diagnosis. You did a great job juggling the special education laws and the criminal laws. I've told other attorneys how well you handled that situation."

"How kind of you. Thanks. Of course I recall you, and that student. Good to see you again, Lieutenant," he said.

"And these are our children, Daniel and Ollie," said Tonya. "This is Lieutenant Todd."

"I helped," Ollie said.

"We all helped," Daniel corrected.

"Happy to meet y'all," smiled Julia. "Can I see the envelope and letter?"

"Absolutely. Thanks so much for coming out. We weren't sure who to call," Josh said as Tonya left the room. He grabbed a section of newspaper and laid it on the coffee table.

"We didn't know if the red stain was blood, so we've been handling it carefully," Tonya said as she returned with the grocery store baggie and a staple remover.

"Smart. Not to mention you also helped to maintain the integrity of the evidence, so to speak. Great pictures, by the way. We should be able to pull some fingerprints off the letter, and maybe the envelope as well. Good work," said Julia, pulling on her latex gloves. Daniel grinned broadly.

"This looks like blood to me," said Julia. "But I can't say if it's human or not. Although this has a bizarre quality about it, it could just be a prank. Any ideas, Josh?"

"I'm clueless. As Tonya said, either one of my old fraternity brothers has come to town, or something is very wrong. It's probably just a prank, don't you think, Lieutenant?"

Julia was watching Ollie. "That's my guess. But it wouldn't hurt to keep your eyes and ears peeled. I'll take this back to the lab to see what they can pull from it. Maybe they've come across something like this before."

Julia excused herself and returned to the Union Station, where she sent the envelope and contents to the lab. Her gut was telling her this was no prank. It was especially troubling since Tonya was a friend. Maybe I can have an officer drive by the Proctor house each day, she thought. And it'd be great if Teresa could track down that other chartreuse envelope. Julia turned her attention to the pile of cases on her desk.

✳✳✳

Teresa had been bothered by the fact she couldn't remember where she'd seen or heard about a chartreuse envelope. Culling through and retaining pieces of information was her strong suit. It wasn't like her to be forgetful. But no matter which mnemonic strategy she used to jar the recesses of her brain, she could not remember. She kept challenging her brain to retrieve the lost information. When did I hear it, or see it, or read it? Where was I? What was I doing? Who was with me? Was there an unusual smell? Noises? Songs? How about going through the alphabet? A...Arrest log—no. B...Lt. Bart Williams—no. C...Coke machine—no. All the way to Z. Nothing.

CHAPTER 2

WAITING FOR THE OTHER SHOE

BRANDON attempted to describe the events of the afternoon to his wife, Jennifer. A bloody chartreuse envelope with their son's name on it, and a visit by a Memphis police officer—these were disconcerting pieces of news. She had plenty of questions, few of which he could answer. She phoned Josh and asked him the same questions. He didn't have any better answers, and he wasn't very convincing when he told her it was probably a practical joke. Jennifer and Brandon didn't sleep well that night or the next, neither did Josh and Tonya. Monday morning the elder Proctors decided to change their planned schedule of activities. By noon they were easing onto Josh's street.

***

May 26 … Hyper-vigilant. Fresh on their minds, that iridescent chartreuse color seemed to be everywhere. Josh was dropping the morning car pool off at the elementary school. Ollie gave him a quick kiss on the cheek and slid out of the car. She was surprised to see one of her classmates wearing a plastic rain coat of that color, with matching plastic shoes and umbrella. Josh turned to drive away, only to be startled by the sight of a crossing guard wearing an iridescent chartreuse safety vest. He felt his heart rate rise and his stomach fall. He was concerned by his overreaction. He'd always considered himself a logical kind of guy, in control of his emotions.

At the high school drop-off there was no show of affection from Daniel. He merely offered an almost indiscernible, but very cool, splay of his fingers as he got out with his friend. Shortly, Daniel saw one of the Goth juniors with an apparent identity crisis, as he was dressed totally in black—black lipstick, dyed black hair, black nail polish, and blackened eyebrows—carrying a notebook with an iridescent chartreuse cover. After dropping everyone off at their schools, Josh began the thirty-minute drive to his office in Olive Branch, Mississippi. His heart rate was still elevated and he was aware of feeling jittery. He just wanted everything back to normal. He thought of his clean desk, organized room, and neatly stacked in-basket. He started to feel better.

Tonya's workday didn't start till 9:30. She again sprayed the kitchen counter and the glass-top coffee table with water and bleach. She had moved from her usual big picture perspective to a decidedly detailed task orientation. Her mind had been racing all night. Is Josh really in danger? Could it have been one of my clients? Adult? Teenager? Male or female? She was afraid this could be her fault. Frustrated as the pain intensified in her stomach she said aloud, "Damn, will I ever get beyond feeling guilty for everything?" Try as she might, she wasn't able to think of a single client who could be responsible for delivering the envelope. She planned to spend as much time as possible today going through client files, just in case.

Josh sat at his desk going over a draft of technical analyses for a client, when an email popped on his PC. He looked over to check it out. It was from an address he didn't recognize, someone using the name *Redstone* with "Did you get it?" in the subject line. He opened it. There was no text. This is odd. Could this email be related to the letter he received Saturday? he wondered. Nah. He returned to his draft.

***

Teresa didn't work Mondays. Her flex schedule gave her a day to sleep in. She found herself in a huge mansion, with more rooms and more glitz than the Chateau at Versailles. There were secret passages, false walls, and hollowed out candle holders. She was furiously searching. She found pictures of relatives, her father's collection of jazz record albums, letters sent by her tenth grade boyfriend, a tricycle with a bent front wheel, her grandmother's perfume, and grade school report cards. She touched each thing found, enjoyed it ever so briefly, and put it aside. The more things she discovered the more energized she became, the faster she moved through the mansion in her quest. She wasn't sure what she was looking for, but she'd know it when she saw it.

Teresa woke with a sense of frustration, failure. Her brain had been awake all night. She didn't feel rested at all. She pulled back the covers, swung her legs over the side of the bed, and sat up. It's that stupid chartreuse envelope, she thought. She rubbed her forehead as she slid her feet into her worn fuzzy slippers, and shuffled off to the bathroom.

Teresa was halfheartedly combing her hair as she stared blankly toward the bathroom mirror. She was working her way through the alphabet for what seemed like the tenth time, and was on "S" when her eyes lit up. "Of course. *Smoking!*" she said out loud. "That's it! I'll be damned." With that cue, her reconstruction of the memory flowed.

***

Julia usually started her day by reading the paper at the neighborhood coffee house—a combination coffee shop and reading library, called the Deliberate Literate. She enjoyed being one of those patrons who chose to take the time to sit down and drink their coffee inside the shop. These people exuded a kind of respectful casualness, even the ones in pinstripe suits. It seemed to be a nice slow-paced way to ease into what was waiting for her at the precinct.

There was certainly no shortage of crime. Memphis can be a tough town. The Bluff City always seemed to rank in the top five of the nation's large cities in per capita violent crimes, occasionally edging out its larger sister cities like Detroit, DC, Los Angeles, or St. Louis. Rape, murder, car theft, and child abuse were perennial hot spots. On the upside, the MPD had one of the better records for solving crimes and making arrests.

But that was little comfort to the vast majority of Memphians who just wished there was less crime, and the captured criminals received longer jail sentences. Julia was a card-carrying member of that group.

As Julia was acclimating to another Monday, her mind wandered from the newspaper she was reading to the chartreuse envelope with its red blotches, the stained handprint on the paper inside. I've still got a bad feeling about this, she thought. Was it a threat? Or just a prank? Will Teresa's steal trap memory yield something useful? She decided she'd try to nudge the lab along with its processing of the envelope. She folded the newspaper and left it on the table for another customer, then headed for her car.

***

Tonya's first family appointment canceled. Though she never liked missed appointments, this gave her the chance to review some client files.

She tried to think through her task. What am I looking for? A history of aggression? That covers a majority of my clients regardless of age. In kids it was called acting out. In adults it was just being mean. How about the idea Josh raised that a client would have formed too close a relationship with me? A good working relationship was always a key to effective therapy. However, with some clients, the way they interacted with the therapist was heavily influenced by that client's personal history with important adults in their own life. In such an instance the client would, to some extent, transfer those feelings and experiences to the therapist as if she were that important person, maybe a parent, relative, teacher, or spouse. When the relationship was based on bad experiences, a positive therapeutic relationship was extremely difficult to establish. There's a low probability such clients could be involved in any jealous actions. However, on the other hand, a client might distort the relationship such that the therapist would be seen in an unrealistically positive light. A client might believe that the therapist was in love with them, or that the therapist somehow belonged to them. These would be the more likely type of client to look for.

Tonya had been a licensed psychologist for thirteen years. That translated into a lot of clients. She racked her brain. *Where do I start?* Beginning therapists are taught to ask a new client *What brings you here today?* or *Why are you coming to see me, now?* It seemed that these questions were applicable here as well. *Why now?* What happened recently that may have triggered such an action? She didn't want to find out that any of her clients had done this. But she had to know.

***

The lab techs promised to pull the iridescent chartreuse envelope higher in the queue. They would get to it by the end of the week. "Thanks," said Julia. A personal face-to-face is always best, and the *très cher* half-dozen French chocolate éclairs from La Baguette didn't hurt.

As Julia walked back into her office the phone rang. She picked it up.

"Todd."

Teresa began talking immediately. "I was out back of the station smoking a cigarette, when some of the guys pulled in. They opened the trunk and began yanking out a bunch of brown grocery bags filled with papers and magazines. One of the bags spilled open. In the middle of the pile in the driveway was this shiny chartreuse envelope. I was thinking how neat the color was. In his usual graceful fashion, especially when viewed from the rear, Marino bent down and scooped it up with all the other papers, stuffed them back in the bag, and went inside. I remember ragging on him for being such a klutz and needing to get rid of that gut. Then he said something about my mother—"

"Never mind *playing the dozens*. How long ago was this?" Julia asked.

"Not long.," said Teresa. "Within the last month, I'm guessing. I don't have clue one as to what was in it, or what case he was working."

"You're incredible, Terry. Thanks." Julia hung up and went to find

Marino. Teresa grinned and lit another cigarette. It was going to be a restful Monday after all.

Sergeant Anthony Marino was a twenty-year veteran of the force. He didn't always have the greatest people skills, but he was a damn good cop, a talented investigator with an exceptional nose for key events and clues. He was a burly guy, about six feet, with a classic Italian demeanor. You always knew his opinion, and he always had your back. His fellow cops nicknamed him *the professor* because he was amazingly well read, and full of seemingly useless tidbits of information. The more complex the case, the more his take on the crime was sought out. Over the years, his riding partners had either benefited from his knowledge, or run screaming for a change of assignment.

"Hey, there you are, professor," said Julia.

"What's up, Lieutenant," said Marino.

"I'm working a case that's right up your alley. Not only that, it may be an alley you've already been working in."

"Shoot," said Marino.

Julia launched into a brief history of the case, starting from Tonya's email and pictures of the bloody iridescent chartreuse envelope, finishing with the fact that the lab should get to the envelope and paper later in the week.

"Sounds interesting," said Marino. "What's the part about me already been working on it?"

"That iridescent chartreuse envelope—it's at the heart of this, somehow. Teresa remembers seeing a similarly colored envelope in a bag of papers you were toting into the station a few weeks back."

"What? Damn Teresa," Marino said. "She's always getting into everyone's business. I don't know anything about … Wait a minute, yeah … I do remember seeing an envelope like that. Damn Teresa. How does she do that?"

"Marino," Julia redirected. "The envelope?"

"Oh, yeah. Sorry, Lieutenant," Marino said, collecting his thoughts. "Let's see. Some big shot scientist for BP Technologies was found dead in a single-car accident. The accident reconstruction boys thought it looked suspicious, but as far as I can recall, they never could validate their hunch. The case was assigned to Tagger to double check, and I volunteered to help him serve a search warrant. We cleaned out everything that might have some relevance from the guy's home and office. I didn't really get involved in the investigation. But, now you've got me curious. I'd like to see the chartreuse envelope I dropped. Keep me in the loop, huh?"

"Be happy to, professor. I could use your help," said Julia, striding down the hall to find Tagger. Her mind was scrambling to make sense of this new piece of information. Lead scientist? What is it that BP Technologies produces? Isn't it medical implant devices? Isn't that what Josh does at R&O? I can't wait to see that envelope.

Later that afternoon, Julia caught sight of Sergeant Johnnie Tagger walking into the station. He was an African American who stood over six-four, as imposing as an NFL lineman. Like other members of Julia's squad, he was a well respected and dedicated cop, with a wealth of experience and remarkable intuition. He was also an invaluable team player, who got along with the variety of personalities in blue.

"Tag!" she called loudly. "Got a minute?"

"Sure, Lieutenant. Let me wash some this crud off my hands and I'll meet you in the squad room," said Tagger. He found her a few minutes later. "Sorry, Lieutenant. We just picked up a vagrant, and he smelled like shit. I mean really like shit. Whatchagot?"

"I'm working a case that may have some tie to one you closed not too long ago," said Julia.

"Which one?"

"The one involving the scientist from BP Technologies."

"Yeah," he said as the full memory began to unfold. "Sturgeon ... Dr. Haverford Sturgeon. Killed in a car crash. Everything pointed away from an accidental death. But we couldn't prove it. What's the tie in?"

"You know Dr. Tonya Proctor, the psychologist who runs the department's debriefings?' He nodded. "On Saturday, a large shiny chartreuse envelope was delivered to her house. There was blood on the envelope, and a bloody handprint on the paper inside. Her husband's name was on both the envelope and the paper."

"Her husband?"

"Yeah. Josh Proctor. He's some kind of engineer. Works at R&O Industries, the bio-medical plant down in Olive Branch."

"What's this have to do with the Sturgeon case?"

"Turns out Marino remembers seeing a bright chartreuse envelope in the bags of papers y'all brought in from the doctor's office and home."

"We went through each piece of paper and found nothing," Tagger said. "I kinda remember a chartreuse colored envelope. But I don't remember what was in it. What's going on here, Lieutenant? Coincidence?"

"You know what I think about coincidences, Tag."

"Yeah. Rare as hen's teeth. Say, last week we returned everything to Dr. Sturgeon's son. Spends a lot time at his father's house in Germantown. I'll get you the address and a cell number."

Julia's hopes for a quick solution for the Proctors seemed to be slipping away. It was already starting to unwind in ways that didn't feel like a fraternity prank.

***

The pace of their lives had been noticeably relaxed since their retirement—Brandon from his law firm, and Jennifer, a licensed clinical social worker, from her position as executive director of a social services agency. They each did volunteer work, but spending time with Josh and his family was their favorite hobby. Now that this bizarre thing had happened to their son, it was important for them to be doing *something* to help.

Brandon parked the car several houses from Josh and Tonya's. He and Jennifer were just close enough to be able to see the mailbox. Jennifer had packed some snacks and drinks. Brandon brought his official Memphis Tigers football binoculars, and she had her digital camera. They'd watched the mail carrier deliver the mail minutes earlier. But it wasn't long before they started to feel conspicuous, as every passing car slowed down to look at them. Maybe they were watching, too. Then a police car. The officer was driving slowly by the mailbox. When he became aware of the elder Proctors' car, he drove directly to it, till they were bumper to bumper. He exited his vehicle and walked to Brandon's side of their car.

"Yes, officer," Brandon said with a smile. He was reasonably confident neither he nor Jennifer looked like criminals, and he didn't want him to think otherwise.

"License and registration," the officer said. Brandon complied. "Brandon Proctor?" he said aloud to himself.

"Yes. We are the parents of Joshua Proctor, whose house and mailbox are just up the street. Is there any chance you know Lieutenant Todd?" he said, thinking a little name dropping couldn't hurt.

"What are you doing here, Mr. Proctor?" the officer asked.

"Well, last Saturday our daughter-in-law found a strange letter in the mailbox, but it didn't come through the U.S. mail. We decided we would watch the kids' mailbox in case the guy came back."

No one spoke for several seconds. Then the officer asked, "Are the snacks good?"

"Oh, yes. Jennifer made the cookies this morning, just a little nourishment. Would you like a few?"

"Only if you think they'll help me stay alert for the rest of my shift."

The officer returned Brandon's license and registration, took the cookies, and left. Jennifer and Brandon turned to each other and let out a collective sigh.

"Maybe this wasn't such a good idea," Jennifer said. "If we're going to do this, we should clear it with Josh to watch the mailbox from inside the house."

"I agree," he said, grabbing another cookie.

***

Tonya didn't know whether to feel relieved or frustrated. She had been thorough in ruling out all her current and recent clients. She was convinced none of them would have delivered the chartreuse envelope to Josh. Now, what about those fraternity brothers?

Josh's day had been uneventful. He hoped someone else had information that might help put this puppy to bed. He'd heard one piece of sad news, however. Haverford Sturgeon had died in an auto accident only a few weeks ago. Josh was upset that he'd missed hearing about it, and that no one had mentioned it before. Hav was a great scientist, an enthusiastic supervisor, and for the last fifteen years, a good friend and mentor. He would've liked to have attended the funeral. Josh recalled Hav talking about his son frequently, not much older than he was. He pulled out the phone book and looked up Dr. Michael Sturgeon.

***

Julia began her drive to Sturgeon's home. It was afternoon rush hour, and the narrow six lanes of Poplar Avenue were swelled with cars, all hurrying to get somewhere, especially the three lanes heading east. Poplar Avenue is one of the major arteries, running from the Mississippi River east through Memphis, continuing with a southeastern dip into the more affluent suburbs of Germantown and Collierville. The stretch within Memphis is notoriously narrow, and buses and SUVs have the impossible chore of staying between their respective white lines, particularly the ones next to the curbs. It is always an exciting drive, but with an astonishingly small number of accidents. The street is bordered by homes and businesses, with churches and schools scattered along the way. Poplar cuts through the poorest of neighborhoods and the wealthiest. The lanes widen after about ten miles from the river, especially after crossing I-240, the branch of I-40 that circles the heart of the city. The small *Welcome to Germantown* marker designates the beginning of more recently constructed business buildings, larger homes, and decidedly smaller business signs, close to eye level.

It was 6:30 by the time Julia made it to Sturgeon's home. His son, Dr. Michael Sturgeon, a general practitioner in family medicine, was waiting for her. He was in his late thirties, with wire rimmed glasses framing a kind face. His posture, his eyes, his voice, and his slowed actions announced his sadness. He was clearly taking the death of his father very hard.

"I'm sorry to bring up sad memories, doctor," Julia began. "As I said on the phone, while reviewing information in an unrelated case, Sergeant Tagger thought he'd come across something similar in your father's papers."

"I don't understand, Lieutenant. Are you suggesting Dad's death wasn't an accident? I thought Sergeant Tagger already straightened all that out," said Sturgeon.

"I want to be clear. We have no evidence your father's death was anything other than an accident. It's just that in the investigation of a different case, something jogged Sergeant Tagger's memory, but he couldn't be sure where he'd read it. Your father's death was one of the cases he recently wrapped up, and he thought it might be in his papers. I'm just trying to double check. Is there any chance you still have them?"

"Actually, I do. I keep coming over here to Dad's, promising myself that I'll go through his effects. I sit down with a pile of things on my left. I pick up each piece to see what can be thrown away, and when I'm through there is an identical pile of his things to be saved on my right. It's just that it's still painful, and getting rid of his belongings would feel so … final." He collected himself. "The papers Sergeant Tagger returned are still in Dad's office, on the floor in piles. His office is just down this hall, on the right."

"Thank you, sir," said Julia, moving toward the office. She found four sloppily stacked piles of papers and journals beside the desk. Nothing chartreuse. Julia pulled on her latex gloves and began sifting through the piles. At the bottom of the third stack she saw it, just a corner. She grasped it carefully and pulled. No blood, no address, no return address, no stamp, only **DR. H. STURGEON** printed in upper case letters with a black marker. Lifting the flap, she retrieved a single sheet of white paper. No blood. The paper had not been crumpled. **DR. S, BE CAREFUL** was printed on two lines using a black marker. She had goose bumps. The printing on the two chartreuse envelopes and papers appeared to have been done by the same person. She replaced the sheet of paper, and slipped the envelope into her messenger bag.

Julia returned to find Sturgeon listening to an opera, a glass of wine and an opened package of French brie on the table. "I'm afraid I wasn't successful in finding what I was looking for," she lied. "Would it be okay if I sent a car to collect your father's papers again? Say by the end of the week?"

"Of course. I still don't understand what you're doing. But I know Dad wouldn't mind. Just have them call first to be sure someone will be here," said Sturgeon as he opened the door for Julia. "Good night, Lieutenant."

"Good night, doctor. And again, I'm sorry to be such a bother at this difficult time."

Julia was making her way back on Poplar Avenue. The sun was bright and low on the horizon making the westerly drive even more challenging than usual. Her mind was popcorning with questions. What was Sturgeon working on? Is there a connection between Sturgeon and Josh? Are there any prints on this envelope, besides those of every cop at Union Station? Who's the chartreuse author? What's up with the color? Is the message a friendly warning or a threatening warning? Was the note for Josh interrupted, so that his too was supposed to say *be careful*? Did the blood mean the writer was injured, or maybe even murdered? What else is in those piles of papers? Can I get the lab to analyze these sooner—like now?

It was after eight when Julia pulled into Union Station. She'd already logged a thirteen-hour day. Tag and the professor had left hours before. I'll wait till tomorrow to take the envelope to the lab so I can speak face-to-face with the techs about the urgency of this case, she thought. I'm getting low on funds. I hope I won't have to buy another box of éclairs. Hell, I'll think it over in the morning. Right now, I need to pick up some food, head for home, and try to clear my brain. She pulled into a Taco Bell drive-through and ordered two Nachos Bell Grandes. It will go perfectly with the beer in the fridge. There'll be hell to pay, she thought. But I'll work it off tomorrow.

CHAPTER 3

EYES PEELED

MAY *27 … Carl Huong.* Tuesday morning came quicker than Julia would have liked, but she made herself get up. This was one of her mornings to run and hit the gym. She didn't always look forward to working out, but she always felt glad to have done it. As usual, she ran 4.7 miles in the neighborhood, then stopped at the Inside Out Gym to work with the strength machines as well as punching and kicking the heavy bag. Afterwards, she ran the 2.4 miles back to her home, cooled down, showered, and dressed. She was a little behind as she pulled into the Deliberate Literate, ready for a cup of coffee, a nutrition bar, and the newspaper. Halfway through her coffee, she could feel her spirits lifting. In fact, she was feeling so good she decided to pick up some of those *très cher* chocolate éclairs for the lab techs after all.

***

"Thanks, y'all. I really appreciate you working on these envelopes," Julia said as she turned to leave the lab. She glanced back. All the techs had their mouths full of éclairs, and their eyes half closed, chewing in slow motion gustatorial splendor. "Good idea, Julia," she murmured, exhaling the words "Now back to the ranch."

***

"Mornin, Lieutenant," said Tagger. "Any luck with the doc's stuff?"
"Yes. I found the iridescent chartreuse envelope. It had writing that

37

looked to be identical to the one I brought in Saturday. I just dropped it at the lab, and I hope to hear something in a day or so. By the way, I think we should bring in all those papers again. I don't know what we're looking for, but I'm thinking there has to be something in there that will help us fill in a few of the missing pieces. Sturgeon's son is expecting your call."

"Got it, Lieutenant. I'll call him and arrange to pick the papers up again."

"Probably be best if you just play dumb. We don't want to jerk Sturgeon's emotions around. I told him we were working another case, and you thought you remembered reading something that sounded familiar, something you'd read somewhere, but you couldn't remember … yadda, yadda. You get the idea. I didn't say anything about the chartreuse envelope, and he didn't see me leave with it," Julia said.

"Mum's the word," said Tagger as he turned to walk away. What the hell is *yadda, yadda*? he thought.

"Any chance you still have the file? I'd like to look it over. Just put it on top of my stack," said Julia.

"It's on my desk. I'll pull the phone number and turn it over to you."

Julia returned from the restroom to find the Sturgeon file on her desk. She could see why the traffic accident investigators had questions. A single car crash with no skid marks, and there didn't seem to have been enough speed to have caused his death. But there was nothing out of line in the autopsy. Tox screen was clear. No alcohol, no drugs, no unaccounted for bruises, and no heart attack. Perhaps he fell asleep? Where's my lab report!

Julia decided to take a break from the chartreuse envelopes, and began to work her way through the rest of the stack. Reading the files made her feel good about the skills of her team. She felt thankful to be working with such a good group of pros. She was almost done, just one more file. It was a missing persons file. "What's this doing here?" she asked. The name on the file was Dr. Carl Huong.

She opened it and began to read:

58 years old, Asian, 5' 5", 130 lbs, black hair, black rimmed glasses. No hist of addict or mentl ill. Did not return home from work this past Friday, has not answ his cell phone. Widower, lives with his only child, a daughter, Mailene Huong age 30. According to daugh, they get along well, & never done anything like this before. Gray, 4 dr 05 Nissan Max. License unknown, No low rider, or other tracking device. Daughter worried, didn't report him missing until the next day, Sat.

She continued to read:

PhD biological engineering. Employed as a

senior scientist at BP Technologies.

"Damn! Another one," she said out loud.

A Monday entry by Officer Roberts indicated Huong had been at work on Friday.

still at office when sec left work. Didn't show up for work today. Sec not know where he was, no entry in his cmptr calendar.

Julia's brain was firing on all cylinders. This can't be a coincidence. Did Huong get a chartreuse envelope, too? Where's my lab report!

"Teresa, find Tagger and Marino," Julia shouted as she reached for her phone. "I need to get to Josh, now."

"Oh, hello, Lieutenant Todd," Josh said when Julia identified herself." … "I appreciate it. Thanks for calling." … "Well, everything's the same-o, same-o." … "No, I haven't been out of the office all day." … "I'll be through about five-thirty." … "Sure. I can drop by the station on my way home, say about six-fifteen?" … "Is there any news? Something I need to be worried about?" … "Okay. I'll give Tonya a call to tell her that it's your fault I'll be late. See you in a few hours."

Josh wasn't convinced Julia's invitation to meet her at the Union Station was a good thing. He wondered what was up.

***

First Ollie, then Daniel bounced through the front door, having been dropped off by their car pool ride. Tonya had just beaten them home.

"Hi, kids. How was school?"

"Fine," they said dully.

"Have you heard anything about the envelope, Mom?" asked Daniel, more concerned than he wanted to let on.

"No," Tonya said. "Nothing. I heard from Dad, though. He's going to meet with Lieutenant Todd tonight to see what the police have found. Did you have any ideas?" asked Tonya. She became aware of Ollie standing silently, but clearly tuned in to the conversation.

"I don't know," said Daniel. Tonya continued to watch him silently. "You know, you said Dad's fraternity brothers might have done this as an adolescent joke. I'm not really sure what a fraternity brother is, but it sounded like maybe a good friend. So, I was just kinda wondering if any of my friends coulda done this. The problem was that people kept asking me why I was looking at them funny. I guess I was trying to see into their minds. I didn't like the feeling. I don't think they did either," he said, dropping his head.

Tonya was impressed with Daniel's sensitivity. He felt worried about his Dad, and he was able to pick up on his own actions and feelings, as well as those of his friends. "Phew! I'm with you, Daniel. I've been concerned too, and I was looking closely at some of my clients to see if they might have sent the envelope. It's funny. We did the exact same thing," said Tonya.

"Me too! Me too!" Ollie said and moved closer. "I was looking at anyone who was wearing that shiny green color, or had that color green umbrella or green notebook. I didn't know any of them. I don't think some of the kindergarteners and first graders would be tall enough to reach into our mailbox."

"Oh, my," Tonya said with a warm smile as she felt her emotions rise. "Aren't we just alike? What a family! We'll have to ask Daddy when he gets home if he did the same thing." She moved to hug them both. Daniel didn't even flinch this time, but he did keep his arms at his side. "Okay, now. Get yourselves a snack, listen to some of your music, then get busy on your homework. I'll get to work on dinner." She watched them trot to the kitchen. Her eyes welled up, and she felt a tear run down her cheek.

She dabbed her eyes on her sleeve, took a slow, deep cleansing breath, and focusing herself she whispered, "Okay, mom, back to work."

CHAPTER 4

FAMILIES: SURVIVING, BUT NOT UNSCATHED

VIOLENT *Beginnings … Charleze.* " 'Mere, girl! I needs ma cigrets," yelled Barbara Washington, stretched out on the couch. "Leezie! Leezie! Where's that stupid girl?"

The front door opened. In walked Thomas Washington and their daughter Charleze Renee, who was struggling with a heavy brown paper grocery bag. The five year-old lugged it to the kitchen.

"Don't you break nuttin," hollered Thomas, "or I'll test that bottom."

"I won't, Daddy. I'm being real careful," said Charleze, as she panted for breath.

"Look what Daddy brung ya," Thomas said enticingly to Barbara. He opened his fist to show several rocks of crack cocaine.

"Oh, you know what I love. Bring the sugar ta momma."

"I got a fool to pay ten dollars to hold him a place with you. He'll be coming in about an hour. Get your pretty face on and do 'im right. Maybe he'll pay extra, maybe come back."

"I'll have his eyes rollin back up in his head," said Barbara, staring at her cocaine.

Charleze's arrival was not welcome—the pregnancy interrupted their primary source of income, and Thomas was convinced he wasn't the father. But Charleze beat the odds. She never experienced the torturous withdrawal typical of babies born to cocaine-addicted mothers. Her only symptoms of fetal drug syndrome was a heightened sensitivity to noise, smells and bright lights. And, thanks to a very concerned and assertive neighbor who regularly checked on her in those important first years, she was able to survive the extreme neglect from her parents.

But those were only her first challenges. Thomas and Barbara resented Charleze for interfering in their lives, for costing them money, for existing. They were emotionally distant, verbally abusive, physically assaultive, and demanding. Charleze owed them, big time.

"Leezie. Where'd you put ma lighter?" yelled Barbara.

"I know where it is, Momma," said Charleze as she ran to the bedroom. "Here it is, Momma."

"What about the bed?" said Barbara. "I've got a man comin'. That bed better look right."

"It's almost done, Momma." said Charleze, running back to the bedroom.

"And spray some of that cologne on the sheets."

"Yes, Momma."

"That damn kid. She'd better start pullin' her weight," said Barbara.

"*Yes, Momma,*" Thomas mimicked. "She jus about screwed up the buy. I told her ta take the money in the back room, and don't come back wid nuttin less than 4 rocks. She up and drops the money, then takes all day ta pick it up. I told her ta bring the money back so I could count it again. Damn. Then she says she's scared and don't want ta go in that room. I gave her a shot. Damn. She needs to be scared of me."

"Leezie! Fix me a sandwich," yelled Thomas.

"Yes, Daddy. The bed's almost done," said Charleze.

"Don't give me none of your lip, girl," said Thomas. "I'm waiting."

"Be right there, Daddy."

***

Charleze thrived at school. She tended to stay to herself, but she was alert, self-motivated and a fast learner. She knew the answers, followed directions, and did her homework. Kindergarten had been good for her social development. But first grade was too easy, too repetitive. She struggled with boredom. That all changed in the second grade as her teacher, Susan Determan, made sure she was being challenged. She arranged for Charleze to join the higher grades for reading and math. The greater the challenge, the harder Charleze worked.

Not long after Charleze's seventh birthday, Ms. Determan noticed a change. Charleze stayed to herself more than usual. She stared frequently, held her lower stomach, and squirmed in her seat.

"What's the matter, Charleze?" asked Determan.

No response.

"Don't you feel well?" she asked, touching the back of her hand to Charleze's forehead. "Does your tummy hurt?"

No answer, but tears formed.

"Oh, sweetie. Tell me what's wrong," said Determan. "I want to help."

Still no response, but Charleze squirmed.

"I'll call your mother—"

"No!" Charleze interrupted. "Don't call Momma. *Please* don't call Momma." More tears.

Determan's concern turned to fear, both for Charleze and for herself. Something bad happened to Charleze. Someone hurt her. She was certain. The signs were too familiar, too personal. She held her breath and closed her eyes. When she opened them Charleze was looking up at her.

"Sweetie. Did someone hurt you?"

Charleze looked down.

Determan bit her lip. She knelt on one knee, and placed her hand on Charleze's back. "Does your bottom hurt?"

Her silent tears turned to sobs.

"Please, sweetie. You don't have to say anything. Just show me with your head. Yes or no. Does your bottom hurt?"

Charleze nodded slowly.

Determan swallowed hard. "Did someone hurt you?"

Again, she nodded. Determan pulled Charleze to her.

Determan left Charleze with the school nurse, and went to the office to discuss her concerns with the principal. They agreed to call Protective Services.

***

A police officer and Child Protective Services social worker went to the Washington home. Both parents were under the influence. Yelling and cussing, they blamed Charleze for being a horrible and ungrateful child. After prolonged questioning in their diminished capacities they began revealing portions of the horror story Charleze had been living. Being low on drug money they decided to expand their sex trade by offering Charleze. Not long ago, they got their first *baby john*. They didn't know his name. But they seemed pleased he'd paid top dollar, and he'd come back. Both parents were arrested for prostituting their little girl.

The social worker tried to calm Charleze. "You're safe now. No one will hurt you again."

"Where's Momma? Where's Daddy? I want to see them," Charleze pleaded.

"Your mommy and daddy are in jail."

"Jail? I want to be with them. Take me to them." Charleze began to cry.

"I'm taking you to live with Mr. and Mrs. Murphy. They're very nice. You'll like them."

"No, I won't. I want my Momma and Daddy."

"Your mommy and daddy won't hurt you anymore."

"They didn't hurt me. I'm sorry. I'll be good. I won't cry when the man comes. I won't tell."

***

Determan, like so many women, and like many teachers in particular, understood all too personally what Charleze was experiencing. It had been a therapist who had helped her work through her own trauma of having been sexually abused by her father. She learned it was perfectly normal to have all those crazy mixed up feelings—fear, shame, guilt, relief, loss. But most importantly, she had to learn the abuse was not *her* fault. As with the majority of adults who were molested as children, Determan was committed to making a difference for other children. She chose to enter one of the helping professions—teaching.

Determan was frantic. She hadn't heard anything about Charleze. She called Protective Services several times—nothing but busy signals. Finally, an answer. Her call was routed to Ms. Byers.

"Hello. This is Susan Determan, Charleze Washington's teacher."

"Ms. Determan? Oh, you reported the abuse," said Byers.

"I've been so worried, said Determan. "And she didn't show up at school today. What happened?"

"Turns out her parents were selling her to men for sex," said Byers.

"No! said Determan. "Oh, my God!"

"The Washingtons were arrested," said Byers.

"What happened to Charleze?" asked Determan.

"She's safe. But she's pretty upset, seems confused," said Byers. "Says she wants to be with her parents."

"Of course she wants to be with them," said Determan. "She's seven years old. She has no idea how parents are supposed to act. They're *just* her parents."

"Parents in name only," said Byers. "They've abused her in everyway possible."

"But the fact remains," said Determan. "No matter how badly they've treated her, it's the only way she's known."

"You'd think she'd be relieved that we're protecting her," said Byers.

"There's no question she wants the sexual assaults to stop," said Determan. "But that's only one piece of it. She's got to be *so* confused, and her emotions *so* mixed up. She's just lost her parents and her home. These are devastating losses. I'm betting she believes this is all *her* fault. If she hadn't said anything to me, she'd still be living at home with her parents. Now, she's feeling even more guilt, on top of everything else. So much emotional pain for anyone to go through, let alone a child. The only supports she has left are here at school, with her friends, with her teachers, with me."

"Well, school is not our priority. Charleze needs to be placed with a family," said Byers. "That's the most important."

"Oh, please," said Determan. "Please don't take her away from her school too. She desperately needs *some* consistency in her life."

***

The Department of Children's Services made the foster home placement. Charleze was enrolled in a new school. Six years, three schools, and four foster homes later, she began the eighth grade. Determan, keeping up with Charleze, convinced state officials and school personnel to find a high school consistent with her intellectual potential. A private boarding school was identified, in its early phase of an affirmative action initiative. Charleze's high scores on national academic tests, combined with her minority status, made her a prime candidate. The prestigious Bovarde College Preparatory High School offered her a full four-year scholarship. The state agreed to the private boarding school placement and assigned Determan as Charleze's foster parent.

The burden shouldered by Charleze and her minority classmates at Bovarde was daunting. They endured on-going harassment and threats, as did the handful of white students and teachers who attempted to befriend them. Charleze's fierce self-sufficiency was born out of her early childhood and a recent history of frequent changes in foster homes and schools. Forming interpersonal attachments had never been easy for her. The hostile environment at Bovarde only served to reinforce a belief that she could trust no one but herself. She continued to seek refuge in her intellectual prowess, at the expense of her emotional development. She threw herself into her studies. Her strategy paid off academically, as Charleze became the first African American to earn valedictorian honors at the school. College scholarship offers poured in.

CHAPTER 5

FROM OUT OF LEFT FIELD

MAY *27 … The List.* It was ten minutes past six when Josh pulled into the midtown Union Station. He parked, walked around to the front of the building, and entered a small waiting area. An officer stood behind a counter at the far side. He crossed to her.

"Can I help you?" the officer said, not looking up.

"Yes, ma'am. My name is Josh Proctor, and I have an appointment with Lieutenant Todd."

"Have a seat. I'll let her know you're here."

Josh found a chair. Ten minutes later, Lieutenant Todd appeared from the hallway on the right. "Hey, Josh. Sorry, I'm running late. Thanks for coming in." They shook hands. "We can meet in here." Josh followed to her office. Julia indicated a stout wooden chair. "Please, have a seat," she said, and walked around her desk to sit in her chair. "Josh. Is there any chance you know a Dr. Haverford Sturgeon?"

"Sure. Dr. S was one of my placement supervisors when I worked on my master's at U of M, back in the early nineties. I learned more from him than any of my other supervisors. He wrote an incredible letter of reference that helped me get hired on at R&O, where I've been ever since. We've stayed in touch over the years, and we even co-authored a few professional articles. I just heard today he died in an auto accident a few weeks ago. I can't believe it. We'd planned to meet at next month's biomedical convention in Chicago. I called his son Mike today to express my condolences. But why did you ask about Hav?"

"You called him Dr. S," said Julia.

"That's what everyone called him. As we got to be friends, I just called him Hav. You didn't answer my question," said Josh.

Julia made eye contact. "I'm not sure of the best way to say this, so I'm just going to say it. Dr. Sturgeon received a note in an iridescent chartreuse envelope just before his death."

Josh froze, his mind in logical overdrive. If Hav received a threat, and Hav is dead, and I received a threat, then I must be next.

"Josh. You heard what I said didn't you?"

No response.

"Josh?"

Josh realized Julia was in the room. "Yeah, yeah, I heard you. But that would mean that I'm—"

"No, it doesn't," said Julia. "But it does mean that we need to be very careful."

Josh rattled off questions. "What about Tonya and the kids? Are they in danger? Do they know about Hav? Do they know that he received a chartreuse envelope? Why is this happening? Oh, Jesus."

"Hold on, Josh. I'm not going to let anything happen to you or Tonya or your kids," said Julia. But she knew better. There was no way she could keep such a promise. She collected herself. "I've already assigned police officers to watch your house. Now, I need to ask a few questions." She waited until Josh nodded. "Do you know a Dr. Carl Huong?"

"Carl too?!" exclaimed Josh. "Of course I know Carl. He's Hav's right arm. He and Hav are, I mean *were*, the best medical implant development team in the country. Is Carl dead too? Did he get a chartreuse envelope like Hav? Like me?"

"Carl is missing. His daughter filed a missing persons report Saturday."

"Carl's missing? Jesus. That's the day I got the letter. Mailene must be going crazy. Oh, Jesus. Hav and Carl, and maybe me. Is there anyone else?"

It had been Tonya who taught Julia how to listen, what to say, and when to say it as they jointly conducted the emotionally laden critical incident stress debriefings. She took an unobtrusive cleansing breath, got a little emotional distance, and began, "Josh, I'm really sorry for the loss of your friend, and having to hear that you may be in danger. Josh, I need to know where you are with all of this. Tell me how you're feeling."

"How am I feeling? I thought you were a cop. You sound like Tonya."

Julia grinned broadly. "You should know. It was Tonya who trained me. Trained me to be a different kind of cop. So, tell me how you're feeling."

Josh forced a slight grin, and began his answer in a staccato, impatient manner, "I'm sad. I'm confused. I'm scared. Damn, am I scared. Oh, yeah, and I'm getting pissed off."

Julia smiled. How the hell does this psychology shit always seem to work, at least eventually? she thought. "What you're experiencing is absolutely normal. Not only that, your getting pissed off means you're not gonna let all these other emotions turn you into jelly. We can work together to focus that anger in the right direction. That means that none of it goes ricocheting around Tonya or the kids. Does that make sense?"

Josh nodded. "I'm working on it. I'm not as touchy-feely as our Memphis cops seem to be." Julia laughed. And with each smile and laugh, Josh began to feel more in control of those overwhelming feelings. "What do I need to do? Give me a one-two-three list of things to concentrate on."

"Oh, a logical man, huh? Okay, here we go. Number one. You need to be very careful. Pay attention to every little detail. Notice people and cars. Keep an eye on your rear view mirror. Check your office and home to see if anything has been disturbed. Put my number on speed dial. Don't go places you don't have to." Josh nodded. "Number two. Write down everything you can remember about Sturgeon and Huong. What were they working on? Where did they go together? Who did they interact with?" Josh nodded again. "And, number three. Get yourself focused for your ride home tonight. What kind of expression, emotion and attitude do you want your family to see, especially Ollie & Daniel? What do you have to do to create a sense of calm for your family? How are you going to explain the police car outside your house? How will you be supportive to your family when they begin to freak out?"

"Enough already. I'm glad I didn't ask for a four or a five. You're lists are longer than mine. I thought you were a touchy-feely kind of cop," said Josh, as he showed that he still had his sense of humor. "Those are terrific directives, ones that I will work on, and act on." He added quietly, "Thanks, Lieutenant."

"Please call me Julia," she said. Julia had the same *limp dishrag* reaction she experienced after the debriefings. She found working on feelings in such intense situations to be exhausting. "Let me walk you out."

CHAPTER 6

FAMILIES: WHEN THEY STRUGGLE TOGETHER

MAY *27…Number Three.* As Josh pulled around the corner he could see a car, which he assumed was an unmarked police car, sitting in front of their house. He'd been thinking of Julia's *number three* all the way home. She was right, and he felt thankful for her advice. Josh mentally rehearsed his strategy. *I'll be setting the tone for the family regardless of what I do. I need to set a positive one. Don't lie to the kids, but don't say things that will scare the bejesus out of them. I'll tell Tonya everything.*

It's a good thing he had prepared, because the second he opened the door, six eyes were all over him. Josh smiled. "Sorry I'm late. I was talking to Lieutenant Todd. The police lab hasn't processed the envelope yet because there were more important cases, but they hoped to have something soon. And Lieutenant Todd has assigned police officers to watch our mailbox for a day or so." Ollie and Daniel seemed to be calmed, and raced to take a look at the unmarked police car.

Tonya turned to him. "Assigned a police car? What's really going on, Josh?" He couldn't tell whether he saw fear or anger in her eyes.

Josh whispered, "I'll tell you everything after the kids are asleep. But I think it's important to keep up a good front for them right now."

Tonya stared. Barely moving her lips she said, "The minute they're asleep."

"Come look, Mommy," yelled Ollie. "He's right there." Tonya turned and walked to the window.

The three of them returned to where Josh sat waiting in the den.

"What did you do today, Daddy?" Ollie asked.

"I was at the office, sweetie."

"No, I mean that me and Mommy and Daniel all tried to look for people with shiny chartreuse clothes and stuff. You know, trying to guess who put the envelope in our mailbox," Ollie said.

"Oh, I see. Yeah. I kept wondering who might've done it. I even thought about my fraternity brothers who might be playing a very unfunny joke," said Josh.

"You were right, Mommy," said Ollie. "The whole family did the same thing. Just like a team," Daniel, Ollie, and Tonya filled Josh in on the day's events.

***

"Okay. What's going on?" asked Tonya, once the kids were settled in their beds.

Josh held both her hands and began at the beginning giving Tonya a blow-by-blow account of his meeting with Julia. Tonya flinched and tensed just as Josh had. He could see it in her face and feel it in her hands. She knew Hav and Carl. She too could follow a logical argument to its natural conclusion.

"Julia learned well from you, hon."

Tonya did a double take. A meek "Huh?" was all she could muster.

"I was scared shitless. She dragged me back to earth, and put me on a quest to do specific things." He went on to describe Julia's recommendations.

Tonya was crying. "I'll have to remember to give her an A." They embraced without speaking. Tonya was caught up in the danger and the fear, and felt grateful for the comfort of his arms and his emotional support. But then something changed. She could feel it. She shifted her attention to the here and now, to being with Josh, to the give and take of their embrace. It was no longer supportive. It was different. Josh was different. She was aware that he was no longer with her. She pulled back. One look into his eyes confirmed what her body had been telling her. Josh had left her. As his own fears resurfaced, he'd shifted his energy to focus on gaining intellectual control of the situation. He was mentally reviewing Julia's first two lists.

"Josh? Where are you?"

He caught the edge in her question. "Huh? I'm right here."

"You're not here with *me*."

Silence.

"Where are you, Josh? What are you thinking about?" Tonya pushed, knowing full well what he was doing, but feeling deserted and left out. Her emotions were changing. They had a new focus. She was angry at Josh.

Josh knew he'd been caught. He felt guilty for abandoning her. But instead of owning up to his actions, he became defensive and presented the front of being annoyed by Tonya's questions. "I just need to think this through."

CHAPTER 7

HELP WEARS GUCCI

MAY 28 ... *Frederick Durnst.* Julia had showered and dressed, and sat quietly in her living room. The events of the last few days, combined with long hours and too much coffee, weighed on her. She could feel the knots in her shoulders and neck, and the beginning of a tension headache. With her eyes closed, she took a few deep breaths and relaxed her body, using a simple technique of muscle tensing and release. Once she felt calm, she began, like Peter Pan, to think *happy thoughts.* She learned this technique from Tonya, and often used it to begin her day. Dwelling on even the smallest good things put her in a more positive zone, which in turn helped her to be a more creative problem solver. This had made a major difference in her insightfulness and decision making on the job.

Julia ordered decaf at the Deliberate Literate. And by the time she finished her coffee, nutrition bar, and paper she was focused. When she got to her office she busied herself in developing the core of a crime board to help her conceptualize the scope of this case, and a focus for finding who was responsible. She began listing the known elements on a sheet of notebook paper.

Two iridescent chartreuse envelopes with threatening/warning notes, one with blood. One dead scientist. One missing scientist. One threatened scientist. Four piles of paper.

In the column of unknowns, Julia listed

Source of the chartreuse envelopes. Meaning of the notes.

Source of the blood. Connection between the scientists. Huong's whereabouts. Motive. Identity of assailant/s.

She concentrated, trying to will something new to jump off the page. Nothing budged.

Time for basic police work, Julia thought. I need a detailed profile on both scientists, including their schedules over the past six months. What were they working on? How is Josh involved? And having fingerprints wouldn't hurt. She left to find Marino and Tagger. On the way she stopped by Teresa's desk.

"Mornin, Lieutenant," bubbled Teresa. "What's goin on?"

"Morning, Terry. I'm just trying to get some heads together to figure this chartreuse envelope thing out."

"Yeah, I hear that case is really taking off. It looked like a teenage prank, and now it's looking more like a double murder. I'm pumped," said Teresa in a smoker's voice.

"What else have you heard?" asked Julia.

"Not much, yet. The guys have been feeling like they've screwed up by missing these connections. Oh, yeah, and that the Proctor guy's mother bakes great cookies," she said, smiling.

"Huh?" said Julia. "Never mind. I probably don't want to know. Say, do me a favor. Be on the lookout for anything that might be connected to this case. It's more frustrating than usual, because we're only finding clues and connections by stumbling over them."

"Sure, Lieutenant. You know how much I love this part of the job. I mean the part that's not in my job description."

"And the part you do so well. Thanks, Terry." Julia left Teresa beaming.

She found Marino and Tagger wearing latex gloves, sitting glassy-eyed amid mounds of letters, papers, articles and journals.

"Bring me up to speed, fellas," she said as she walked into the room.

"This is way more than I ever wanted to know about joint replacements. I probably could have handled it better without the drawings and pictures. Do you have any idea what they do to you before they put in one of those things?" bemoaned Tagger. "And then, it's more like carpentry than surgery. My bones hurt."

"He's right, Lieutenant. I have a new sense of empathy when I watch them cut up a whole chicken on the Food Channel. This is some gruesome stuff," said Marino.

"It's a good thing men will never have to give birth," Julia said, shaking her head. "I'm truly sorry about your pain, but what about our case?"

"Sorry, Lieutenant. Didn't mean to get all misty," said Marino. "We're not much farther than we were yesterday. We don't know what we're looking for, so I'm not sure we'd know it if we saw it. Kinda like this whole case."

Tagger said, "We put out an all-points on Huong's Maxima, but nothing's turned up. We checked the airlines—nothing. We did a walk around the parking lot at BP Technologies—nothing. We asked to view their security DVDs, but were told we needed a search warrant. Durnst was not a very helpful guy."

"Who's Durnst?" Julia asked. "He's new."

"Dr. Frederick Durnst"—Tagger checked his notepad—"is the CEO of BP Tech. He was hired three years ago, and Sturgeon used to report directly to him. Since they haven't replaced Sturgeon, he's Huong's new boss. It's funny, though. He doesn't seem all that bothered by Huong's disappearance. He just kept talking shit about top secret this and top secret that. Call me silly, but I think he deserves a look."

Marino chimed in. "There's been nothing from the stakeout at the house. How long we going to keep that up?"

"Maybe twenty-four hours more. I can't justify it, and we can't afford it," Julia said. "I was hoping to have something from the lab by now. Put Durnst on your to-do list, Tag."

Julia filled them in on her meeting with Josh, including her request to spend some quality time thinking about what the two docs have been working on, and how it tied to him. "I can't shake the feeling this thing is a whole lot bigger than one, or two homicides," she said. "Okay, professor, you keep working your way through these papers. There has to be a clue in there somewhere. Tag, you learn a little more about Durnst, and keep on top of the all-points. It'd be good to get prints for Sturgeon and Huong. If they're not in the data base, go out to their homes and pick up something with their prints on it. I'm going to follow-up with the lab, and keep tabs on Proctor. I'll work on a search warrant for BL Technologies' security DVDs, and for Huong's office and computer."

***

Julia decided she wanted to meet Durnst for herself. She took Poplar Avenue to BP Technologies, on the outskirts of Collierville. The buildings were set at the rear of a large neatly landscaped area of manicured lawns, with dozens of flowering pink crepe myrtles bordering the wide walkway to the front door. Trees of varying size dotted the property, smaller ones in clusters of three, larger ones standing in isolation. Low, square-cut hedges bordered the front of the lawn. Flowers bloomed everywhere. The main building was a two-storey square, yet modern structure covered with rectangular pieces of pale marble-like stone, and large windows. The first floor appeared to be about twenty feet high. A taller, nondescript windowless structure attached to the main building at the northeast corner. She took this to be the warehouse, or the production area.

Julia made her way up the walk, through the automatic sliding glass doors. The lobby was large, open, and made good use of sunlight. Brightly colored lighting fixtures in the shape of flowers hung on long green chains from the ceiling. Small trees stood in large planters. Abstract art hung from the walls. Plush chairs were scattered around. The overall effect was a blend of ecology and professionalism.

She stopped at the guard station, about twenty-five feet from the entrance. After checking in and receiving directions, she headed for the CEO's office on the second floor. It was a few minutes before she found it. After a thrust and parry with the secretary, a Ms. Maureen Lister according to her engraved brass on walnut name plate, she was ushered in.

His office was nothing like Julia had ever seen. *Plush* was an understatement. Light rust carpeting so thick she wasn't sure her feet made contact with the floor. Flat gold walls adorned with what looked to be gallery quality original paintings, each individually lit. Figures jumped out of the carved wooden panels of the end tables, with inlaid mother of pearl tops. A large matching armoire stood in the front corner, down from the door. The *piece de résistance* was his desk—huge, dominating the room, though it sat at the far end. Unimpeded sunlight streamed off the starkly bare desktop. Aunt Louise always told me that all my taste was in my mouth when it came to decorating, Julia thought. But those big red leather chairs set in front of the desk just didn't belong. Neither did Durnst's similarly appointed chair behind the desk. She fought the urge to check the soles of her shoes for mud or worse. She crossed the room and stopped at the back of one of the red leather chairs.

Durnst, who had been standing when she came in, took a seat at his desk without speaking. He was in his mid-fifties, with thinning brown hair that he combed straight back, leaving an occasional single hair sticking up where his hair used to be. He wore stylish tortoise shell glasses, a blue lab coat over blue pin-striped trousers, and a mauve and purple tie. Julia felt her cheeks flush as she braced against his arrogance.

"I'm investigating the disappearance of Dr. Carl Huong. As I'm sure you know, he never made it home after work last Friday."

No acknowledgement.

"I understand you refused to allow my officer to go into his office, or to view your security DVDs," said Julia more loudly.

"Well … Lieutenant, is it? I do not see how I can allow you or anyone else to go through Dr. Huong's office or look at our security DVDs. The work of this company, and companies like it, is top secret. I am sure you are familiar with industrial espionage," Durnst pontificated. "There are people who would kill to know what goes on in these companies. Nonetheless, I will be happy to give you our attorney's number." He pushed an unseen button under the lip of his desk.

"Yes, Dr. Durnst," came the secretary's reply.

"Please give the Lieutenant one of Mr. Stanford's cards on her way out," he said without looking at Julia.

The flush in Julia's cheeks spread to her neck. She wasn't sure what she'd expected, but it wasn't this kind of treatment. "Perhaps a search warrant would help?" was her best comeback.

"I am sure you will be able to discuss such things with our attorney, Mr. Stanford," Durnst said as he continued to focus on something in the drawer.

Julia realized she'd been squeezing the top of the red chair. She looked down to see her hand print had become part of the decor. She wiped her hand on her trouser leg, turned and left. Once off the plush carpet Julia felt more secure, as if actually feeling the floor again gave her a sense of being grounded. To her left, she could see Ms. Lister holding out a business card. Without a word, she walked over, took the card, opened the door and headed back to the lobby, leaving the door wide open.

That went well, Julia thought as she slid into her car. What an asshole. I really want to know just what secrets he's protecting.

***

May 28 ... Myrna Taylor. As Julia approached downtown Memphis the tallest buildings became visible. The sun reflected off the silver-gray steel facade of the Pyramid to the right, making it difficult to see at times. The handful of tall buildings in the downtown area top out at just over thirty-five stories. Nothing like the New York City skyline, but just the same, it stands out in stark contrast to the surrounding flat land of the delta. Julia turned left on Danny Thomas Boulevard, and pulled in behind the Shelby County Criminal Justice Complex, located at 201 Poplar Avenue. The large complex houses the Memphis Police Department, the Shelby County Sherriff's Department, the District Attorney General's offices, the Public Defender's offices, and criminal and felony courts, all attached to the County Jail. When it was built, the jail was known as the glamour slammer. Now, it's simply *201*. She entered the building and took the elevator to the office of the Assistant District Attorney General.

"I'm Lieutenant Julia Todd. I know I don't have an appointment, but is Attorney General Taylor in?"

The secretary wrinkled her nose up as if someone had just farted. "Assistant Attorney General Taylor doesn't see anyone without an appointment."

"Attorney General Taylor and I have worked on several cases. I know she'll want to see me."

Grudgingly the secretary buzzed in. "There is someone here who says she needs to be seen."

"I know. I've told her," the secretary said. "I'll check."

Looking up, she said, "What did you say your name was?" Julia repeated her name loudly. The secretary raised her eyebrows, "She'll be right out."

"Julia," said an attractive, well proportioned woman in her late forties, opening the office door. She was dressed in a dark blue power suit, with a mid-calf length skirt, large diamond studs in her ears, yellow gold bangles on her left wrist, and understated patent leather pumps by Gucci. Her green eyes were prominent. Her red hair was short, wavy, and worn combed back in what was called a *DA* in Elvis's day. "To what do I owe this pleasant surprise?"

"Hi, Myrna. I've got a tiger by the tail, and I think it's time to bring you up to speed," said Julia.

"Well, by all means come on in. Ms. Van Peebles, would you be so kind as to hold my calls, please," said a smiling Taylor with a slow, gentile, southern accent. Inside her office, Taylor turned two leather chairs to face each other. "Sit. Tell me what you have."

Julia explained the unfolding case of the iridescent chartreuse envelopes, with the possibility of two deaths, and her concern that others might follow. She described Durnst's response to her earlier that morning.

"Julia, only you could put these isolated events together with a piece of colored paper. So, you really think there's something here?"

"I can feel it. Way too many coincidences."

"I've learned to pay attention to your instincts. What can my office do to help? Other than get another secretary," she added with a smile.

"For starters, I thought I should alert you in case anything pops. Second, I need a search warrant to look at the BP Technologies security DVDs and Huong's office."

"I'm not convinced that you have enough for a search warrant, especially if we have to do battle with a staff of corporate attorneys. But I'll check into it. I'll get back to you this afternoon. You still at the midtown station?"

"Yes. I think they're going to have to carry me out of there feet first. Thanks, Myrna. I'll keep you posted," Julia said as she opened the office door. She made a point of being unusually grateful to Ms. Van Peebles on her way out.

CHAPTER 8

LET'S HEAR IT FOR THE ÉCLAIRS AND GUCCI

MAY 28 ... *Going the Extra Mile Pays Off.* Julia made the ten minute drive from downtown to Union Station. This was definitely not her favorite time. She had to sit tight, and depend on other people to come in with useful information. She was waiting on the lab results, a call from the Assistant Attorney General regarding a search warrant, updates from Tagger and Marino, any juicy tidbits from Teresa, and a call from Josh with his information on Sturgeon and Huong. She jumped when her phone rang. It was Teresa telling her the lab results were in.

"Well, don't just sit there. Bring the report in," Julia said.

Teresa knew the Lieutenant had been dying for these results. So, it was with a big smile that she delivered them. "Here they are, boss. Can I hang around and have a look?"

"You shittin me?" Julia challenged. "You know you've already read through this report at least twice."

"Oh, no, ma'am. I only read it once." Still smiling, she returned to her desk.

Julia devoured the report.

First envelope and paper positive for male human blood. Size of bloody prints infers a male adolescent or male adult. Non-bloody finger prints from same person on the paper and on the envelope. A second set of finger prints on both the bloody envelope and the letter. Second prints are noticeably smaller, implying an adolescent or adult female. Second prints not in the data base. A third set of finger prints, infers an adult male, on the envelope only. None of prints in database. The second envelope and sheet of paper have prints from at least six different persons, all of whom appear to be adult males. One of them is a match to the bloody finger print of the index finger found on the first envelope. One print belongs to Sergeant Anthony Marino, one to Sergeant Johnnie Tagger. Other three are unknown. Printing on both envelopes and both papers written by the same person using the same type of black marker, purchasable at any office supplies store. The iridescent chartreuse envelopes are produced primarily by one company in Austin, Texas. They are sold locally at Davis-Kidd Bookstore, and at Bongs R Us, in the midtown area. They are also sold online from several sites, including one directly from the company. P.S. Please send more éclairs.

Julia digested all she had just read, hoping to fill in some blanks. She rehashed the information. The same man addressed both envelopes and wrote both notes. A female was involved in handling both the note and envelope with a man's blood stains. Neither the male's nor the female's prints are in the governmental or law enforcement data bases. The third prints on the first envelope probably belong to Josh. Sturgeon and his son probably account for two of the three unidentified prints on his envelope. Need to send someone out to Davis-Kidd and Bongs R Us to check into purchases of the chartreuse envelopes. We still don't know if Huong also received a chartreuse envelope.

Okay, this is good, Julia thought. New leads. New questions. Are there other chartreuse envelopes floating around? Sounds as if we're looking for a man and a woman, of which the woman may have killed, or wounded the man. Did she assault him before he could finish Josh's note? In addition to the lab report, she just noticed that the author used nicknames on both notes, *Dr. S* and *Josh*. Did that mean the author knew them personally?

***

May 28 … Allison White. The promise of a new day lay silent as ill feelings smoldered. Neither Josh nor Tonya said a word as they readied themselves for work. Somewhere within each of them was an aching readiness to start afresh, and each was hoping that the other would break the silence. But their mutual stubbornness won out, as neither wanted to be the first to give in.

Ollie and Daniel were eating breakfast. Something was different. Mom was not her usual talkative self. Then Dad came to the table. Mom stopped speaking. Dad never started. Ollie and Daniel felt the chill and recognized the situation. They knew their roles. They made sure they did nothing to contribute to the problem, and limited their comments to *Yes, please* and *No, thanks.* Ollie's eyes were expressive and fearful, as they pleaded with Josh and Tonya to fix this problem and get back to normal. Daniel kept his distance.

The ride to school was quiet. The carpooling classmates had experienced the chill upon entering the car. They too followed the rule of silence. Josh did kiss Ollie goodbye. But Daniel left the car without any acknowledgement. Josh muttered to himself, "Jesus. What the hell am I doing?" as he grappled with how to protect his kids in the wake of his personal distress.

He took a deep breath and shifted from his stomach to his head, focusing on Julia's *number one*—be on the alert. This made the drive to R&O seem longer. He constantly looked in his rear view mirror. He noticed things and cars and people for the first time. When he finally pulled into the parking lot, he was amazed. I didn't know there were purple flowers growing in pots outside the R&O building. When did they put those there?

Walking to the building he shifted to Julia's *number two*—focus on Hav and Carl. When he got to his desk he grabbed a pen and paper, and brainstormed one-and two-word descriptors of things that linked the two men. Then he began to flesh out the entries. He was concentrating so hard on the list that he neglected *number one*. He heard his name called. A tall, slender blond stood at his left shoulder.

"Oh, hey, Allison," said Josh, startled. "I didn't see you there. Sorry, I was just doing some brainstorming. What's up?"

Allison White was a gifted engineer who had joined R&O Industries some eight years after Josh. Although attractive, she did not always attend to her appearance. Her short, straight, natural blonde hair routinely hung in her face when she bent forward. She shied away from make-up, stylish clothes and jewelry. She was comfortable working with staff, but not so in social contexts. Like Josh, she had a supervised field placement at BP Technologies while a U of M graduate student in the Engineering program. Huong had been Allison's supervisor.

"Josh, isn't it awful about Carl?" said Allison. "I talked to Mailene last night. He's been missing since Friday. She's so scared something terrible has happened."

"I just heard last night, myself. I sure hope he turns up soon. You and Mailene are friends aren't you?"

"Yes. Mailene and I went to school together. In fact, Mailene's mother used to drive the car pool. Every once in a while her dad, I mean Carl, would take us. He was my favorite placement supervisor."

"I'd forgotten that," said Josh. "Had you been working on any projects with him?"

"Well, I'm not supposed to be talking about it. You know, competing companies and all that."

"Over the years, I've done some things with both Hav and Carl. We had such mutual respect and trust that we were able to work together without violating our companies' business boundaries. Heck, I knew about some of Hav's discoveries and special projects before they saw the light of day, and he mine. We used each other like consultants. Is that how it was with you and Carl?" asked Josh.

"That was so sad about Dr. S," said Allison. "Actually, your relationship with Dr. S was more collegial than the one I have with Carl. He's still my mentor, and he gives me a lot more help than I could ever give him. But a few weeks ago he did ask my opinion of the Forest Brothers' work. I guess he was considering using their manufacturing services in one of his prototype replacement joints. I told him about the problems we've had with their shoddy work, and the fact that we terminated our contract with Forest Brothers Industries."

"Now that you mention it, Hav asked me a similar question. I told him the same thing you told Carl," Josh said. He hesitated, but decided to ask. "Is there any chance that you've seen any iridescent chartreuse envelopes around?"

Allison felt perplexed. "What an odd question … But the answer is yes. I saw one in Carl's office just last week. I didn't think anything of it at the time, but it was a little psychedelic for Carl. What made you ask that?"

"I saw one the other day. I'd never seen anything like it before," said Josh. Just then someone called for Allison. She looked up, and excused herself. Josh called after her, "Please let me know when you hear anything about Carl." Josh pulled his BlackBerry from his belt and hit number nine for Lieutenant Todd.

***

Julia had just hung up from talking to Josh when her phone rang again.

"Hi, Myrna," said Julia. "That's great news. I'll be at your office in twenty minutes to pick it up. By the way, I have new information. One of the engineers says she saw an iridescent chartreuse envelope in Huong's office last week. I hope we're not too late."

Julia met Tagger and Marino in the BP Technologies parking lot. Search warrant in hand, they marched directly to Durnst's office, where they found him in conference with the company attorney. After the introductions Julia handed the search warrant to Durnst, who handed it to his attorney without looking.

"Everything seems to be in order, Dr. Durnst. We need to let them do their work," Stanford advised.

They split up, Tagger going to pick up the security DVDs, while Julia and Marino headed for Huong's office.

Snapping on her latex gloves, Julia said, "I'll take the desk and computer. You take the files and bookshelves. Remember, look for anything we might be able to pull a print from." They proceeded to go through Huong's office inch by inch.

Shortly, Marino said, "Got a coffee mug that should have a print on it." He continued his inspection, pulling out each book. Dustless books were opened. Not long into this process he let out a "Bingo!" Marino held up a large volume, the word **ENGINEERING** visible. "Looky here," he enticed, slowly opening the book to reveal a hollowed-out five by eight-inch hiding place, about two inches deep. Julia bounced up and seized it. Inside was a blue plastic CD case. They exchanged looks. Marino with a big smile as if he'd won the lottery, and Julia wide-eyed and dying to know what was on it.

"Bag and tag," said Julia. "Good work, professor. Now, find me another one."

Julia returned to Huong's desk. She was looking for a chartreuse envelope, and for any reference to Forest Brothers Industries.

"What the hell do you mean you can't find the security DVD for last Friday?" Tagger yelled, raising himself and looming over the five-foot five-inch chief of security. "I don't like being jerked around. Do you understand the meaning of a search warrant? You'd better find that DVD, or I'm hauling your ass to 201." Tagger had his full attention.

Torrance Lacy had always wanted to be a police officer, but he repeatedly had the crap beat out of him in the self-defense classes before he dropped out of the Police Training Academy program. Beads of sweat formed on his forehead. He didn't want to be taken to the *glamour slammer* at 201 Poplar. "I'll be right back, Sergeant, sir," he said as he left to get help finding the missing DVD.

Tagger reached for his two-way. "Lieutenant, got a problem here."

Julia headed for Durnst's office, taking the steps two at a time. She was working on fanning the slow burn that began in his office that morning. She checked her shoes before entering his office in hopes of finding some dog crap, or a wad of gum. Nothing. Damn.

"I would strongly recommend you get your attorney back here to explain the legal system to you," Julia said to Durnst as they stood face to face in his office. "This is totally unacceptable. You knew we were interested in seeing the security DVD from last Friday, and now it's *missing?*"

Durnst looked unconcerned. He stepped back to buzz his secretary, and directed her to have the company lawyer return to his office immediately. "There. Is that better, Lieutenant?" he asked. "I can assure you I know nothing about any missing security DVD. I am sure it was simply misplaced, and the chief of our security force will find it post haste," he said in a supercilious tone.

Julia worked on containing her anger. She sneaked in a cleansing breath and tried to step back emotionally, moving from the churning in her stomach to the thought processes of her brain.

What an asshole, she thought. He's jerking my chain, and loving it. And, he's feeling supremely confident. What does he know that we don't? A phone buzzed.

"Attorney Stanford is here, Dr. Durnst," said his secretary. "I'll send him right in."

"Mr. Stanford, and none too soon. Lieutenant Todd is making some rather radical charges. I think you are precisely the person to hear them," said Durnst, as he flauntingly turned his back and took a seat in the large ugly red leather chair behind his desk.

Stanford turned to Julia for an explanation, which she provided. After she finished presenting a clear picture of events, Stanford said, "That certainly is a problem, Lieutenant. But of course, you know better than I that unless you have probable cause to substantiate your allegations, the company and employees of BP Technologies must be assumed guiltless."

Jesus, she thought. These clowns must have graduated from the same school, majoring in the art of arrogant bullshit. Addressing both men, Julia said, "You've both been apprised of the situation. I assure you that at the first hint of probable cause I will personally be hauling somebody's tight little ass to jail. In the meantime, we will continue our searches." She wheeled and moved quickly from the room. Guess I needed just one more cleansing breath, she told herself.

Marino had finished sweeping Huong's office. He found no other secret hiding places. He had loaded a box containing Huong's computer, an assortment of CDs, the coffee cup, and the book with the hidden CD in the blue plastic case. Tagger had pushed Lacy about as far as he could. He was pretty sure Lacy had nothing to do with a cover-up. For his part, Lacy promised he would be continuing his search for the security DVD until it was found. He was still sweating.

They met in the parking lot.

"We're being jacked around, Lieutenant," Tagger grumbled.

"Tell me something I don't know," Julia said.

"Sounds as if I missed all the good stuff," said Marino.

Julia spoke over her shoulder as she was getting into her car. "See y'all back at the ranch. Let me know the lab techs' timetable for going over this stuff. I can't wait to see what's on that CD."

She thought she'd make just one more visit to La Baguette tomorrow morning.

CHAPTER 9

NUMBER TWO, OR IS IT NUMBER ONE?

MAY 28 ... *The Ford Explorer.* Josh returned to his brainstorming list after alerting Lieutenant Todd to the information he received from Allison. His mind kept going to that chartreuse envelope in Carl's office, but he forced himself to stay on task. Josh considered his list of one and two-word links. Normally, a person would simply go to the first entry on the page and work down from there. But something disrupted that process today. He began with the third entry on the list, *recent projects.*

Josh knew Hav and Carl had been working on a prototype for an ingenious variation of extant artificial hip replacement devices. Their goal was a design that would not only be an improved joint, but one that could be adjusted or upgraded easily, as conditions required. In lay terms, it was like being able to expand computer memory simply by replacing the memory card. Theoretically, the procedure could be conducted on a simple outpatient basis. What a breakthrough for the industry and for those who will need an artificial hip. Not to mention the fact they would make an absolute ton of money for BP Technologies.

Josh continued working on his list. His email chimed. He looked up to see another email from Redstone—subject line "Be Careful." Again, no text. He stepped to his office door and looked at the bank of cubicles, as if he could find the person who had been sending the strange emails. What if this is connected to the chartreuse envelope? he thought. He returned to his desk, and attempted to track Redstone's email address. After twenty frustrating minutes he was convinced Redstone knew his way around computers, because he was unable to nail down the originating email address. He attempted to reply to the email, but when he clicked on **REPLY**, he received a neatly boxed error message. Reflecting on *number one*, he punched nine on his BlackBerry.

Josh described the emails from Redstone, and his inability to track them down. Then he told Julia what Hav and Carl had been working on.

"Their new artificial hip device would be so dramatically different that they'd have to take extraordinary steps to assure its safety and durability," he said. "Too many companies had lost billions of dollars on law suits and recalls because they rushed their device to market, only to discover a serious flaw one or two years later. I'm guessing Hav and Carl had reached the end of the final research phase, and were preparing for production and marketing. But I still don't understand how Forest Brothers Industries fits in."

"Thanks, Josh," Julia said. "Every new piece of information gets us closer to solving this case. Stay with it, and keep me posted."

Josh was pumped, juices flowing. He was aware of a strong compulsion to jump headlong into this, instead of running away from it. He returned to his list of ideas, intrigued with the link involving *mutual colleagues*. He jotted down Allison's name.

Then he considered the scores of graduate students who had worked with Hav and Carl. Josh decided to divide them into current employees, current students, and former students. He pulled up the BP Technologies webpage, and identified the employees who worked in Hav's and Carl's department. He found eleven. He checked his professional association member listing. He identified ninety-one with graduate training at Memphis or Ole Miss, nineteen of whom lived in the mid-south. Just over one hundred people. He photo copied the association membership listings on which he'd red-marked each of the identified persons, and printed off the employee list from the BP Technologies webpage.

Josh realized it was very quiet. He walked to his doorway. Almost everyone had left for the day. He put his copies in an envelope, wrote Lieutenant Todd's name on the outside, dropped it in his briefcase, turned off his computer and headed for the exit. He would leave the envelope for Lieutenant Todd on his way home.

Josh scanned the parking lot. Few cars remained. People were in the process of finding keys, loading trunks, fastening seat belts, and driving away. He saw a black Ford Explorer parked at the edge of the lot. He could tell there was a person at the wheel, but it was too far away to identify the driver. He thought he could see a number of cigarette butts on the blacktop outside of the driver's door. Had he been there waiting for someone? Did he just clean out his ash tray? Were the butts someone else's trash? Josh pulled out his key fob and pushed the unlock button. His car flashed acknowledgement. He opened the door, taking a surreptitious peek over his shoulder as he got in. The Explorer hadn't moved. He turned the key, backed out of his space, put the car in drive, and drove out of the lot. He glanced in the rear view mirror. He had chills. The Explorer was turning onto the street just a few cars behind him.

Oh, great! he thought. Why didn't I ever sign up for karate classes? Enough! Get organized. If I drive to the station I'll be safe, but he'll know I've been talking to the cops. If I drive home, I'll be taking him straight to Tonya and the kids. I need a plan … Okay … One, I keep driving and watching him. Two, I don't stop the car unless I'm in a busy traffic area. Three, I make a few turns to see if he's really following me. Four, I'd sure like to get a look at him, and maybe even a license plate number. Whoa! Where'd that come from? That must be the pissed off part coming out again. Oh shit. My job is to get away, not be a hero.

The traffic was building up as Josh approached the Mississippi state line. He could still see the Explorer in his rearview. After crossing the state line he turned right, on a side street. The Explorer turned right. He made a quick left at the next corner and made another left bringing him back to the main street. He continued on the main street. No sign of the Explorer. He returned his eyes from the rearview mirror just in time to see the Explorer entering from the upcoming side street he was about to pass. In that instant he was able to get a glimpse of the driver.

"A woman!" he said out loud, feeling a sense of relief, followed quickly by bravery. He pulled into a bagel shop parking lot hoping she'd follow. She did not. He set out after her. Maybe a tag number. No such luck. She was consumed in the heavy traffic. Josh headed for the midtown station. Maybe Julia would be there.

***

Ollie and Daniel were in their rooms, ostensibly doing their homework. Tonya was in the kitchen monitoring three pans at varying stages of cooking, hoping they would finish in a timely stepwise fashion. Today was a long day. She wasn't used to being angry with Josh, certainly not for so long. And she was feeling guilty for allowing herself to feel hurt, or worse, for choosing to feel hurt. She thought back to the qualities that had made Josh so attractive to her. He was confident, competent, organized, logical, solution-focused, punctual, and thrived on being in control. He was always predictable, and she found that comforting. It was clear he was coping with this craziness the best way he knew how—thinking his way through logically. It's just that he was also using the logic to deny the fear-related emotions. This was not helping him. She heard Josh open the door, and made a point of smiling as she turned towards him. But her countenance quickly turned to one of concern upon seeing Josh's expression. Her stomach jumped.

"What's wrong?"

Josh paused, then said, "Something strange happened today." He told her about his drive home from work, the Ford Explorer, the woman, and his subsequent visit with Julia.

"Josh. I'm scared. What's going on? Who's doing this? When's Julia going to solve this thing, so we can get back to normal?"

"How the hell should I know?" he said, more gruffly than he'd intended. His uncontrolled emotional response surprised him. But instead of acknowledging his underlying fear, he chose to continue to show anger. Tonya turned back to the stove, squeezing the spatula so hard it vibrated.

Conversation at the dinner table was minimal. Daniel and Ollie were unsettled by the chilly atmosphere, and the unusually heavy way plates and utensils were set on the table. They hated it when their mom and dad were at odds with one another. They just wanted to be assured that everything was okay with the foundation of their lives—their parents. They wanted them to always be predictably positive. The kids kept their eyes down, only Ollie snuck a few peeks. She didn't like what she saw.

There was no thaw in the coolness that night. Tonya and Josh slipped into bed without speaking.

CHAPTER 10

THE OPENING BELL: THE PRELUDE

DECEMBER *1997 ... The Internship.* Two young adults sat in a plush outer office. Both were dressed neatly in their best business attire. The rich decor and furnishings were impressive. They sat on the edge of their seats as if something from their inferior clothing might flake off and get the chairs dirty. The male squirmed frequently. His eyes darted about the room anxiously, while he dug his thumbnail into the handle of his briefcase. In contrast, the female sitting beside him was composed, a sense of anticipation lighting up her face. She sat with perfect posture, which, if possible, was at the same time controlled and relaxed. She casually held her purse in her lap, turning her head slightly as she took in every detail of the room.

A stylishly attired secretary sat behind a large mahogany desk. Her presence did nothing to detract from the gestalt of the room. The phone buzzed softly.

"Yes, sir," she said.

"Yes, sir."

"Mr. Goldman will see you now," she said, gesturing toward the double doors. "He has ten minutes."

The young man leaped from his chair. He was first to the doors, opening one and walking in ahead of his companion. Once inside he stopped. The intimidation of the waiting room could not compare to that of Mr. Goldman's office. The young woman slipped gracefully around him and confidently moved passed the highly polished boardroom-sized table toward the man standing behind the desk on the room's far side.

"You must be Miss Mitchell," he said, smiling, holding out his right hand.

"Yes, sir," she said. "Charleze Mitchell. It's so good to meet you, Mr. Goldman." She saw his gaze turn and heard the sound of shuffling footsteps on the plush carpet.

"And you must be Mr. Watson." He released Charleze and extended his hand to greet the young man.

"Yes, sir," he said. "Thornton Watson."

Having made the impression he'd intended, Goldman said, "Why don't we move to the table where we'll be more comfortable."

Goldman sat at the head of the table, and they took the seats right and left. Pulling two resumes from a file folder he said, "We're always glad to have Harvard interns here at Bear Stearns. Charleze, I see you've spent some time at Lehman Brothers. And, Thornton, it looks like this is your first placement on Wall Street." Thornton nodded, looking nervous and chancing a glance at the young woman seated across from him. "Okay. Charleze, since you were at Lehman, why don't you tell me what you know about the stock market."

"Well, sir," answered Charleze. "The stock market is one of the ways publically traded companies raise money. The market can be played in a variety of ways, from fairly straight forward to very complicated. Most people follow the least complicated route. They focus on making money when the price of a given stock goes up."

"The old *buy low-sell high* strategy," Goldman said. "And what is that strategy called?" he asked aggressively.

"Being *long* the market," said Charleze.

"Yes, that's right," said Goldman. "Have you heard that term, Thornton?" He thought the name Thornton sounded pretentious, and so he demeaned it by over pronouncing it.

"Being long the market?" Thornton squirmed and sat up straighter. "No, sir. I have never heard that terminology before."

"Well, if you haven't heard of being long the market, I'm sure you've never heard of being *short* the market." Still looking at Thornton, Goldman said, "Tell him about being short, or *shorting* the market, Charleze."

"I don't pretend to understand the complexities. But in general, a person who is long the market is trying to make money when the price of a given stock goes up, hence, buy low-sell high. On the other side of that coin, a person who is short the market is trying to make money when the price of a given stock goes down," Charleze took a breath and watched for Goldman's reaction.

"Don't stop now. You're on a roll," said Goldman. "How does an investor lose money?"

"Again, they're just the opposite. A person who is long a given stock loses money when the price of that stock goes down. Whereas, a person who is short a given stock loses money when the price of that stock goes up."

"Correct," said Goldman. "A stock picker who is long a stock buys at the current price, and after it goes up, sells at a higher price, pocketing the difference. And, yes, the process of shorting a stock is more complicated. First an investor identifies a stock he believes will decrease significantly in price. With the help of a broker, he borrows shares of that stock, and sells them at price Y. When the price of the targeted stock falls, the investor buys shares of that same stock at a lower price X. He is then able to return the shares he borrowed. The investor keeps the difference between what he obtained when he sold the borrowed stock at price Y, and what he spent when he bought the same stock at the lower price X."

"Oh, God. I think I'll stick to being long a stock," said Thornton, not realizing he'd verbalized his thoughts.

Goldman raised his eyebrows. "Thornton, I'm going to assign you to one of our people who specialize in being long the market." Thornton relaxed. Gesturing to the door, he directed, "Ask my secretary to give you a letter of introduction for Mr. Wykowski." He waited until Thornton left. Turning to Charleze he said, "Now, what do you know about hedge funds?"

"From what I've seen, that's where the action is," Charleze said. "Managing a hedge fund is the most challenging, the most complicated, the most difficult, the most intensive, the most risky, and the most lucrative. Hedge funds can make money whether the market goes up or down." Her eyes were shining. "People have told me that working in a hedge fund is measured like dog years. One year's work equates to seven years of experience." She paused, gathering her thoughts. "Hedge funds hold a large number of stocks in their portfolio. They use both long and short strategies, hence the term *hedge*. The manager's income is in part tied to gains and losses in the fund," she paused, her eyes alive as she thought. "Hedge funds have been called money market funds for the excessively wealthy. And individual hedge funds can be worth billions."

"I'm impressed, Charleze. I'll bet you even know what *two and twenty* means."

"Hedge funds typically charge their investors two percent of the entire investment plus twenty percent of the gain. Thus, two and twenty. Really successful hedge fund managers with impressive returns for their investors can demand more."

"Our hedge funds get three and thirty," boasted Goldman as he leaned back in his chair. "Of course, you know that hedge funds often make or lose millions of dollars every day. Like Darwin, it's survival of the fittest. The stress is indescribable, and scores of hedge funds go under each year. But the top managers thrive on the stress, and earn some of the most exorbitant salaries on Wall Street," he paused for effect. "Look around, Charleze. Who knows. This could be yours in five years."

Charleze could barely contain herself. She'd never had any money of her own and she ached for the security that wealth could bring, but she'd never dreamed of being this rich. "I can't wait," she breathed.

"I read through your resume and letters of reference. They're even better than mine were at your age—valedictorian from Bovarde, summa cum laude from Brown in economics, a masters with honors in business economics from Harvard, and you've almost completed your doctorate there as well." He whistled.

Charleze smiled modestly.

"I see a name change. You get married?"

"No, sir. I just had it changed when I graduated from high school," she said matter of factly.

Goldman chose not to pursue the issue. Looking at his notes, he said, "they say you are, 'bright, articulate, intense, a fast learner, hard working,' and, I like this one, 'clearly ambitious.' From what I've seen this afternoon, I believe them. I'm assigning you to one of our more successful hedge fund managers, and I'll be keeping a close eye on you. If you progress as I believe you can, I'll have a sweet offer for you when you graduate in the spring."

Charleze was ecstatic. "Thank you, sir. I'll work very, very hard. You will *not* regret this."

✳✳✳

"We want to welcome our new interns," the man said. "Over the years we've found it useful to orient interns to Wall Street jargon, sometimes called *street talk*. In your handouts you'll find an alphabetized listing of the terms used most frequently around here. It's like a foreign language, but you can't work effectively without mastering it."

Charleze skimmed the listing. She was comforted to see she already knew many of them—*accretive, asset class, balance sheet, bids, book value, BRIC, commodities, dilutive, dollar cost averaging, ETFs, futures market, limit orders, liquidity, market orders, market cap, moving averages, multiples, PE ratio, PEG ratio,* and *trailing stop loss.* But there were many others she wasn't sure about—*credit default swaps, derivatives, leveraging, margin calls, naked shorts, non-securitized debt, options market, puts and calls, second offerings, short squeeze, structured asset-backed securities, synthetic collateralized debt obligations,* and *uptick rule.* She also was not familiar with the foreign markets.

The man was saying, "... and so I encourage you to memorize these terms, even if you don't understand what they mean. Not all of these terms will apply to your particular placement, but you need to know them just the same. I'll do a few with you. Let's begin with *accretive.*"

***

"I'm Derrick Orz," he said extending his hand. "You'll be assigned to my office for the duration of the internship. You have lots to learn. This isn't a classroom. My team and I are not here to be your teachers. We're here to make money—all day, every day. There's always a market open somewhere in the world. And there's always something happening that affects those markets—a crisis, a major discovery, a war, or some other event," he said looking at his watch. "You're expected to study the manuals thoroughly, observe the process, and only ask questions when you know enough to ask *intelligent* questions. We'll answer questions and explain procedures as we can. The more you learn, the more we'll teach you. In the initial weeks, you'll be assigned to different components of the business every few days. My secretary has the manuals, the phones, and your schedule for the first week."

"Excuse me, sir. Phones?" asked Charleze.

"Yes. You'll carry three phones with you at all times. One for customers, one for brokers and bankers, and one for me. I must be answered by the second ring, regardless of what you're doing, or who you're talking to." Charleze nodded. "Look me up in three days. I expect you'll have a few intelligent questions to ask." He walked from his office leaving Charleze standing in front of his desk.

Charleze had been an exceptional student for the last twenty years. Studying the manuals was easy, and organizing her time came naturally. She devoured the literature provided, and searched out related articles on the internet. She familiarized herself with the unique computer programs designed to make market predictions based on the application of probability theory, and to secure instantaneous buy-sell orders. In between, she kept up with significant events of the world—weather, strikes, governmental coups, crop failures, bank failures, commodity shortages, ruptured oil pipelines, legislation, interest rates. By the third day she was ready for Orz. She had a list of *intelligent* questions, and she knew his schedule for the day. She would look him up.

***

May 1998 … Oh, My God. "Charleze. Charleze. Good to see you. Have a seat," said Ben Goldman as he gestured to a leather chair in front of his desk. Charleze sat.

"I've heard nothing but glowing reports from Orz. Not only have you performed exceptionally in your internship, but I understand you finished writing your dissertation in your *spare* time?"

"Yes, sir," Charleze said. "All I have to do is defend it next week, and I'll have all my requirements for graduation."

Goldman shook his head "Amazing." He paused. "You recall the promise I made when you began your internship with us?"

"Yes, sir. I do, sir."

"Well, the offer stands. I have an assistant hedge fund manager vacancy that I'd like you to fill. I won't take no for an answer."

"I consider it an honor, sir."

"Great! Now, I want you to have some transition time … get moved in, see a play, have a vacation. How about starting one month from today?"

"Yes. Oh, yes. Thank you, sir."

"And just so you don't forget us over these four weeks, I have a little something for you." He handed her an envelope. "Call it a signing bonus."

Charleze opened the envelope slowly to find a check for $50,000. She gasped.

"Not enough?" he teased.

"Oh, no, sir. This is enough … I mean, this is more than enough … I mean, this is wonderful. Thank you so much."

Goldman laughed. He'd guessed right. She didn't come from money. She would work hard for it.

CHAPTER 11

THE OPENING BELL: HER ADDICTION

JUNE *1998 ... Power.* Dr. Charleze Mitchell reported to Bear Stearns. Her new assistant manager position was assigned to their hottest hedge fund. She inhaled the opportunity, nestled quickly and adeptly into her new duties. But there was something she had not fully anticipated—stress. As an intern she had been insulated from the intense stress of having her livelihood on the line every minute of every day. Charleze adjusted, and soon learned to make stress her ally, giving her an edge. Her accuracy and timing were uncanny, especially with the riskiest and most lucrative stock selections. She mastered the plate-spinning skills of hedge fund management, being both long and short the market, making judicious use of leverage, and juggling other people's money. As for her own money, there was more than she'd ever dared imagine. And the more she made, the further she shielded herself from the pain of that never quite forgotten seven year-old girl.

But there was a dark side. Charleze became addicted to stress, to risk, and to power. Her addiction was not that different from a drug addiction, as her neurotransmitters provided a euphoric state. And she always craved more. Making more money became her raison d'être, regardless of how it was accomplished or who was hurt. She learned how to use the power of a multi-billion dollar hedge fund, speedier computers, and well-planted rumors to manipulate the market. She shorted companies and drove stock prices low enough to bankrupt them, collecting money all the way down.

In the summer of 2003, Charleze left Bear Stearns to open her own hedge fund, Tornadic Growth Investments. The market was on fire, and she rocketed to the top of her new game. At thirty-four, she cut a striking figure—tall, light brown skin, a very short afro, fine facial features, engaging eyes, and a signature walk. She made the most of these attributes by wearing short skirts and revealing blouses. Her status and appearance belied her ghastly childhood.

Charleze hired Willie "Mac" McMillan as her second in command. Mac had been schooled on the street. There was nothing academic, refined, or articulate about him. He loved to play hardball, in every respect. He was an in-your-face, action kind of guy, with an intuitive sense about the stock market. He was ruthless, with a great track record of picking winners. He clearly enhanced Charleze's place on the Street. She loved him for that, but not in the romantic, attached sense. Mac, though wealthy, did not belong in the same class of people she aspired to. No. She loved him for what he had been able to give her—more power, more money. For his part, he understood he had no chance of being involved romantically with this uptight, smiling in your face, back stabbing bitch. Yet he, too, thrived on their relationship, cementing their bond.

For four years Tornadic Growth Investments was highly successful. But all was not well on Wall Street. In 2007 the subprime mortgage crisis tsunami revved up. Over one hundred hedge funds had folded during the previous eighteen months, with a combined value of some forty-five billion dollars. The initial wave of an estimated eight million affected homeowners defaulted on their loans. In June of that year, Charleze's old firm, Bear Stearns, announced it was liquidating over three billion dollars of its assets to bail out two of its hedge funds created specifically to invest in subprime mortgage-backed securities. By August both those hedge funds had filed for bankruptcy.

The old investment strategies were no longer working. Tornadic Growth Investments was heavily leveraged. Lenders were demanding cash to offset the declines in the value of their subprime-based collateral. Investors were screaming for their money. Charleze scrambled to liquidate holdings in order to cover investment losses. This was a different kind of stress. She and her hedge fund were in big trouble. In December, 2007, she sat down with Mac for a serious tête-à-tête.

"How far are you willing to go to keep us afloat?" Charleze asked.

"I'll do *anything*." Mac said.

That's all the incentive Charleze needed. She laid out an audacious six-month plan to recoup hundreds of millions of dollars. But the cost for others would be high—personal pain, jobs, financial ruin, and, if necessary, death.

CHAPTER 12

FAMILIES: WHEN THE LEGACY OF VIOLENCE CONTINUES

VIOLENT *Beginnings … Mac.* Willie McMillan leaned back in his office chair, blowing smoke rings, staring emptily into them. It don't get no better than this, he thought. Well, maybe a broad. That's not a bad idea. I'll have to get out my little black book later.

He couldn't believe the last years. What a lucky break to team up with the wicked witch of the west—or was it the east? She knows how to play the game. She don't take shit from nobody, and she's smart as a whip. Yup, I was lucky. Of course, I've done good too. I've made both of us a boatload of money. And I'll make us even more once this deal goes through.

Ever since he was eleven Mac had felt lucky. He began to physically tighten up as childhood memories came flooding in. He remembered the stories his mother, Shelly McMillan, had told him.

His mother came from a middle class family. Grandpa was the local television news anchor. He smiled from the tube, but never at home. At home he regularly beat Mom and Grandma. Mom said it was a terrifying life. He was controlling, threatening and demanding. He insisted on an unlisted phone number, and banned them from using the phone. Except for school and grocery shopping, Grandpa rarely allowed Mom or Grandma to leave the house. Mom could not have friends over, and she was forbidden to go to her friends' homes. Grandpa was fond of using a doubled up extension cord, so Mom had horseshoe shaped bruises on her back, buttocks, legs and arms. She wore long sleeves and pants to school. He kept his slaps and punches away from her face, most of the time.

In the craziness of her life, she learned to know *love* only when she was being hit. Mom said it was better to be hit than ignored. Sometimes afterward, Grandpa would say he was sorry, give her a hug, and maybe a piece of candy. She learned how to set him off so he would hit her, and sometimes hug her. Mom fell for a guy just like Grandpa ... Brian was that guy. He always seemed to be angry about something.

"Shut that damned kid up or I will!" shouted Brian McMillan. He blamed Shelly for getting knocked up, for having a baby that cried, and for being less available to him sexually.

Shelly McMillan held her two month-old son closer and rocked him faster, "Shh, Willie. Nice and quiet, Willie. Rock-a-bye baby ..."

She remembered all too well when Brian had said the same thing before grabbing their first child. He picked up their infant daughter and shook her, yelling at her to shut up. Then she did—permanently. He acted as if his ten week-old daughter had been defective, as if he'd had nothing to do with her death. But the doctors in the ER didn't believe her when she told them, as Brian threatened her to say, that she'd dropped her baby. The autopsy confirmed bleeding behind her lovely brown eyes, and a swollen brain. Shaken Baby Syndrome was easily determined as the cause of death. They locked Brian up for three whole years.

Shelly struggled financially, taking jobs as a waitress and housekeeper. Brian kept writing her from prison telling her how sorry he was, how he loved her, how he was looking forward to being with her, and that they would make another baby. She so ached to be loved. She consumed his letters with unbridled denial and an indefensible sense of hope. Neither history nor reality played a role in this delusion. She convinced herself he truly meant it this time. And, in fact, the day he came home was wonderful. It was like a first date. They were anxious, excited. He moved more slowly than she'd ever remembered. Shelly welcomed him home.

Brian had been a mechanic, and even with his prison record, was able to find a job fairly easily. He made Shelly quit work, stay at home and serve him. Brian had to have dinner on the table when he came home from work. Sometimes he came home early. When dinner wasn't waiting for him he blew up, throwing things, then hitting Shelly. Sometimes he would take out his revolver and threaten her until he had extracted every ounce of fear from her. Later came the apologies and the promises to never do it again, followed by the love making. Baby Willie came along in short order. Shelly walked on eggshells constantly, and tried to teach Willie to do the same. The pattern was so familiar she would sometimes be confused. Was she the little girl who was being beaten by her abusive father, or, had she become her mother, powerless to protect her child?

Brian controlled his drinking during the week so he could maintain his job. When Willie was six or seven, he began to drink more heavily. He took to buying a few bottles of Jack Daniels on Fridays after work. At first he used a glass, but soon he was drinking straight from the bottle. He was a mean drunk, more terrifying than when he was sober. He would never just sit there, drink and fall asleep. He always came after Shelly or Willie. Once, Willie stepped between them to protect his mother. Brian really did a number on him, breaking several ribs. But Brian would not allow a trip to the ER. He just kept Willie out of school for a few weeks. Worried about the consequences, Brian repeatedly warned Shelly to keep her mouth shut, while he nervously made frequent apologies to Willie, promised never to do it again, and bought him toys.

Willie soon began to imitate Brian. He yelled at Shelly, belittled her, made angry demands. He pushed her several times, and once slapped her in the face with his open hand. He seemed to be surprised at his own behavior that day, and left the room. It wasn't long before teachers were sending reports home about Willie being a bully, beating up on boys and girls alike. There were stories about him torturing animals, and he was suspected of setting fires. Another generation of violent and assaultive perpetrators had been assured.

At first Brian seemed satisfied, almost proud to see that Willie had begun to emulate him. They joked as they made fun of Shelly. But it wasn't long before the weekend beatings were back on for both of them. By the time Willie was 11, Brian had settled into a predictable routine. Willie's senses would be on full alert. He could smell the alcohol two rooms away, and knew how much was left in the whiskey bottle by the intensity of the odor. He recognized the point when his father's speech was slurred just far enough, signaling that he would soon be coming for him. He could hear the floor boards make their first complaint when his father turned his attention to the back of the house where his bedroom was. And he could hear that damn song he used to hum as he looked for something to hit them with.

The temperature was cool in his Wall Street office, but Mac was dripping with sweat as the images came even more vividly.

Well, he wasn't going to get me that night, Mac thought, clenching his fists as he relived the pivotal event in his life. He was a big SOB and I was just a little guy. But I had a plan. Not tonight. It would stop tonight. I was ready for him. I opened my window, tied a sheet to my bed, and hung the other end through the open window. When he came in yelling my name like he always did, he staggered right over to the open window. I was hiding in the closet, watching through a small crack in the partially opened door. As soon as he bent down to look out the window I ran from the closet as fast as I could with my baseball bat in my hands. He never heard me coming. I whipped that bat around and hit him on the back of the head. He fell out of the window and landed three stories down on the sidewalk. The bastard was dead.

I couldn't believe it. I was so happy he was dead. I ran to tell Mom. But when I told her, she started screaming at me.

"What have you done?" she yelled. "What are we going to do with no money? What the hell were you thinking? You had no right to ruin my life."

My own mother turned on me. I hauled off and let her have it with my fist right in the mouth. I grabbed some clothes and ran out of the house, never looked back. All the foster homes and juvenile halls were a piece of cake after what I'd been through. At least I had food to eat.

Yeah, mine and anyone else's I wanted. I made sure every kid I ran into knew I'd killed my old man, and I'd kill them too if they crossed me.

Mac calmed as his thoughts shifted to his last foster home with Bob and Thelma Lawrence. At sixteen I was big and mean, but they gave me my space. Unlike my other foster parents, they treated me decently, and bought me nice clothes. Mr. Lawrence was a retired stock broker. He was always talking about the market. I didn't pay much attention. I thought it was a stupid waste of time. Mr. Lawrence took me to one of the brokerage houses. He told me to watch everything, but not to say a word. What I saw and learned had nothing to do with the stock market. I was totally blown away by the kind of clothes those guys wore, their suits, their shoes, their watches, and their fast cars. I wanted what they had.

Mac sighed. I tried to learn how to study the stocks, but I wasn't able to do all that reading and math. Instead, I learned to rely on my powers of observation and on my memory. It wasn't long before I was able to tune into the market. I didn't understand the mumbo-jumbo of the company balance sheets, but was able to read the psychology of the market, the panic selling, the lemming buying, and best of all, the timing. Many people describe the market in human terms, like *impulsive, ready, resistant, testing,* and *whimsical.* It was that part of the market I learned to read real well.

Once, while the Lawrences were out for the evening, I found their stash of bills. The next morning I went to the brokerage house and bought fifty shares of IBM stock. I really got off watching it go up. Within a year, the price of a share of IBM stock had doubled. I sold my shares and pocketed over five hundred dollars' profit. The Lawrences had always done right by me, so I returned their money to its hiding place. I used the profit as my bank roll, and within three years I grew it into six figures. I bought their clothes, their shoes, their watch, and eventually their car. I've worked Wall Street for twenty-six years, and working with the doc is my best gig so far.

I understand Mitchell real well. She may have gone to the fanciest schools and have all those initials after her name, but on the inside we're peas in a pod. We came from the same lousy home life, we live to take care of number one, and we don't trust nobody.

CHAPTER 13

THE FBI

MAY 28 ... *Maria Lopez*. My first assignment, and man, did I screw up, she thought. Not only was I so obvious that Proctor knew I was following him, but he actually saw me. Masterson will have my ass. Well, I did lose him when I ducked into that store parking lot. Listen to me. *I lost him*. I'm supposed to be tailing him, not the other way around. Oh, I wish I was back on desk duty at the Crimes Unit, thought Special Agent Maria Louisa Lopez.

Maria was a twenty-five year-old with a spanking new master's in criminology. Her brother was an MP, on his second tour in Iraq. Over the years he had told her story after story. She couldn't help herself. She wanted to be in law enforcement, too. She had always been into athletics, could take care of herself, used to hunt rattle snakes in the central Texas hill country, had a pretty good academic record, and was unusually good on the firing range. She applied to the graduate school in criminology at UT Austin. She was so excited when she was accepted, and her brother was so proud when she graduated. Then she read this shiny ad in the trade magazine touting the joys of working for the Federal Bureau of Investigation. She applied and was invited to attend the Academy. She sailed through the training at Quantico, as well as an orientation to the Financial Crimes Section, and was promptly assigned to Memphis.

Hell, she wasn't even sure where Memphis was. The Bureau had secured a furnished apartment for her. As instructed, she took a twenty minute cab ride from the airport to an apartment complex in east

Memphis, off Park Avenue. She picked up the keys at the manager's office, along with a *Welcome To Memphis* bag of treats, ads, and information. An SUV was parked in her assigned parking spot. The keys were on the kitchen counter, with a note that said she was to report to her supervisor Monday morning at eight sharp. That gave her almost a week. She spent the time learning her way around the city, and grocery shopping.

***

May 26 ... Lawrence Masterson. The newly assigned Memphis area field supervisor was Special Agent Lawrence W. Masterson, a veteran with the Economic Crimes Unit of the FBI's Financial Crimes Section. The ECU worked closely with the Securities and Exchange Commission. Ten days ago he had been uprooted from his long time office in New York City and, to quote him, was "shipped to this backwater town in the middle of two cotton fields where the only hill is a flat street named Mount Moriah. All you need to know in Memphis is Elvis Presley, Federal Express, pork barbecue, and Northwest Airlines. And the Civil War may be over, but the war of the black and white races remains in full swing. Oh, yeah. It's hotter than hell."

He recently received word that his first and only staff person was being assigned. He was reading a description of his soon-to-be very own special investigator. He'd rolled his eyes so much they hurt. What the hell is this? he thought. I'm not ready for retirement yet, but I bet Special Agent Maria Louisa Lopez will help me get there. He picked up the letter and started to read it for fourth time, hoping it would be different this go-round.

Maria stands all of 5' ½". She has curly black hair that she wears just off the shoulder. She is fun-loving, outgoing, enthusiastic, and has extremely high energy. She always seems to be eating something, yet never gains an ounce. She can be a tad ditzy now and then, but she is a crack shot.

"Who writes this shit?" he said aloud. "It sounds like something written in a high school year book by a favorite sorority sister. I can hardly wait."

***

At precisely eight o'clock Maria knocked on the door.

"Come on in," Masterson bellowed. "It's the hallway door. It's not locked."

Maria lost her enthusiastic smile. She blew out a long breath upwards, fluttering her free-spirited bangs, turned the knob, and walked in. She found herself in what appeared to be a reception area, but with no furniture, no receptionist. The walls were the classic moveable beige metal ones. She could see a light to the right and moved in that direction. Rounding the corner, she came face to face with a huge Black man, beads of sweat glistening on the top of his balding head, and a full mustache. It was not that he was tall, he wasn't. But he seemed to fill the room. He had a rather large stomach which was placing a serious strain on the three lower buttons of his sweat stained shirt, and a scowl that made the rolls on his forehead fold over on one another. She screwed up her courage, and with her best posture and in her most assertive voice said,

"Sir. Special Agent Lopez reporting." There was a long silence. Maria smiled slightly.

"Well don't just stand there with that shit-eatin' grin. Sit down," said Masterson, and he took a seat behind a large wooden desk. "We are it," he announced.

"Sir?" questioned Maria, as she took a seat.

"We're it." Masterson said again, as if saying it twice would make it more understandable. Then reconsidering, he clarified, "Ain't nobody here but us chickens."

Maria made a face, her mouth hung open.

"Close your mouth, Lopez, and return your eyebrows to their full, upright and locked position," Masterson said. He leaned forward, placing his forearms on the desk, as if in a football stance. "Here's the

deal. This is a shit assignment. Me and you are gonna make the best of
it. We have only one investigation underway, and we already have two
dead bodies."

Maria felt as if she had just been zapped with a lightening bolt. She
couldn't even mouth the words *two dead bodies* that were screaming in
her brain.

Masterson continued. "The SEC had been receiving complaints
about a hedge fund named Tornadic Growth Investments, managed by
Charleze Mitchell. The complaints allege illegal manipulation of individual stock prices. I was working the case back in New York. Mitchell is
one smart cookie. It turns out that her second in command is someone
the authorities have known for quite a while, one Willie McMillan,
aka Mac. He's been in trouble with the law ever since he was a kid.
In fact, there's an unsubstantiated rumor that he killed his own father
when he was only nine or ten. Find something dirty on Wall Street,
and chances are that Mac is lurking somewhere in the bushes. But there
never seems to be any hard evidence. Then we received a seemingly
unrelated complaint out of Memphis from a Dr. Haverford Sturgeon.
He is, correction, *was* the lead engineer at BP Technologies. His department was completing the final R&D phase for a new artificial hip joint.
What I hear is this joint is so advanced it'll revolutionize the industry."

He took a long drink from the bottle of water sitting on his desk.
"Anyway, the boss sent me to parley with him. We met two hundred
miles away in Nashville, because he was concerned about being seen
talking to the feds. He told me that all he had were bad feelings. He
was really quite jazzed, and I didn't know if he was some kinda nut
scientist or what." After another long pull on the water bottle, he went
on. "So, I'm sitting there thinking I could have called this one in while
watching reruns of Gilligan's Island, and I'm still waiting for the punch
line. That's when Sturgeon starts to talk about Wall Street. He says that
BP Technologies is preparing for a monster spike in their stock price as
soon as they announce the results of the R&D and their timetable for
production of this new hip. He tells me that it's pretty common for a few
investors to short a company after an announcement like this because

of the high probability of unforeseen problems in the device, and the resulting recalls and lawsuits, which would drive down the price of the stock. Okay, I'm still waiting, but I'm more interested. He says there are rumors one particular hedge fund has been making inquiries at several brokerage houses about being first in line to short his company's stock after it pops. So, I start to play connect the dots, and Sturgeon is looking a lot less loony tunes, and a lot smarter."

Maria hadn't been paying attention. She was still stuck back at *two dead bodies*. I joined the ECU precisely because stock brokers' worst injuries were carpal tunnel syndrome and paper cuts, she thought. Nobody ever got murdered. This isn't happening—

"Lopez! Hello! Anyone home? Lopez!"

She became aware of Masterson yelling at her.

"Did I put you to sleep? Don't tell me. They didn't teach you any of this basic stock market shit in your shake 'n bake training program? Or maybe you slept through that lecture?"

Maria just sat there with a glassy eyed stare.

"Oh, my God! It's even worse than I thought," he said.

Masterson got up and left the room.

"I'm gonna find a razor," he said.

CHAPTER 14

THE SMILE

VIOLENT *Beginnings … A Coping Strategy.* Charleze had learned long ago how to use a smile, how to hide behind it, how to disarm someone with it. Aside from her intelligence, the smile was just about the only survival tool she'd had at her disposal as a young child coping with her parents. Refusing to do something resulted in her being screamed at, demeaned, and threatened. Mouthing off brought a slap. Hiding only meant more of the same. So it was early on that she discovered the smile.

No matter how scared she was, she smiled. No matter how much she hated to do something, she smiled. And certainly, no matter what she was thinking about someone, she smiled. As a cute child, and now as an attractive woman, the smile had the most potent impact on people. They didn't get as mad, or they didn't stay as mad, or they didn't realize what she was really up to, or they thought she was interested in them.

Charleze grew up associating pain with a smile, exploitation with a smile, belittlement with a smile, rejection with a smile, and rage with a smile. A smile was supposed to reflect emotions like joy, happiness, satisfaction, perhaps even love. Despite all her intellectual attributes, she had never been able to disconnect the associations of those emotional opposites. At some level, Charleze understood the confusion. Yet, without help, she never had the energy or motivation to do something about it. Besides, the smile was still one of her best tools. It was an easy substitute for a positive social or emotional response, and, it projected social acceptability. But, when at her worst, the smile obscured the figurative knife she could drive into someone's back, without their ever knowing it was coming, or from where it had come. Those very few who understood her, like Mac, knew to be aware of the smile, as it too often signaled deceit.

Her human need to be held had been frustrated as an infant, a toddler, a child, an adolescent, and now as an adult. Her most gratifying interpersonal experiences had been with Susan Determan, but she hadn't allowed herself to get too close. Her primary emotional focus was self. Attachment and empathy remained light years away. Charleze hadn't learned to trust her emotions, and, at the slightest exposure, retreated to her intellectual world where she was competent, where she was somebody, where she was safe.

Longing for safe companionship, she convinced herself to buy a dog. It was like trying to walk after having been in a full body cast—difficult, painful, and foreign. Kiska, an off-white Alaskan Husky with one blue eye and one green, was the perfect dog. He thrived on being around Charleze. He loved touching her and being touched by her, and he tolerated her crazy schedule. She dared to experience emotional ties to another being for the first time. She cared for Kiska, and enjoyed taking care of him. She looked forward to being with him. She felt pain when he was hurt. And, she allowed herself to become attached to him. She was aware of feelings she had never let herself experience before.

After six years, Kiska died. Charleze, like a three year old, couldn't forgive Kiska for leaving her, and at the same time believed she was to blame. It would be years before she dared open herself up to another being.

CHAPTER 15

THE NEW YORK – MEMPHIS CONNECTION

M AY *28 ... Monitoring from Afar.* Mac's iPhone was buzzing. He checked the screen and smiled.

"Speak good words to me," Mac said as he answered the phone ... "When?" ... "What did they find?" ... "What did Durnst do?" ... "I'll bet the cops were shitting on themselves having to deal with Durnst." ... "Lacy did *what*? That pipsqueak." ... "The video's been melted down, right?" ... "Good." ... "They still haven't found him, have they?" ... "Yeah, yeah. I know you told me, but I'm naturally the nervous type. How are we on the Forest Brothers merchandise?" ... "Yes, I'll wire your money tomorrow." ... "Keep me posted. I don't want to have to come down there again."

Mac knew he would be going to Memphis at least once more. He left to meet with Mitchell.

***

"Where are we on taking care of that problem?" smiled Charleze, masking a cauldron of intensity. "Everything is riding on our pulling this off."

Mac ignored the smile, and went to the heart of her question. "Don't get your panties in a wad, doc. I took care of Sturgeon personally, and nobody's the wiser."

"Yes, but Sturgeon isn't the only one who's been putting the pieces together," she said, maintaining her composure, almost singing as she emphasized key words. "Your man screwed up. From what I've heard, he was running and bleeding all over the place. Someone must have seen something."

Still in sync with Charleze's message, Mac glared. "From what you've heard? Who the hell've you been talking to? You got someone on the inside that I don't know about? Don't you even think about crossing me?"

"I wouldn't dream of it, Mac. But like you, I don't trust anybody. And I need to have as many ears on the ground as possible," said Mitchell, pretending to have been hurt by a misinterpretation of her motives.

"I'm telling you not to worry about my part of the plan. That's what you pay me for. Nobody's gonna find him. All traces of blood were cleaned up, and the security video was melted. No trace. No problem," said Mac.

"What about White, Osborne, and Proctor?" asked Mitchell.

"They don't even know what it is that they know. They won't be a problem. And, if they are, they won't be a problem for long," said Mac with a smile of his own, though a menacing one.

"You'll see to it personally?"

"Damn straight." He was matching her jab for jab. Except Charleze had definitely outclassed and out finessed him in this round. She was Mohamed Ali, floating like a butterfly and stinging like a bee, to his incredible Hulk of raw anger and aggression.

"And BPTX?" she asked, using the stock ticker symbol for BP Technologies.

"My man on the inside will do his thing as soon as they go into production. And he's very hungry. He'll do what I tell him, and he'll do us a good job."

"No screw-ups, Mac."

"Don't worry about me. You just take care of your part, and make damn sure you're ready to short the hell out of their stock," he said as he locked eyes with her. Neither one blinked.

*****

The man was smoking as an expression of his agitation, taking deep drags followed by a forced exhaling of smoke. His thoughts were coming rapidly. *So he thinks it's my fault. He thinks I screwed up. He thinks I don't know how to handle things on the ground. Well I've got news for him. When it's all over, I'll be waiting right here. His 5th Avenue duds don't impress me a bit. I knew him back in the day. I know how he thinks. I know how he acts.* "Here, Macky Macky. Come to papa, you son of a bitch," said Cory "Sneak" Roberts, as he patted his compact Smith & Wesson semi-automatic.

Sneak and Mac had done a stretch in a juvenile corrections facility together. They learned how to survive in the kiddy joint. Sneak's specialty was doing odd jobs. He never went anywhere without his good luck charms, his Smith & Wesson and his brown pocket spiral notebook. They were his trademarks. At five-seven and nondescript, he easily blended into any crowd. He was an accomplished pick pocket. He was very observant, would patiently spend days on a stakeout, and had been known to have wasted a few people when the money was right. Mac had waved seventy-five thousand dollars in front of him when he asked him to take care of a little problem. Sneak agreed, but he didn't trust Mac, and had expected all along that he would be on Mac's to-do list.

Mac had a second man in Memphis who had two jobs. One was his own, and the other was watching Sneak. Mac had called in some personal markers. He arranged for false papers and false letters of reference so that *Paul Chisholm* would present as an extraordinary candidate for the newly vacated buyer position at BP Technologies. The telephone calls from well connected people were a special touch, and helped seal the deal. Of course, Mac also helped by arranging a little accident for the previous buyer. Arranging accidents had been his specialty since he was eleven. For his part, Paul was good on his feet. He'd made his reputation as a con man extraordinaire. He was extremely personable and could fit in just about anywhere. He was accepted quickly into the social side of the organization, and soon identified the behind the scenes power people he could go to when he needed something. Companies were not that different from the military. There was always an effective supply sergeant type who could scrounge anything, and he would make good use of that connection.

CHAPTER 16

FBI: TAKE TWO

MAY *26 ... Starting Over.* Maria had not moved since Masterson left. She wasn't sure whether he was looking for a razor to cut her throat or to slit his wrist. She didn't blame Masterson for freaking out. She was mortified by her actions. She deserved it. After the longest ten minutes on record, he returned. He had obviously regained whatever composure he'd had. Without a word, he walked around his desk and sat down with obvious slowness. He stretched his arms forward, again placing his forearms on the desk. He cleared his throat. Quietly and slowly he said, "What if you tell me what it is that you think you've heard this morning."

Maria began, equally quietly, but carefully. "Well, sir, I heard that we are the only ECU staff in this region. We have one open case, and we have two dead bodies." She took a few breaths. "You were in New York investigating complaints on a hedge fund run by someone named Trapeze? And she works with a very bad person named Max? Then you came to Memphis, no, Nashville to meet with some nut engineer about a telephone call he'd overheard? You met for drinks in a snazzy hip joint. And I kinda got lost after that ... sir."

Masterson exhaled. "The mind boggles." He rolled his eyes, again. "You may want to write some of this down." Maria took out a pad and pen.

"Okay, yes, it's just the two of us in this office," he said. "I'm not expecting them to send anyone else. Yes, we are only working one case.

Yes, there are two bodies—that I know of. The New York hedge fund is called Tornadic Growth Investments and is managed by a woman named Charleze, Charleze Mitchell. And, her right hand man is Willie McMillan, also known as Mac. And yes, he is a bad dude. Allegedly killed his father at age nine or ten, remember?" Maria's eyes widened and she nodded. "Stay with me, now. Sturgeon from BP Technologies here in the Memphis area was a brilliant man. He's the second one to have been killed. He and his assistant developed a new type of artificial replacement joint for hips. It's expected to revolutionize the business. Nod every once in a while, Lopez, so I know you're still with me."

Maria looked up from her note pad and nodded. Masterson then walked slowly through the key points of this investigation,

"One, BP Technologies plans to announce very good news about its new artificial hip joint. Two, many investors, hoping to make money, will buy stock symbol BPTX, expecting it to rise considerably thereby increasing the value of their shares. Three, a few investors will be betting against the stock, and will short BPTX when it reaches the top of its climb in hopes it will drop big time afterwards, thus making them lots of money. Four, and, the point that Sturgeon was making, someone is actively planning to gamble an unusually large sum of money in betting against the BPTX stock, implying that they have some advance information the stock will drop."

"Oh, that's not fair, is it?" Maria said.

Masterson had been trying so hard to maintain his composure—no small feat. "It's called *illegal*, Lopez." But, at least he could tell she was listening, and just maybe she had some grasp of the situation.

"And, that would mean that the person who's been contacting all those brokerage houses in preparation to short BPTX stock must have some way of knowing that the joints will fail," said Maria, wide-eyed.

"There *is* a God! Yes Lopez, that's exactly the key to this crime. And, in the meantime two people are already dead, which makes me think that McMillan is somewhere in the mid-south bushes. Now we need to find the evidence and nail these crooks."

"Where do we start?" asked Maria.

"Well, it so happens, Sturgeon's assistant Dr. Carl Huong called me just after Sturgeon was killed in a car accident. He expressed the same concerns as his boss. He gave me the names of three people who had some technical dealings with the two of them, and might have knowledge of what has been happening. One is a current graduate student who Huong is supervising in a field placement. The other two are former students who trained under the two docs several years ago. My biggest concern now is that Huong has gone missing. I'm afraid he could be victim number three."

"Have you been in contact with the police?" asked Maria.

"Good question, Lopez. No, not yet. Mostly because the police declared that Michael Tibett's and Sturgeon's deaths were accidental. And I didn't have any evidence that some big crime is about to be committed."

"Who is Michael Tibett, and why do you think he and Sturgeon were murdered?" asked Maria, reading from her note pad.

"Tibett was the lead buyer in the purchasing department of BP Technologies. The belief that he and Sturgeon were both killed is just based on twenty-seven years of investigative experience. It's only a hunch," said Masterson. "But, if you follow my logic, and you've been hanging in there pretty good so far, Lopez, getting rid of a buyer could improve the chances of purchasing some inferior merchandise." He paused. "I know it's a stretch, but that's my thinking right now."

"What about the three people that Huong named?" asked Maria.

"I don't know what I think about them. I haven't been able to find the first one, Dorothy Osborne. The other two, Joshua Proctor and Allison White work for a competing medical device company here in the area. But according to Huong, they are very trustworthy. So, it could be that whatever they know may be an issue for whoever is masterminding this thing."

"Like Mac and Charleze," said Maria.

"Bingo! You get the stuffed bear," said Masterson. "Sounds as if you're ready to do something. I think you should keep tabs on Proctor.

Just follow him for now. See if anyone else seems to be interested in him. I'll look after White. We don't want either one of them to be next."

***

The Proctors live in a small Memphis neighborhood called Hein Park, which abuts the east side of the Rhodes College campus. Rhodes is a small private college with a well maintained campus and uniquely designed buildings, all covered with stone harvested from their own quarry. The majority of houses in Hein Park are large two story brick homes, built in the 1920s. The lots tend to be expansive and covered with large trees, shrubs and flowers. The streets are narrow, with parallel drainage cuts, and no curbs or sidewalks, lending a sense of quiet and charm. The Proctors' home is located on a side street just north of an abundantly treed six lane boulevard named, North Parkway. On the south side of North Parkway is Overton Park, a large urban park.

Down on one knee in the heavily wooded northeast corner of Overton Park was Sneak. He was looking across North Parkway into the Hein Park subdivision. His binoculars were trained on the Proctors' house, as he watched a team of tree trimmers work in a large willow oak. "Come on, guys," encouraged Sneak. "Just cut those two limbs to the right. Yeah, there goes one." A short time later, "and there goes the other. Perfect. Now I can see straight into the side window." He smiled as he jotted down land marks in his brown spiral pocket notebook.

CHAPTER 17

FAMILIES: A SECOND CHANCE

VIOLENT *Beginnings ... Julia.* The only light came from a fat maroon candle. Billy Joel sang mournfully in the background. She was swallowed up in a large cloth bean bag chair, with a cold bottle of Michelob in her hand, and a towel around her sweaty neck. Still wearing the tattered pair of the old fashioned cotton sweat pants and a faded Dallas Cowboy's sweatshirt from her evening yoga workout. Her big toe peaked out from the sweat sock on her right foot. Julia Todd was feeling existential.

The meaning of life according to Billy Joel? Hell, no. He even walked away from Christie Brinkley. What was *he* thinking? The real question is what is the meaning of *my* life? Just look at me. I'm a mess. Julia Todd was having a bad hair night as her thoughts tumbled out. Getting involved with the Proctors was like getting too close to the flame. What a couple. What a family. Those are two things that have eluded me, and in some ways, have defined me.

She looked over at her bookshelf, and found the outlines of three framed pictures. She couldn't see the faces for the candle flame reflected in their glass covers, but she knew them by heart. The smallest one was of a family with two parents and two preschoolers, a boy and a girl. Everyone was smiling. Except for the more modern dress and hairdos, it looked like a Norman Rockwell family. Yet behind the all-American smiles were a physically and emotionally abusive mother, and a father who was rarely around. Everything got worse after the divorce. Julia and her younger brother Wayne endured broken bones, boiling water, welts, bruises, belittlement, and shame. She was ten and her brother seven when protective services took them out of Arizona and placed them with Aunt Louise. She'd never paid much attention to Aunt Louise before. She looked in the direction of a larger second framed picture she knew to be of an older woman and two young children. No one was smiling. Aunt Louise was her father's sister. She lived half way across the country, in Memphis. She had no husband, no children. She'd agreed to take them, but not without resentment.

Julia continued her memory trip. Aunt Louise was probably in her late forties or early fifties when she took us in. We thought she was so old back then. She'd never married. She wore her hair in a bun, and rarely smiled. She lived in a large house in east Memphis, and was a librarian at the main branch of the Public Library on Peabody Street. Never married, never smiled, a librarian. So cliché. But so, Aunt Louise. A laugh exhaled through her nose as she imagined Aunt Louise with her index finger to her lips shushing someone.

It was a rocky first few months as the three of us struggled to adjust to our new lives. I suppose part of it was the shock of one day being in Mommy's dominating and often scary presence, and then the next day being in Aunt Louise's house where everything was unknown. As for Aunt Louise, I'm certain she was overwhelmed by our invasion of her perfectly structured, labeled and organized world.

Julia took a slow sip of her beer. I admit, Wayne and I did push the limits of Aunt Louise's patience. One day she really got mad at Wayne. She pulled her hand back to whack him, and I jumped in and grabbed her arm with both hands. I told her she would not hit my brother. I remember that we looked at each other for a long time, mostly just trying to understand the situation we both found ourselves in. She didn't pull her arm away from me, and I didn't let go of her. We just sort of both began to relax. She brought her arm down and I released my grip. Aunt Louise dropped into a nearby large overstuffed chair, still looking at me, and then at Wayne, who knew better than to say anything.

"Come here, child," she said in a quiet, gentle way.

I'm not sure why, but I wasn't afraid. I walked over to her, and she scooped me on her lap. We looked at each other a little longer. "Come here my little guardian," she said, as she gently pulled me into her and held me, and I let her.

It wasn't long before Wayne was inching his way over to the big chair. Aunt Louise reached down and picked him up as well. The three of us stayed there for what seemed a long time. Everything changed that day. We became a family. Aunt Louise never hit either one of us. Julia looked again at the framed pictures until she found the largest one. She knew there were three smiling people in that picture. She felt warmed.

But the feeling cooled as she considered her single status. I've never seemed to find the right guy. Of course, what guy wants to spend the rest of his life with a pistol packin momma, who's used to giving men orders and expecting them to be followed, keeps crazy ass hours, and loves to hit a workout bag? Oh, there have been a few who were brave enough to try, but it just never seemed to work out.

Anderson was a dream. His eyes, his smile, his chest, his body … Ooh. She closed her eyes and imagined the two of them at the beach, and then, afterwards. She moaned softly. Then her eyes flew open. The lights were always on, but nobody was home. He had no opinions on politics, no concept of people who lived outside Memphis, let alone on the other side of the world. He couldn't carry on an intelligent conversation. He was amazingly sexist in his beliefs. His idea of speaking another language was talking Bubba speak to his drunk buddies at the local bar. He watched nothing but sports on television. He never read anything except the Sunday funnies. And, kids. Forget it. How in the world did I get hooked up with Anderson?

Oh, yeah, the body.

"Ooh."

Travis was a renaissance man. He had two master's degrees, one in English, one in political science, and a PhD in British analytic philosophy. He could hold an intelligent conversation with anyone about anything. He had opinions he hadn't even thought about yet. Her smile faded. Oh, yeah—the opinions. I never seemed to agree with his ideas. And of course, my opinions were always wrong. And he had a well thought out rationalization for everything he wanted to do, even if it was illegal. He never seemed to know how to hold me, or treat me as an equal. How in the world did I get hooked up with Travis?

Oh, yeah, his mind.

"Ooh."

Worthington Whozits the third was high society. He came from generations of Old South cotton money. He'd attended only the most exclusive schools. And he helped run the family business. He loved his cars, his horses, and his high society parties. He always looked like he just stepped out of a magazine, the clothes, the shoes, and the bling. She shook her head. But I never really fit in with his family or with his crowd. After all, I was an impoverished foreigner from Arizona, *for god sakes*. At first, having a cop around was unique, and interesting. I was the flavor of the month. But, I could never figure out where to carry my pistol, and the newness of me soon faded as his friends worried about where to stash their drugs. He exchanged me for a leggy, blondish accessory. How in the world did I get hooked up with Worthington?

Oh, yeah, the excitement of his money.

"Ooh."

I need a man who is just a little of each of those guys—reasonably good looking, intelligent and gainfully employed. A man who appreciates me as a woman and as a cop. A man who is a good lover, and a best friend. A man who wants to have children. There must be a man like that out there somewhere. "The Piano Man" was playing. Maybe this year? she mused.

"Ooh."

CHAPTER 18

WORKING THROUGH IT: A BEGINNING

MAY 29 ... *The Talk*. The alarm went off at 4:30. Josh and Tonya set aside early Thursday and Saturday mornings to workout at the YWCA. They were tired of being mad, and besides, they truly missed one another. And so their silence just naturally broke.

"Wanna go?"

"I guess. You?"

"Okay."

They pulled on their sweats, collected their exercise bags, and piled into the car for the eight-minute trip.

At six, he watched as she swam her final laps. Tonya had been a competitive swimmer in her pre-college days. Her strokes were fluid and strong, and she still had remarkable endurance. Kind of how she approached life, it occurred to him. Her confidence and poise only made her appear taller than her five-six. She still looked good in a bathing suit, and he still liked watching her hips pop up as she did her flip turns at each end of the pool. Except for the addition of a smallish tummy, there was no evidence of her having born two children. If anything, the last seventeen years had added a sexy maturity to her figure. She tended more to the practical, as she preferred to wear pants so she could get on the floor with her young clients. She wore little make-up, and often just pulled her long hair into a ponytail.

Tonya pulled herself from the water, grabbed a towel, and began to dry off as she walked back to her flip flops. She caught sight of Josh sitting in the raised bleachers that lined one side of the pool. She acknowledged him with a small wave. Josh had been working-out in the weight room. His favorite holey T-shirt was soaked with sweat, and his muscles were still a little pumped up from the workout. He looked good. Though he was not too happy about losing some of his hair, she found his retreating hairline made him even more attractive, especially now that he had begun having his barber cut his remaining hair shorter. He still had it.

Josh worked his way down the bleachers to the bottom corner, and Tonya climbed the three steps to meet him. They sat together.

"You look great," Josh said.

"You too," she said.

They sat in silence a while. Tonya broke in, "I hate it when we don't talk."

"Me, too."

"And we haven't really talked since this thing began."

Josh started to question her comment, but then understood she meant that *other* kind of talking. Staring into the sparkling waters of the pool, he managed a small, tight lipped smile of agreement, but did not offer to lead off. In these kinds of talks, he was not unlike Daniel, whose comfort level precluded his initiating hugs, but he was quite willing to passively accept them.

"Have you seen the notes from the schools?" she asked. Josh looked lost, shook his head. "Daniel was sent to the office for fighting, and Ollie has been crying a lot, for no apparent reason."

"What's going on with Daniel? He knows better than that."

"Daniel's scared. They're both scared. They're afraid for you."

"They seem okay, to me," he said, still considering his point about fighting.

"That's because they're trying to show you what they think you want to see. They don't want to upset you." She took his hand. "You've been acting differently around us."

"Different? I'm not acting different. I think I've been doing really well. I'm dealing with a lot of crap. But still, I talk. I listen. I try to be strong," Josh said defensively.

"It may feel like that to you, but, that's not what I see." Tonya said. "And I'm sure that's not what the kids see."

Josh rolled his eyes, shook his head and exhaled loudly. "What is it I'm supposed to be doing?" he said, pulling his hand back.

"You don't talk to us. And when you do, you're impatient and angry, like now."

"Like now?"

"Josh, I know you're scared. We are too. But it feels like you're mad at us. We've been walking on eggshells." She could feel her eyes welling up, her throat closing. "Ollie asked me if you still love her." Josh looked up to see Tonya's tears.

"I ... I've never stopped loving Ollie. Or Daniel. Or you," he said. Silence.

When he spoke again, his fist was clenched, his voice loud. "What am I supposed

to do? I can't get on top of this. I'm so frustrated. I can't solve it. And my emotions ... I can feel anger raging in me. I can't control it. I'm afraid. And I'm afraid for all of you." For a moment, he surrendered. Tears formed.

Tonya grabbed hold of him, sweaty T-shirt and all.

CHAPTER 19

THE BLOODY FINGERPRINT

MAY *29 ... New Information, More Questions.* Six éclairs and $14.78 later, Julia had Huong's hidden CD, and the lab's findings from his computer and coffee cup. She was so excited she didn't know which to look at first. She chose the lab's report, saving the CD for later. The computer address book, as well as a list of incoming and sent email addresses was printed out. Good, she could cross check the names against the ones she received from Josh last night. There were lots of emails back and forth between Huong and Sturgeon, and several to Allison and Josh. That only made sense. She scanned the report, as it listed several websites. One of the most frequently accessed was a brokerage site that displayed information about stocks. Others included the Securities and Exchange Commission, and Tornadic Growth Investments, a hedge fund.

There was a handwritten notation in the report:

Finger prints pulled from coffee cup match those found on both chartreuse envelopes, including the ones found in blood.

Julia stared. She tried to pull her thoughts together. "Huong is the chartreuse envelope guy?" she said to herself. That's why Allison White saw an iridescent chartreuse envelope in his office. Is it Huong's blood that's on Joshua's envelope? Is he the man who was shot or stabbed by an unknown woman, probably the same woman who followed Josh last night in a black Ford Explorer? Was Huong trying to warn or threaten

Sturgeon and Josh? Is Huong dead? Did the mystery woman deliver the bloody envelope to Josh? If so, why?

She put down the lab report and retrieved the CD from its blue plastic case slipping it into her computer. "Whoa! This is way over my head," she whispered as she scrolled through pages of technical drawings and specifications, chart after chart of statistical research data. Maybe I can get Josh to interpret this. I bet the lab techs are not the only ones who work for food. Any éclairs left? She picked up the phone. "Tag could you grab the professor and come in here?"

Tagger and Marino appeared. "You wanted to see us, Lieutenant?"

Julia pushed the lab report over to them. "Take a look at this." She waited till they got to the good stuff.

"Oowee!" Tagger exclaimed. "I didn't see that one coming."

"It's like dumping everything out and starting all over," Marino said. "Is Huong one of the good guys, or does he wear a black hat?"

"That's the sixty-four million dollar question," Julia said. "Help me walk through these scenarios. Tag, you take the argument for Huong being the good guy. Marino, you take the bad guy perspective." They worked for a good ten minutes. Each had reasonable arguments. Each argument had holes.

"Why do we always seem to be getting blindsided by new information?" asked Julia. "It feels like we're in a puppet show, and someone else is pulling the strings. This is a lot bigger than we've been thinking. What're we missing?"

No response.

"Where do we go from here?" Marino asked.

"I keep saying that in the face of not knowing, we're better off just chipping away with basic knock on every door police work. Marino you go to Huong's house and collect some hair samples that we can use to compare DNA with the blood on the envelope. Then we'll know for sure if it is Huong's. I know I don't have to tell you to be gentle with his daughter. Tag, see if you can run down that black Ford Explorer that was following Josh last night."

"That should be easy. Let's see. Do we know which state's plate? No.

Do we have a tag number? No. Do we have an approximate age, race, size, or description of the woman? No."

"If it were that easy, I'd have given it to Marino," Julia said.

Tagger smiled.

"I'll get with Josh and see what he can make of the CD you found, professor," she said. "I may also want to tail Josh a few times myself to see if I can pick up anything or anyone."

"Say, Lieutenant," said Marino. "I'm seeing quite a bit of stuff on the stock market in Sturgeon's papers. I don't know if it means anything, but I noticed that the lab report indicated lots of hits by Huong on stock related websites. Maybe it's nothing more than a mutually keen interest in watching BPTX stock go up, but it is something. I want to check Huong's computer to see if there might be any overlap."

"Go for it."

CHAPTER 20

THE DEVICE

MAY 29 ... *A Texas State Trooper.* Josh's eyes were wide and he wore a big grin as he read through the contents of Huong's CD. "This is amazing ... Oh, that's how they resolved that tension problem ... Yes, of course ... That is so creatively simplistic ... What a beautiful design ... Oh, not there ... Yes, there ..."

Josh felt in awe of what his mentor Hav and Carl had put together. It was without a doubt the best piece of work he'd ever seen. He reviewed the statistical outcome data on the new device. That looks good, he thought ... Yes ... At the .01 level of statistical significance ... The control groups didn't have near the flexibility ...

"Everything looks great here," he said. "Same down here." He read aloud. "All superior materials, parts and adhesives. New surgical instruments and surgical techniques shown to be far superior." He followed an asterisk to its corresponding footnote heading, *Use of materials, devices, adhesives from any of the following companies must be prohibited.*

"Here's Forest Brothers Industries listed as having substandard surgical screws," he said. "I remember a recall notice on those."

"So, is there anything we can use?" asked Julia.

"Not unless you need a total hip replacement," said Josh. "You can't imagine how brilliant this device is. I've never seen anything like it."

"Thanks for driving in and being our expert. Any idea why Huong would have hidden this CD?"

"If I ever accomplish anything like this I'm going to hide the plans in at least six places," said Josh.

Teresa buzzed in. "Lieutenant, I have a State Trooper from Texas on line two. I think you'll want to talk to him." Julia picked up.

"Lieutenant Todd," she said … "Yes, Trooper Daniels. What can I do for you?" … "Carl Huong. Yes, I am interested. He's been missing since last Friday." … "You found it *where*?" … "Juarez, Mexico." … "Yes, I see. Any sign of Huong?" … "Any sign of foul play?" … "Really, totally stripped?" … "This is helpful. I appreciate you doing this. Anything I can do for you?" … "Are you kidding?" … "Okay. Where do I send them?" … "You got it. Thanks again."

"They found Carl's car in Mexico?" Josh asked. "Any sign of him?"

"A few state troopers were involved in some kind of El Paso-Juarez law enforcement exchange exercise, and they came on a totally vandalized car. Trooper Daniel wrote down the VIN number, and looked it up when he got back to the states. It's registered to Carl Huong. No sign of Huong. The car was so completely stripped and torched there would be no way for forensics to find anything useful."

"What'd he ask you to send him?"

"A pair of Elvis Presley silver-rimmed sunglasses, for his kid," Julia said..

"Thank you very much," Josh imitated.

"Needs work," she said. "Hey, I almost forgot. I cross checked the names you gave me with the more frequently used email addresses from Huong's computer. We came up with Allison and someone named Dorothy R. Osborne. You know her?"

"New name on me. Was she listed as a program graduate or as a graduate student?"

"She's a student in the U of M masters program. But when we checked, no one's seen her since last Friday. That's the same day Huong went missing. Lives alone, half a block north of the university. Nobody's home. No car in the garage. Mail stuffed in the mailbox from the last five days."

"Any chance she drives a Ford Explorer?" Josh asked.

"We had the same thought. No, she drives a 2005 baby blue Volkswagen beetle, with an *Engineers Make Better Lovers Logically* bumper sicker. I'm not even sure what that means."

Josh laughed. "You'll have to ask Tonya. Well, I think I'd better get to work. My in-basket is full."

"Thanks again, Josh." Julia gave him time to pull out of the lot. She reached in her pocket for her keys as she walked to her car. Leaving the driveway, she drove in the direction she thought Josh would be taking. It wasn't long before she spotted him several cars ahead. "Let's see if anyone is watching. Now where's that Explorer?" Julia said to herself.

Two cars behind Julia was a gray Buick LeSabre.

CHAPTER 21

THE CRIME BOARD

MAY *29 … The Iridescent Chartreuse Envelopes.* Marino and Tagger entered the squad room with a cup of coffee in their hands. Julia was already there. She had been scrutinizing the items on the crime board.

"Afternoon, gentlemen," greeted Julia. They acknowledged her greeting with a combination of murmurs and slurps, and took a seat.

"Let's fill in some of these gaps. Professor, where are we on your side?" asked Julia

"I haven't read this much stuff since I was in college. It's a lot tougher with age," said Marino.

"And it's a lot tougher without all those drugs. Or, is it a lot tougher *with* all those drugs?" said Tagger.

"As I was saying before I was rudely interrupted by the trash talkin from the peanut gallery," said Marino. "I've read almost all the documents in the Sturgeon stacks, and I've pulled the stock related stuff from Huong's computer. These guys seem to have been interested in a New York hedge fund called Tornadic Growth Investments, managed by a Charleze Mitchell, as well as with the Securities and Exchange Commission. One scenario is that the docs were getting into insider trading involving this hedge fund, and were worried about the SEC. My gut tells me that these guys were above board. So, another scenario is that they were checking out the fine details of the SEC laws and regulations to see if this hedge fund was in violation."

"Or," Julia said, "they were thinking about blowing the SEC whistle on Mitchell."

"Yeah, that would work as scenario number three," added Marino, feeling miffed at being trumped after all the work he'd put in.

"What's the status on collecting a sample for a DNA comparison on Huong?" Julia asked, ignoring Marino's pouty comment.

"That turned out to be a challenge. Mailene Huong is a basket case. She machine-gunned me with questions about her father's whereabouts, and when I told her what I wanted, she was convinced that meant I thought he was dead," lamented Marino. "Anyway, I pulled some hair from his comb and took it to the lab. I told the techs that we suspected that this DNA would match that of the blood on the envelope. They seemed quite willing to get right on it, and kept talking about éclairs. Whatever the hell that means."

"Dealing with the families is always a bitch. Thanks for handling that," Julia said, and watched as Marino's mood softened. Turning to Tagger, she asked. "How about the envelopes?"

"Turns out they ain't big sellers," said Tagger. "The dudes and dudettes at Bongs R Us freaked when I walked in. People were diving into the back room. Items were crashing as they fell from the shelves and tables, and there was a lot of flushing going on."

"Don't take it personal, old buddy," said Marino.

"Ahem!" Tagger cleared his throat. Julia rolled her eyes. "This store did have the envelopes on display, but the clerk wasn't very helpful. He said he was surprised to see they even sold them. And would you believe they had no electronic record keeping system. All the purchases are made in cash, recorded by hand, and kept in a cigar box. I was shocked. On the other hand, Davis-Kidd hasn't sold any of these envelopes over the last twelve months, but, their electronic records go back decades. They gave me a print out of all credit card purchases of these envelopes for the last three years. Guess whose name I found."

"Carl Huong," Julia and Marino said in unison.

"Close, but no cigar," said Tagger. "Try Mailene Huong."

"What now?" said Marino, taken aback by the prospect Mailene could be the mystery woman. "Don't tell me she owns a black Ford Explorer."

"Have you questioned her about the envelopes, Tag?" Julia asked.

"It's on my list," Tagger said.

"And what about Sturgeon's prints and the background check on Durnst?" she asked as she wrote Mailene's name on the crime board.

"I had a similar experience with Sturgeon's son. Our repeated visits have convinced him that his father's death was no accident. I took his can of shaving cream to the lab for prints. But no one said anything to me about éclairs," Tagger said as he looked pointedly at Marino. "I'm waiting on responses from the FBI and the TBI on Durnst. He's been in Tennessee for the past six years. Though he sounds like he's from England, he was born and raised in Cleveland, Mississippi. Go figure. Since he's been here, he doesn't have as much as a single moving violation. Not even a parking ticket."

"You ready for this?" Julia teased. "I received a call from El Paso earlier this morning."

"As in Texas?" asked Marino.

"Yup. Yahoo and giddy up," Julia came back. "It seems one of their State Troopers found Huong's Maxima, stripped and torched."

"In El Paso?" asked Tagger, surprised.

"No. In Juarez, Mexico," answered Julia, feeling pretty good about how well she'd strung out this piece of information.

Marino and Tag started talking to no one in particular. "Juarez … torched Texas Rangers … stripped … Mexico …"

"Okay, pardners. Let's rein them thar horses in a mite," Julia said. "El Paso and Juarez had some kind of law enforcement exchange going on. There was nothing left for forensics, no sign of foul play, and no sign of Huong."

"Juarez?" said Marino one more time.

"Moving on," she said. "Josh reviewed Huong's CD. He was blown away by what the docs had developed, and at how positive the research results had been. He did find a reference to inferior products from Forest Brothers Industries. Nothing else we could use." Changing her tone, "I followed Josh to his office at R&O Industries this morning. I saw plenty of black Ford Explorers, but none with a woman driver, unless you count the ones filled with kids. I did catch a glimpse of a gray LeSabre with heavily tinted glass in my rearview that seemed to be going our way. But it turned off shortly after crossing into Mississippi."

There was a silence. Each one was looking at the crime board trying to make it make sense. Julia spoke first.

"Rest your eyes Marino, then expand your investigation beyond the stacks of papers. See if there's any chance this case does involve that hedge fund." Marino nodded. "Tag, keep dogging the FBI and TBI about those records on Durnst. And find Dorothy Osborne." Tagger acknowledged affirmatively. "I'm going to check on Josh again when he heads home after work."

CHAPTER 22

THE PATENT

MAY 29 ... *Plan B.* Durnst was in deep concentration as he read every word of the final patent application for the new artificial hip joint developed by Sturgeon and Huong. This is going to make all us rich, he thought as he turned over page 23. These damned lawyers. I can not believe they actually go to school to learn how to write this indecipherable dribble. I am sure they do it so no one, except members of their exclusive club, can understand what they are talking about. Then he smiled, but I understand this part. The device belongs to us.

Durnst reached inside his lab coat, pulled out a Mont Blanc fountain pen, and signed as Chief Executive Officer on the last page of all six copies. There were other signature lines reserved for the Chief Financial Officer, and the President of the Board. Now that he had signed, he could take the document to collect their signatures.

Attorney Stanford knocked on his door, and then entered. "Any questions?" he asked.

Durnst shook his head. "I have signed all the copies, and I am ready to take them to the CFO and the Board President for their signatures."

"Let me know when you have all the signatures. I'll make copies for everyone before hand delivering them to D.C.," said Stanford.

***

Charleze's BlackBerry buzzed. It had a 901 area code—Memphis.

"Hello," she said … "That's good news. Let me know when the others have signed the form."

CHAPTER 23

THE CARPET

MAY 29 … *Tonka.* At a Pilot Travel Center in West Memphis, Arkansas, an eighteen-wheeler was pulling into the truck stop for the night. The driver was Nancy Nichol. She had driven from Georgia with a load of carpet. Her one hundred twenty-five pound mixed pit bull-boxer companion sat on the passenger seat next to her. He was jet black with a white paint brush tail. Tonka was antsy.

"I know, I know. It'll be just a few minutes more, Tonka, till I can park this rig." Nancy said. "Then you can take your leak."

It was after eleven and the parking area looked full. Each truck's side window was hooked to a combination electricity and air conditioning unit, as if in a drive-in movie theatre for super-sized vehicles. Flickering lights flashing from several of the cabs indicated the drivers were watching a video they had probably rented from the Travel Center. Other drivers were most likely sleeping.

They rumbled slowly through the maze of parked tractor trailers until Nancy spotted a vacant space. She made a wide turn as a set up to back into it. She enjoyed being able to show off her driving skills, and she didn't hesitate as she shifted into reverse and eased in perfectly on her first try. She had been driving for two years. The driving wasn't bad, and she enjoyed the money and benefits the company provided. She was always being hit on by the male of the species, but she could handle that. The biggest downside was stopping to spend the night. Her first nights had been pretty nerve-racking, as she worried about what may be lurking just outside her door. Threading the seat belts through the arm rests of the doors was only minimally reassuring.

Finding Tonka made a big difference. He offered the security she needed. Having had an abusive male owner, Tonka was distrustful of men. Once he even went off on a passing truck that had a picture of the Marlboro Man on the side. The men along the route soon learned not to come anywhere near her parked rig. And the CBs crackled with stories of men wetting themselves when they had.

Now, it was even more clear. Tonka had to pee. Nancy would stretch her legs as she walked the quarter mile to the combination restaurant-service center to rent her hookups, while Tonka did his business. She didn't get five steps before barking snapped her back. Now what? she thought. Probably a snake or a coon. She unlocked the door to her tractor, climbed back up, and after a few seconds re-emerged with a mega-flashlight—a fifteen million candle power RoadPro. She climbed down and relocked her door, then proceeded somewhat cautiously down the side of her trailer towards Tonka's continued barking. She wasn't looking forward to this.

"Shut that goddamned hound up! I'm trying to sleep here. Christ!" a fellow driver yelled from his window.

Nancy jumped, and the beam of the flash light found a passing jet. She regained her composure and followed the barking. Tonka had left the parking area and was in the adjacent field. The weeds were about waist high, and the ground was strewn with golf ball and baseball-size rocks, making it difficult to walk across.

"Jesus, there's no telling what's hiding in here," she mumbled. "Tonka, knock it off. I'm coming," she said in a loud whisper.

The white tip of Tonka's black tail showed in the flashlight's ray. She adjusted her direction slightly and moved closer. She shined the beam in a circle around him just in case some animal was there. Nothing. Nancy took a few more steps. The ground was becoming uneven, and she jarred her insides as she stepped in an unseen hole.

"Damn it!" As she recovered, her field of vision had opened up. Tonka seemed to be barking at a roll of carpet.

"Tonka, I'm right here. Calm down."

Tonka wheeled and bounded to Nancy, then returned just as quickly to the carpet. "I feel like I'm in the middle of an episode of *Lassie*," she muttered.

"Tonka, what the hell are you doing?" She walked carefully toward the carpet. I hate snakes, she thought, remembering a line from *Indiana Jones*. What is this—old movie night? Maybe I'm more scared than I know.

She spotted what appeared to be a dark four-foot tree branch and, hoping it wasn't a snake, moved slowly toward it. On her second step the snake popped up, and in one quick motion, turned and struck. Nancy scrambled to adjust her weight, leaning backward. It missed. She lost her balance, falling squarely on her butt. The flashlight went flying. She thought she'd seen a flash of white. Cottonmouth moccasins are aggressive as hell—and deadly poisonous. They'll come after you. Still sitting, her legs churned, like riding a bicycle in reverse. Her heart was pounding against her ribs. Her mouth was bone dry, and she struggled to get on top of her short, rapid breaths. She raised up on her hands to crabwalk, though her feet kept slipping, as the heels of her running shoes found only occasional traction on the grass and stones. Despite her all-out effort, she only managed to move inches away. Her senses where on full alert. Where'd it go? I can't see shit.

"Tonka!" she yelled. "C'mere! Get this snake!"

Tonka was concentrating on the carpet. He turned sharply, and in three bounds landed on top of Nancy.

"Not me, stupid," she pointed. "The snake!"

Tonka turned, lunged, and sunk his teeth into the thin black shadow. Dutifully he returned to Nancy with his prize. She stretched for the flashlight, and directed it at Tonka.

"It's a damned tree branch," she gasped. "I'm such a dipshit." She reached to hug Tonka in a full bear hug. "Thank you, baby. Thank you."

Tonka dropped the branch, returned to the carpet, and began barking again. Nancy stood, and tried to compose herself. For the first time she was aware of pain in her hands. The flashlight revealed blood, pieces of glass, and small cuts. She picked out the glass, and wiped her hands on her jeans. Grabbing the branch, she moved behind Tonka, stroking him and talking as calmly as she could manage.

"Let's see what you've found."

Using her stick, and shifting her weight to her back foot in case she had to get out fast, she poked into the roll.

Nothing.

Tonka barked again. She lifted the flap of the carpet with the branch and tried to peal off one layer. The carpet was wet and heavy, snapping the branch. "Phew. This sure does stink," she said as she gathered her courage. She grabbed the edge of the top flap with her right hand, while keeping the light beam focused so as to be able to see what was under it.

"One ... two ... THREE!" She yanked the top layer up and over. It slapped the ground on the other side with a thud. She moved the light to explore every inch of the still rolled carpet, but she couldn't see any snakes.

"Oh, hell, I don't need to be out here doing this," she said. "Let's go, Tonka."

Nancy began walking back to civilization, but Tonka didn't budge. He barked again. "What?" she yelled. He looked back at her and then again at the carpet. "I hate you. You know I hate you," she said as she considered the prospect of having to unroll the carpet. "This better be buried treasure. Otherwise, it's back to the pound for you," she said as she returned to the carpet.

Nancy moved slowly, placing both feet on the open top flap. Her shoes made a squishing sound. "Oh, great! Now I'll have to burn my new Air Jordans just to get rid of the smell," she said. "Okay, Tonka, get ready. If anything moves, you kill it."

Nancy put her right foot on the remaining roll of carpet, and gave it a strong push. It started to give way, but rolled back. She took a deep breath. She inched closer and pushed again with the same foot, harder. The carpet unrolled another quarter of a turn. She could see and feel something rolled up in the carpet—something lumpy, heavy. Two more pushes should do it. And they did. Nancy stood with her mouth agape and eyes wide. Tonka had begun to bark again, but was staying back. At her feet was the body of a small person. Maybe a man, by the clothes.

She heard Tonka growl and turned to see one of the truckers moving quickly in their direction. "I told you to shut that damned dog up!" The man was yelling at the top of his voice. "Now I'm going to...Jesus Christ! What'd you do, kill somebody?"

***

It took the West Memphis police almost four hours to work the scene and remove the body to the coroner's wagon. Nancy sat on one of the cement parking stops behind the neighboring McDonald's. She was staring at the black topped parking lot. She'd been interviewed no fewer than three times about what she had been doing out in the weeds.

"Coffee?"

She looked up and saw that the sleeping, swearing, threatening, out of control driver had come with a peace offering.

"Thanks," she said.

Tonka growled as he lay next to her. Nancy petted him slowly. "Shh, boy. He's okay."

***

Julia got the call at 3:07 AM. She splashed some water on her face, pulled on her clothes and drove west on I-40 across the Hernando de Soto Bridge and into West Memphis. About four miles on the other side of the Mississippi River, she turned off the interstate and looped back under I-40 to the crime scene at the Pilot truck stop, which sat just south of the eastbound lanes. This was going to be a long, tough day.

"Still had his wallet, credit cards, a hundred 'n six dollars, and a nice watch. We called y'all since he's got a Memphis address on his Tennessee driver's license," said the officer. "Prelim looks like he was shot once in the stomach. No exit wound. Doc says he's got enough to keep him busy, and he'd be happy to transport him to your shop and sign him over to y'all."

"Thanks," said Julia. "Chances are good he was killed on our side of the river anyway. He was reported missing a week ago. I was still holding out some hope. Damn."

CHAPTER 24

EMOTIONAL SUPPORT

MAY *30 ... Giving and Getting.* Julia pulled out of the Pilot Travel Center, turned right to the stop sign, and turning right again, negotiated the poorly lighted entrance to the expressway. Just east of this area, congestion builds as I-55, coming from the north, jogs over to join I-40 and together they approach the Mississippi River, where they split. One takes the newer bridge at the northern edge of downtown Memphis, and other takes the older bridge at the southern edge. Julia dodged a few eighteen-wheelers and rows of orange road-repair barrels as she moved to the left hand lane, retracing her path on I-40. Usually it was comforting to see the lights of downtown Memphis and the lights on the arched "M" pattern of the supports that rise above the bridge. But not this day. Instead of seeing the lights in this figure-ground scene, Julia found herself focusing on the darkness of the river, the sky between the buildings, and the sense of emptiness she felt. On the other side of that darkness was the rather rundown, undersized, and ill equipped morgue which would be housing the body of Dr. Carl Huong. But then, it was probably better than the wet, smelly carpet that had been his resting place for the past week.

Julia checked in at the Shelby County Morgue located just east of downtown, on the edge of the medical center. The backlog was sizeable. Huong was already number four that day. Dr. Johnson would be performing the autopsy, but she didn't come on duty until nine. Julia would get a call later in the day. She drove to Huong's home, and pulled in the driveway at five-thirty. Instead of banging on the front door, Julia woke Mailene with a telephone call to let her know they had found her father's body, and that she was at her front door to answer all her questions. Mailene appeared in her robe, blurry eyed and hysterical. She grabbed Julia in a bear hug and cried. Julia walked her back into the house where she eased her down to the couch.

"Why?" Mailene kept asking.

"We don't know yet," Julia said softly.

The questions came rapid-fire from Mailene. "How did he die? Where did you find him? Did he suffer? When did this happen? Who found him? Who did this to my Daddy? Why? Can I see him?"

Julia made an attempt to answer each of her questions. Then she had a few questions of her own. "Mailene, tell me about these iridescent chartreuse envelopes."

Mailene's expression was blank. "The chartreuse envelopes? I don't understand."

Julia remained silent but used her eyes to convey that she was expecting an answer.

"I bought some of them last year for Daddy's birthday as a joke. He was always so out of it, only wearing dull colors. Why? Do they have something to do with his being killed?"

"We don't know. It's just that we came across some of these envelopes in our investigation. I thought you could shed some light on them." She shifted gears. Again, gently. "Tell me about your father and Dr. Sturgeon."

"Oh, Daddy loved Dr. S. He always said that teaming up with him was the best thing, after Mom and me, that ever happened to him. Dr. S. was always so nice." Her voice trailed off. "Now both of them are gone."

"Did your father talk about the project he and Dr. Sturgeon were working on?" prodded Julia.

"Daddy only said that it was something very, very big. He was so excited. I don't know what it was."

Julia pushed on, "Do you have any idea why he might be interested in the Securities and Exchange Commission?"

Mailene made a face. "Doesn't that have something to do with the stock market?" Julia nodded. "Daddy never played the stock market. The only stocks we have are the ones in his IRAs and his retirement package from BP Tech. He always said that stocks were just another way to gamble away our money."

"Almost done," said Julia. "Does the name Dorothy Osborne ring a bell?"

"Dorothy? Sure. She was Daddy's intern for the last four or five months. He was impressed with her, and spoke highly of her abilities. He was hoping she'd come to work for BP Tech after she graduated. Why do you ask?"

"Dorothy went missing the same day as your father," answered Julia. There was silence as Mailene attempted to digest this latest bizarre piece of information.

"Can I see my father now?" Mailene asked.

"The answer is yes." Julia said, "But you need to know that he no longer looks

like you remember him. We think he was shot last week, and his body has begun to decompose. A decomposing body is not pretty, and it smells. But, if you want to see him, I can take you right now."

"Yes, I have to see him no matter what he looks like. Let me get dressed," said Mailene, sounding a more composed.

***

After dropping Mailene back at her home, Julia picked up a large coffee at the McDonald's drive-through, just up the street from the midtown station. She was drained. Being sleep deprived didn't help. Breaking the news to the surviving family members was arguably the most difficult part of being a cop. She fumbled with the top, as she waited for the traffic to break. "Damn. That's hot," she said brushing the drops of coffee off her leg. She took a careful sip, then made an elongated u-turn as she pulled out of McDonald's and, after a short drive on Union, pulled into the Union Station. She was nursing her coffee as she managed her way to her office. Marino and Tagger were waiting for her.

"Excuse my French, Lieutenant, but you look like shit," said Marino.

"Teresa filled us in," added Tagger before Julia could marshall a come back. "We have éclairs."

Julia brought them up to speed. It was clear Mailene was not the mystery woman. And, it was a good guess that the blood stain on the chartreuse envelope would turn out to be Huong's.

"So, it's looking more like Huong was a good guy. Who and where is the mystery woman?" Julia challenged.

Teresa buzzed in. "Lieutenant, call on line two. The FBI." They looked at one another. Julia picked up.

"Lieutenant Todd. Who am I speaking with?"

"Special Agent Masterson," he said. "I believe we've been working on the same case."

"We have?" she said. "Which case is that?"

"The one involving the murders of Haverford Sturgeon and Carl Huong," he said. "I think we need to meet."

"Absolutely," she said. "I'm at your disposal."

"How about one-thirty today, at your shop?" he said.

"See you in a few hours, special agent." Julia hung up the phone. "And the hits just keep on coming."

***

"Mommy! There's a picture of Daddy's friend on TV!" yelled Ollie. The local early morning television stations had been running their respective versions of the *breaking news* segue as they called attention to the discovery of Carl Huong's body in West Memphis.

Tonya's heart sank. She plopped down on the edge of the bed. Tears filled her eyes. Josh walked from the bathroom and saw her.

"What's wrong?" Tonya could only point. Josh turned to look at the TV, all the air sucked out of him. "No!" he shouted.

Tonya stood and pulled him back. They sat on the bed watching the report, the pictures of the Pilot truck stop, a picture of Carl, and a video of last year's interview for a story on artificial joints. The feelings were coming so fast they couldn't be labeled, and were barely recognizable. Their worst fears as to what might have happened to Carl were realized. He was a friend and colleague. There was a profound sense of loss and sadness, then came anger. At the same time, the knowledge that Josh appeared to be next after Hav and Carl evoked intense fear. They were both overwhelmed. Tonya sat frozen. Josh bounced up and began to pace the floor, muttering to himself, and looking around jerkily.

"Josh," Tonya said more loudly than she had intended, "stop pacing. You're making me nervous."

"Making *you* nervous," he said loudly. "How do you think I feel? I don't have a clue as to what I've done to make me a target of a killer. I don't know how to protect myself. I don't know if I have to protect my family. And if I do, I don't know how to do that either."

"Quit talking like that," she demanded.

"What is it you want me to do?" Josh snapped. He turned and finished getting ready to go into work.

Tonya was still trying to sort out the barrage of feelings, and was aware that there was a new one. Josh had just shut her out, again. He was pissing her off. So it was with pursed lips, fiery eyes, lots of banging of things, slamming of drawers, and muttering under her breath, that Tonya also prepared for work.

***

A parallel scene was unfolding at the grandparents' house, as Jennifer and Brandon were having their coffee and watching the early morning show on Channel 5.

"My God! Josh is in real danger, isn't he?" asked Jennifer. She grabbed Brandon's hand. They were thinking the same thing, "We need to go over there, now."

It was usually a twenty-five minute drive, but during morning rush hour, it took them an agonizing thirty-five minutes from driveway to driveway. They moved quickly to the front door, and Ollie let them in.

"Nana! Grandpa! What are you doing here?" asked Ollie with a smile and hugs all around.

It was at that moment they realized they hadn't thought this visit through, especially its impact on the children. Daniel appeared on the stairs plugged into his iPod. It seemed apparent neither Ollie nor Daniel was aware of the news, or at least of its relevance. Jennifer shifted into her old clinical social worker mode and took the lead. She walked over to Daniel, who still hadn't seen them. She touched his arm. He startled, but eased into accepting a hug. Jennifer put her right arm around him and held her left arm open to Ollie to join her. She walked the children into the den, where they settled on the couch. Brandon fell in behind them, choosing the easy chair located at one end of the couch. In a soft, gentle tone Jennifer said, "Something bad has happened. Grandpa and I came over to see if we could help. One of your daddy's friends has died."

"I saw him talking on the television this morning, and I told Mommy to watch," said Ollie. "He wasn't dead."

"Who's dead?" asked Daniel. "Do we know him?"

"It's Dr. Carl Huong." Jennifer turned to Ollie, "I'm pretty sure you were watching an old video of Dr. Huong. And, yes, he died. We know that Daddy and Mommy are very sad."

"What happened to him?" asked Daniel. "Did he have a heart attack?"

"No, someone shot him," Jennifer continued in her same soothing voice, her eyes glued to the children.

"With a gun?" asked Ollie.

"Of course with a gun, you ninny. How else do you shoot someone?" Daniel chided.

Brushing aside Daniel's comment, Jennifer said, "Yes, Ollie. He was shot with a gun. We don't know who shot him."

And then it happened. No fanfare. No hesitation. The kids simply put it together.

"Does this have anything to do with the bloody envelope?" asked Daniel.

"Is he going to come here and shoot Daddy?" asked Ollie.

Brandon gasped. Once more, Jennifer stepped up. She knew the kids had to be told the truth, but they didn't need to be scared senseless. She kept her same calm voice, which seemed to do wonders for the kids. For ten minutes all questions were addressed and answered as accurately as possible. The children's voices began to mimic Jennifer's calm. They sounded as if they were gaining control over their personal terror. Everyone looked up to see Josh and Tonya standing at the archway of the den. Tonya was crying, but mouthed the words to Jennifer,

"Thanks Mom. I can learn a lot from you."

Ollie jumped up and ran to Tonya, and reached for Josh. Daniel rose more slowly and joined his sister, hugging both parents. Brandon slid onto the couch and squeezed Jennifer's hand as they watched their little family. Josh was struggling with his own emotions, knowing he had to shelve them for the time being in order to set a moderate tone for the children. He pushed his fears down deep. He caught his mother looking at him, then became aware of Tonya talking.

"So sad," she said. "We'll miss him very much."

Daniel sang out, "Hey, there's a car in front of our house." They rushed to see Lieutenant Todd striding up the front walk.

"Julia. You look as if you've been up all night," greeted Tonya as she opened the door.

"Yeah, I seem to be giving that impression to everyone this morning," said Julia.

Tonya, realizing what had probably transpired asked, "Did you make the scene in West Memphis?" Julia dropped her head in acknowledgement. "Oh Julia …" she caught herself. This was not the time to discuss the details—not in front of the kids. She changed the subject. "We've been talking about how sad we are about Carl, and, we've been trying to figure out what to do to increase our vigilance. Any ideas?"

Turning to the children, Julia said, "You know, I can't recall ever seeing a family work so well together like y'all've been doing. I'd say, just keep doing it."

Tonya glanced at Jennifer, who understood. "Who's ready for breakfast?" she said, ushering Daniel, Ollie, and Brandon into the kitchen.

"Oh, Julia. You were there? You saw Carl?" asked Tonya with an emotional cocktail of sympathy, empathy, sadness and fear.

"Yeah. I got the call a little after three this morning. After we wrapped up, I drove to Mailene's to break the news, and took her to the morgue to see her father."

"My God." was all Tonya could manage, and she moved to embrace Julia, offering what little supportive emotion she had left. Julia relaxed in her arms. Josh watched while emotions erupted inside of him. There was simply no way to tell which emotions they were, only that his psyche and stomach were awash with them. He didn't like the feeling, but was incapable of doing anything but yield to it. Julia saw him first, and then Tonya was attracted to Julia's gaze. The two women moved to Josh and escorted him to the couch, where they sat on either side of him. It was a safe place. Each had their own reasons. And each let down their guard, allowing a few tears to come.

Jennifer appeared at the opening of the den with a spatula in her hand. She stopped in her tracks. What she saw made her heart ache. A part of her wanted to take them all in her arms. But a different part wanted to take her magic spatula and make everything okay. So, in her cheeriest voice with her spatula held high, she asked,

"Pancakes, anyone?"

The three looked up as if they had been caught doing something wrong. They looked away and adjusted themselves. Julia managed a weak, "I ... I do." And, after some half-hearted attempts to compose themselves, they all followed Jennifer into the kitchen.

Eating breakfast did wonders. The noise level returned to normal as the children readied themselves for school. Julia told them she'd be following along behind their Dad as he dropped them off at school and as he went on to his office.

The elder Proctors watched as the three cars pulled away.

"I'll do dishes," Brandon said.

CHAPTER 25

THE MPD MEETS THE FBI

MAY *30 … Shared Turf.* After following Josh to the elementary school, the high school, and R&O, Julia returned to the precinct. She saw no single women driving black Ford Explorers, no gray LeSabres. She would go back to tail him for his return trip home. She went to the ladies room and attempted to repair herself.

"Pardon my French indeed," she grumbled to herself. "But the éclairs were fabulous."

It wasn't long before one-thirty rolled around. Upon seeing Masterson, Julia quickly scoured the building for a larger chair. After introductions, the four sat down to business. Julia spoke first,

"So, what brings you here, Agent Masterson?"

"As I said on the phone, I think we may have been working different sides of the same case. Sturgeon and Huong had both contacted me with an SEC complaint. You probably didn't know, but they've been working on the development of a prototype artificial joint. They'd gotten wind of some possible manipulation of BP Technologies stock, by a New York hedge fund. Now, both of them are dead. I believe they were both murdered, as I believe was Michael Tibett."

"Okay, let's back up a bit," said Julia. "Yes, we got a missing persons complaint on Huong. Our investigation raised some red flags that Sturgeon's death might not be an accident. But we still don't have any proof. We also found a link between the two doctors and a third man."

"Joshua Proctor?" Masterson said.

All three MPD officers looked at one another. "How did you know that?" demanded Julia.

"It was a guess, but an educated guess. Huong identified three people who've been working closely with one or both of the docs. The only male is Proctor," said Masterson.

"And the two women are Allison White and Dorothy Osborne," said Julia. Masterson nodded. "Now, who's Michael Tibett?"

"Tibett was the lead buyer for BP Technologies. He was found dead in a single car accident not unlike the one that supposedly killed Sturgeon," said Masterson.

"Why'd you wait so long to contact us?" Tagger asked aggressively.

"Because, Sergeant Tagger, all I had were hunches. And, in fact, your own police department certified both of these deaths as accidents. I didn't have anything for sure until Huong showed up dead this morning with a slug in his stomach," said Masterson with equal aggression.

There was a pause as testosterone levels dropped. Marino was first to speak. "I've been reading papers and emails from both docs. I've seen lots of interest in the stock market, a hedge fund, and the SEC. We just don't understand the stock market enough to know what we're up against. And, frankly, we don't know what a hedge fund is."

Masterson took this as a peace offering, and went on to share the history of his involvement with Tornadic Growth Investments. He gave the same explanation he had given to Maria about the rationale of short selling and the potential for making major money, especially when you can manipulate the status quo.

"So you believe these murders have been committed by, or on behalf of, this hedge fund?" asked Julia. "I'm sorry to sound so poor little ole me southern bellish, but that feels like quite a stretch. Why would they be interested in coming all the way down here to kill people?"

"There are three very important points," responded Masterson, holding up three thick fingers, and pulling one down for dramatic effect. "One is that we could be talking about hundreds of millions of dollars."

Tagger whistled. "Oh, *that* point."

"The second point," he said pulling down another finger, "is that

Dr. Charleze Mitchell, the hedge fund manager of Tornadic Growth Investments, is incredibly bright, and could easily have selected BP Technologies for the very reason that it was based so far away from New York. And, the third point is that her second in command is one very bad actor named Willie McMillan. I wouldn't put any of this past him. If he didn't do the killing himself, he had it done. I feel it in my bones."

The group continued until they had mapped out a coordinated plan to protect Josh and Allison, and to continue fact gathering. Masterson requested that he and Special Agent Lopez be involved in the 24/7 tailing rotations. Julia agreed. Lopez was assigned to the team guarding Josh, while Masterson was assigned to help protect Allison. Masterson further offered to clear the way with the SEC Inspector General for a coordinated FBI-SEC-MPD investigation of this crime.

CHAPTER 26

DOROTHY

MAY *30 … The Bloody Hand.* Dorothy Osborne was an emotional wreck. She was watching the morning news about the discovery of Carl Huong's body. Last Friday her engineering supervisor warned her that she could be in grave danger. Then, she heard him get shot. She saw him lying dead in the parking lot. The recurring dreams of Huong waving a bloody hand at her has kept her from sleeping more than a few hours at a time. She's hypersensitive to noises, jumping whenever she hears one. She's convinced she will be next to die, and remains constantly on the look out. She gets angry at the drop of a hat.

I never used to be like this, she thought. Life was exciting. Life was great. The master's program in engineering at The University of Memphis was the perfect choice. I had a scholarship and a teaching assistantship. And the icing on the cake—a field placement with the renowned Dr. Carl Huong at BP Technologies. God, I adore … I mean, I adored, Dr. Huong. He was like a father to me. He was brilliant. He challenged me, and he treated me like a colleague. I always felt so energized around him, so on fire. His prototype artificial hip … what a breakthrough … so creative … so ahead of its time. It's the cutting edge of biomedical engineering. Thanks to Huong, I've been a part of it.

May 23 … My World Turned Upside-Down. Last week, Huong had asked her to develop a password protected website, a piece of cake for Dorothy who's an accomplished practitioner of the computer. She can do anything with a PC, including making it sing *Hound Dog.* She jumped at the opportunity to do something for him. She knocked it out in an afternoon, leaving a disc and instructions in his inbox. Two days later, on Friday, she was working late. She dropped by his office, expecting to hear how excited he was with his new website. But that's not what happened. Huong was not himself.

"My dear, what I am about to tell you will make little sense, but you must believe me. And, for your own safety, you must not ask any questions," he said.

"Of course, Dr. Huong. I'll believe whatever you tell me," said Dorothy, puzzled.

Huong talked in rapid bursts. Dorothy had trouble keeping up, and even though she wasn't supposed to ask questions, they kept popping from her mouth.

"Something bad is happening," Huong said. "Got to be careful. They've bugged my phone, maybe yours too. They've broken into my computer. I think they're watching me. Maybe you too. And probably Josh Proctor and Allison White."

"What? Who's bugging your phone? M … My phone?" asked Dorothy.

"They're trying to sabotage our new hip—"

"What? Who's trying to sabotage the new hip?"

"No time to explain. We're in danger."

"Danger? From who? Why?"

"I believe they've murdered people."

"Murdered? Who?"

"Police don't believe it. FBI thinks I'm crazy."

"FBI?"

"He said I'd be next."

"Who said—"

"He told me to be careful. He told me to leave. I have to leave. You have to leave. You have to leave town immediately. Mailene won't answer her phone."

"Dr Huong. Slow down. What are you talking about? Who are *they*?"

"No time. I wrote everything down and put it on the webpage you created."

"The one I just did for you?" Dorothy only caught slivers of what he said next.

"... broken into my laptop ... special password ... sent email ... Josh and Allison at R&O. *Only* they will be able to figure it out."

Dorothy couldn't move. No words came. Dr. Huong sounded paranoid, delusional.

He pointed to a large iridescent chartreuse envelope with the name JOSH printed on the outside, and a sheet of typing paper with the name JOSH printed at the top.

"Josh and Allison are in danger. Have to warn them," he said.

He gave Dorothy a hug, and told her to get out of town immediately. Dorothy couldn't believe her ears. Tears flowed as he ushered her out of his office.

But Dorothy did not leave the building. It never dawned on her to be concerned for her life. She was distraught about Huong loosing his mind. He hadn't ever shown the slightest sign of mental illness. Dorothy regained her composure. She needed to talk to Huong, but this time she would not leave until he answered her questions. She strode down the hall. Voices were coming from the direction of Huong's office. She stopped, just having rounded the corner. She would have to find another time. She turned to walk back to her office. That's when she heard it. She froze. Then she heard a soft click, and another. There was the thud of something or someone falling to the floor, and maybe a chair overturning as well. She cleared the corner in time to see Huong stumbling from his office, bent over and holding his stomach. He saw her and waved a bloody hand for her to get away. She stumbled back, aghast. Daring to peek around the corner she saw a short white man with a small pistol in his hand running from the office in the direction Huong had gone.

She forced back her shock and fear, and ran to Huong's office. From his window she saw Huong lying motionless in the parking lot, near his car. The other man came running over, bent down and checked his pulse.

He pulled a set of keys from Huong's pocket, unlocked the trunk of the Nissan and, with some difficulty, loaded him into it. After closing the lid, he ran to another car and retrieved a plastic jug and some rags. He returned to Huong's Maxima and began cleaning up the blood. He was working his way toward the building. Dorothy realized he was coming back to the office. She looked down and saw a blood-covered chartreuse envelope and the bloody crumpled paper bearing Josh's name. She grabbed them, and ran. Once around the corner Dorothy stopped and listened hard. She heard the man walking, not walking and cussing, and again walking, not walking and cussing. She assumed he was cleaning up Huong's blood. She hurried to her office, closed and locked the door.

Dorothy sat at her desk crying. The words of Huong were echoing in her ears—*in danger ... leave town immediately*. The vision exploded in her mind of his bloody hand waving her away. She grabbed her cramping stomach.

Ten minutes passed. Dorothy gathered herself and ventured from her office. Listening hard, she made her way to Huong's office, slowly. No sound. At his door she dared to look in. Empty. She tiptoed to his window and cautiously peered out. Huong's car was gone, but the man's car remained. Fear overwhelmed her. She had to leave before he came for her. Her car was parked on the back side of the building. She stopped at her office and collected as many things as she could carry, including her laptop.

Dorothy knew she must be logical and efficient. There would be plenty of time later for emotion. She was used to walling off her test anxieties in order to focus when she had four exams in the same week. However, this was far more difficult. She had to distance herself from the emotion and shock of what she had just seen, as well as the terror of being hunted down and killed herself. She willed herself to focus on the importance of getting away from Memphis as soon possible. She needed a plan, a damned good one.

Dorothy's mind was calculating as she settled behind the wheel. I can't go home. That man could be waiting for me. Is he high-tech? Can he track my credit card use? My cell phone? Gas is almost four dollars a gallon. I only have a few bucks on me. The banks will be on their Saturday half-day schedule tomorrow. Where can I go? It has to be some place close. Where can I stay tonight? She lowered her gaze through the windshield. Oh, my God! This baby blue veedub is way too easy to spot. I need to stay off the main streets. Maybe I can crash in my university office for the night.

Her mind raced through names of friends and relatives. No—too easy to find. Hey, Millie lives around her somewhere. I haven't seen her since high school. What's her married name? Barry … no. Burns … no. Barnes. Yes, that's it. Barnes. I'll find her.

Dorothy drove south into Mississippi to avoid being spotted on the more heavily travelled Poplar Avenue. She looped over to Highway 78 and back into Memphis. She drove to the southern edge of the university campus, the side opposite from her home. It was getting dark. There were only two parking garages on campus. She chose the one furthest from where she lived. Near the stairway on the second level, a car sat with an all-weather cover. It was not uncommon for professors to leave their covered cars in the garage while they were out of town. Dorothy drove to a spot three spaces down. She pulled the cover and draped it over her VW. She took the stairs to the ground floor, and hiked across campus to the Engineering Technology Building and her office. Dorothy waited until the guard was talking to a small group of students, before walking in. She pretended to sign in, and, using the stairs, headed to her room on the third floor. After assuring herself that no one was around, she unlocked the door and went in without turning on the lights. She quietly closed the door and threw the lock. She crossed to the windows, closed the blinds, and with her eyes wide open and heart racing, collapsed in her chair. She'd made it this far.

***

May 24 … Delivering the Mail. Dorothy didn't sleep well, sitting in her chair with her head on the desk. She'd been awakened several times by dreams of Huong waving at her with his bloody hand. The sun broke through narrow slits in the window blinds, waking her from her most recent thirty-minute sleep. She was groggy and disoriented, but it didn't take long for her to wake-up as a mounting fear gave her focus. She walked down the hall to the woman's restroom, used the facilities, threw water on her face and made an attempt at combing the snarls out of her long brown hair. She didn't recognize the mirrored face looking back. She was a disaster—bags under her puffy red eyes, smeared eye make-up, hair in disarray, and wrinkled clothes. She gave her eyes another splash of water, and made one more pass at her hair before returning to her office. Clicking away on her laptop, she found the addresses for Josh Proctor and Millie Barnes. She gave Millie a call from the payphone in the hall.

The building normally opened at noon on Saturdays for professors who came to conduct research, along with their graduate assistants. Shortly after twelve, she left the building, returned to the parking garage, replaced the all-weather cover, climbed into her car, and drove to the bank to withdraw her savings of $894.32. She grabbed a burger on her way to the Proctor house, where she dropped off the chartreuse envelope. She jumped over to Watkins Street, taking it north through the city, beyond the entrance to Shelby Forest, to the small town of Millington, by the less travelled rural roads.

CHAPTER 27

THE NEW YORK-MEMPHIS CONNECTIONS

MAY 30 ... *The First Setback.* Charleze was awakened by her cell phone. She checked the incoming number.

"Yes," said Charleze. "Tell me." ... "They what?" ... "West Memphis?" ... "Juarez? You mean the one in Mexico?" ... "Wait a minute, where the hell is West Memphis?" ... "Just across the Mississippi River?" ... "That idiot doesn't have the brains God gave a goat." ... "What's the fallout?" ... "Are you sure?" ... "We can't afford anymore sloppy jobs." ... "How many men does he have down there?" ... "Yeah, I'm thinking the same thing." ... "What do you need?" ... "I can do that." ... "Call me when you know."

***

Mac was shaving. His iPhone buzzed.

"Yeah," Mac said. "Nooo!" ... "God damn it!" ... "I *am* calm!" ... "Okay, okay. Tell me." ... "And you *believed* the little shit?" ... "Yeah, Yeah." ... "Tried to get the gun away?" ... "And it jammed?" ... "Twice!" ... "I told him a hundred times to get rid of that piece of junk." ... "Yeah, I'm still here." ... "With a stapler. Good. I'd a hit him with the damn desk." ... "Did you check to make sure he cleaned all of it up?" ... "What about the guards?" ... "Good. They bought your story?" ... "Okay. So the guards were running around in the warehouse with their

161

thumbs up their ass. You're sure you melted the security tape." … "Okay! Security *DVD*!" … "Let me know the minute you hear anything."

Mac hung up and dialed another number.

***

Sneak had had a long night of partying. He forced his eyes open, and shut them again against the morning sun streaming through a large opening in the drape. He felt like hell. He turned slightly, rubbed his eyes, and tried again. Things were coming into focus too slowly. He opened his eyes wider and was confused by the pile of sheets next to him. He rubbed his eyes yet again and lifted his head to get a better look. He jerked back. It wasn't a pile of sheets—it was a person covered with a sheet. What the …? Oh yeah … the broad in the bar. He sat up quickly and looked towards the hotel's wall safe where he had put his seventy-five thousand dollars from Mac, minus the thousand he took with him last night. The safe door was closed. He turned back to the woman in his bed. He couldn't see her face since she was lying on her side, her back to him. However, he did take some time to admire the outline of the body draped by the sheet. He smiled, "Nice ass."

Not bothering to put anything on, Sneak eased himself off the bed and walked softly to the safe. He looked back at his sleeping partner. She hadn't moved. He slowly spun the tumbler clockwise, stopping on fourteen, a reverse spin and on to twenty-three, and a short half turn back to the right, stopping on two. He pulled down on the handle and opened the safe quietly confirming the money was still inside. He leafed through the stack of large bills to reassure himself it was all still there. The click of the closing safe was loud enough to rouse her. He returned and sat on the bed as she adjusted to the light and to her surroundings. She startled when she saw him.

"Oh," she said. "I remember … What a night." She reached down and pulled her purse and clothes to her in a big wad. She got out of bed covering her front with her clothes and stumbled to the bathroom. Sneak smiled, "Yeah, nice ass."

Sneak pulled on yesterday's clothes and turned on the TV. His stomach flip-flopped as he watched the news about Dr. Carl Huong. He began talking to the TV.

"How the hell did they find the car in Juarez? You mean some dumb shit was wandering around in those weeds at night and found the body? Who does that?"

He was engrossed in the news story, thinking about what Mac would do, when the bathroom door opened. He jumped. He'd forgotten she was still there. She was looking for her shoes, not paying attention to him. She found the shoes near the door and slipped her feet into them. She walked up to him, kissed him on the cheek, and gave him a weak smile. He pulled some bills out of his pants pocket and peeled off four hundred dollars. "Get yourself a cab, sweetie." He slapped her on the derriere.

After she left, Sneak grabbed his compact Smith & Wesson and proceeded to disassemble, clean, and oil it. He was certain that Mac would be coming and he would only get one shot. He couldn't afford to have his good luck charm misfire this time. He emptied the bullets from the clip, and made certain that the bullets and the clip were clean, and the spring loading action was working smoothly. He reloaded the clip, shoved it into the pistol grip, chambered a round, and carefully slid it in the holster of his shoulder rig.

The next order of business was to stow his cash in the money belt he wore under his shirt. Sneak figured he had to disappear and soon. He wouldn't use the telephone in his room because he didn't want to leave any kind of trail. He slipped into his shoulder holster and oversized jacket, and left the room heading for a nearby laundromat. It had both a change machine and a pay phone. He secured a handful of quarters, and made a few calls. There was a Greyhound bus leaving this afternoon at 2:38 for Fort Worth. He reserved a cab for 11:30, allowing plenty of time for travel and purchasing a ticket in cash. On the way back, he stopped in at a Perkins Restaurant and ordered one of their large blueberry muffins and two coffees to go. At ten, he walked back to his room to pack his bag and wait for the cab.

Sneak jumped as the phone rang. He was dreading this call. He waited until the sixth ring before answering.

"Yeah," Sneak said … "Oh, hiya, Mac." … "No I wasn't dissin you." … "Look, I—" … "No, I just—" … "No, I don't think you're a—" … "How was I supposed to know some chick on eighteen wheels was gonna—" … "I *was* real careful." … "No, I ditched the gun." … "I am *not* that stupid." … "Don't cash the check?" … "You're not coming down here, are you?" … "What do you mean, you don't have to?"

Sneak's stomach felt as if he were in an elevator that had suddenly dropped three floors. Then he heard it—the slightest hint of a sound as the door to his closet opened just a hair. His blood turned to ice.

He was dead before he hit the floor.

***

Pacing helped her to think when she was angry or anxious. Back and forth in her bedroom. Quickly, back and forth. "This isn't happening," Charleze said out loud. "I've worked so hard for too long." Her BlackBerry rang again. She checked caller id. It was Mac. She was so pissed.

"Yes Mac," she said with honey oozing from her lips … "What's that? The police found Huong's body?" … "Me? No, I'm not upset. Why would I be upset?" … "That's your responsibility, isn't it? It's your mess. I'm sure you'll clean it up." … "It's already done?" … "Hopefully, I won't be hearing how the police have traced Sneak back to you, and then *back to me*." … "Yeah, call me any time you have such good news, Mac. Good-bye."

Charleze gritted her teeth. "I told him not to screw this up. I'm *not* going to be the one holding the bag if this goes south." And she wasn't smiling.

***

Mac looked down at the paper copy of the emails Chisholm had taken from Huong's PC after the hit. I don't know what this bullshit poem is supposed to mean, he thought, but I'm sure those geeks will be able to figure it out. I can't take any chances. His iPhone began to buzz. He noted the incoming number.

"Yeah," said Mac. "By the numbers. No gun. No notebook. No witnesses" ... "He still had his little Smith & Wesson didn't he?" ... "I knew it. You have his notebook?" ... "Who's he been tailing?" ... "Had he made any contact?" ... "When you've checked everywhere, and I mean everywhere, go after him yourself." ... "No. I want it to look like an accident." ... "Don't worry about your money. It'll be in your account tomorrow, and I know you've already pocketed Sneak's seventy-five K." ... "I wanna know the second everything is cleaned up."

CHAPTER 28

LOGIC TAKES A HOLIDAY

MAY *30 … The Illusion of Control.* Josh looked up, surprised to see the R&O Industries complex. It took a few seconds for him to realize he was sitting in his car, parked in his usual space. The gear shift was in park, the motor off, and the keys in his right hand. His mind scrambled to make sense of this. The more he tried, the less he understood. He was aware of an *oh-oh* sensation in his stomach, and started to feel afraid. He had questions, self-control questions. How did I get here? Did I drive all the way to work? I don't remember a thing. Am I losing my mind? Did I hit anyone? How long have I been sitting here? He got out and walked around the car to check for signs of an accident. He moved slowly, afraid of what he might find. The bumpers, fenders and doors were fine. No cracks or pits in the windshield. The tires showed no sign of having hit a curb. The hub caps were still on. Okay, he thought. I didn't hit anyone. That's good. Maybe I fell asleep? Whoa. That's not good either.

The psychologist and social worker in the extended Proctor family would have easily identified the power of trauma and subsequent distress. However, for the engineer in the family, who was always in control, or at least was under the illusion of being in control, none of this made sense. He would just have to suck it up and head for his office. He would be on top of this thing in no time.

Josh entered the offices of R&O Industries. He was aware of walking slower than usual, but he wasn't in tune with how his entire body belied his self-image of being in control. His shoulders were rounded, his back was stooped forward, and his eyes were downcast as if he were carrying a great burden. His vision was becoming tunneled, and his ears were ringing with silence. He became aware of foot steps getting increasingly louder. He looked up to see Allison coming closer, and then launching herself at him. What the …? He felt her arms around him and his name being called. She was holding him up. Others gathered and moved him to a chair.

"Get him some water," one directed.

"Give him air," said another.

"No, put his head between his knees to get the blood back into his brain," said a third. He felt his head being pushed down.

He could feel a curtain being parted and his senses returning as he heard talking around him. The return blood flow was reviving his brain. Yet, he remained in a weakened state. His senses had not recovered fully. Similarly, his thought process was not executing with its usual precision, and, he was bombarded with illogical thoughts which triggered very real and intense feelings. Along with the physical recovery, was the pervasive sense of embarrassment at having been so weak as to have fainted, in front of everyone. He could not turn off the negative irrational self-talk, coming from an unknown source deep within his brain, *They will never see me as a strong person again.*

His well organized and logical brain was turning on him. His strength was becoming his weakness, as it surged to convince him that he was less than a man, because he was not strong enough to stave off fainting. He wanted so much to disappear, or for everyone else to disappear. Thankfully, along with the physical recovery, came the cognitive recovery. He saw and felt the genuine concern of his colleagues. This sense of being cared for and accepted helped him to marshall equally strong logical positive self-talk. And the intensity of his embarrassment began to subside.

"Here, have a drink of juice. It'll help," said Allison. He took a drink from the bottle of O.J.

"Thanks. Sorry I did a swan dive on you back there."

"Don't be silly. The news about Carl hit me like a hammer, too. It has affected us all. We haven't been able to talk about anything else this morning. None of us, including you, are statues of stone," she scolded gently.

Josh looked around making eye contact with each person. He smiled meekly and nodded minimally to thank them and let them know he was alright now. They began to move back to their desks.

"Do you want to stand up?" asked a familiar voice. It was the *head between his knees* voice. He didn't trust that voice before, but he did now. And with hands on each arm he made it to his feet. He felt a slight wooziness, but his head soon cleared. Josh was the kind of person who was always ready to help others. But needing others' help implied weakness, and accepting help had always been difficult for him. Nevertheless, with sincerity he said,

"Thanks y'all. I really appreciate it."

Allison walked with him to his office. Josh had accepted the fact that he needed help, and he was appreciative of Allison, and her logical, assertive, and uncomplicated assistance. He hadn't noticed that side of her before. She continued to look after him.

"It would probably be good if you ate something. I don't think the break room donuts would be helpful. Did you bring your lunch today?" she said.

"I think so," Josh said as he opened his briefcase. "Yes here it is," he said blankly without touching it. It never dawned on him to eat something now that had clearly been intended for lunch.

"I think you should eat your sandwich, *now*," she said.

The sandwich was a good idea. Josh could feel his strength returning. Allison remained with him.

"Josh. Why would anyone want to kill Carl?" she asked. "I can't think of anyone who didn't like him."

"I don't know," he answered. "But I'm thinking it has something to do with BP Tech, and their new artificial hip joint. I don't want to think this, but maybe Hav's death wasn't an accident."

Allison gasped. "I haven't wanted to believe that, but the thought has been rattling around in my head since I saw the news this morning." There was a lengthy pause before she spoke again without looking up, "If that were true, what's the probability those people in their inner circle are also in danger?"

Josh thought a bit, and said, "I suppose that could follow." He waited until Allison looked up and made eye contact. "Were you in Carl's inner circle?"

She winced. "No … Maybe … I don't really know. Carl and I had frequent telephone conversations and a handful of emails that were about their device. I didn't tell anyone because he told me not to. Do you think that would put me in his inner circle?" she asked.

Josh again took his time, then avoided her question. "Hav and Carl used to talk to me about their device as well. And what about Dorothy Osborne?"

"I never met her. But Carl used to brag about her. I'd be surprised if she didn't know more than the two of us. Do you know her?" asked Allison.

"No, I just heard the name," said Josh.

Another pause, as Allison tried to determine just how much information to share with Josh. "Have you ever heard the name, Redstone?" she asked hesitantly.

Josh's eyes flashed. "Yes. I've received a few emails from someone calling themself Redstone. You, too?"

Allison became animated. "Did it only ask you to read your email?"

"I've got two emails from Redstone. Neither one had any text, only an entry in the subject line. The first was, *Did you get it?* and the second—"

"Said, *Be careful*," Allison interrupted, "and the third came today saying to, *Read your emails*."

Josh realized he hadn't turned his computer on yet. He swiveled his chair around and clicked the mouse to wake up his machine. After some hemming and hawing, the screen came up. Josh clicked on email. Several new emails loaded. One was from Redstone, with the subject line *Did you get it?* Allison moved closer.

"Open it, Josh," she said. Josh complied. *Read your emails* appeared in the text. They both stared at it.

"Do you have any idea what this means?" asked Josh.

"I wish I did," said Allison.

"Sounds as if Redstone thinks we've received some kind of message that we were supposed to have acted on," said Josh. "Let's think about what type of message from which person. I don't recall having any earlier emails from Redstone. Since we've both received these three, is it too much of a reach to think this might be tied to Carl's death? And if so, the emails in question would have been sent by Hav and Carl. Or, if you didn't receive any emails from Hav, maybe just Carl?"

"I'm with you," said Allison. "To take your thinking further, it would seem logical that we're talking about having the same emails. Then it would be a matter of matching our email files to see which ones were the same, or maybe at least sent on the same day by the same person. And since I use a laptop, I can bring my Mac in here and we can go down our emails one by one."

"I like the way you think," Josh smiled.

"I have appointments the rest of the day. What if I meet you here tomorrow morning, on Saturday, say at around ten?" suggested Allison.

"That dog'll hunt. See you then," said Josh. After Allison left, he reached for his BlackBerry and punched nine.

CHAPTER 29

THE **GET SMART** SHOE

MAY *30 … Teresa Does It Again.* Teresa was frustrated. Lieutenant Todd had invited her to investigate, to do police work, to be one of the team. But she hadn't turned up a thing. She began to expand her search of MPD bulletins, as her duties would allow. Later that day, she skimmed through the logs of the various precincts.

Cory Roberts found dead. One bullet, behind the right ear. Hotel room was in shambles. The deceased had been searched. One empty holster and one empty money belt. Crime scene investigators discovered a loose heel on his shoe. When they twisted the heel they found a hollowed area containing a piece of paper with a phone number. It had a New York City area code.

Now this looks interesting, she thought as she picked up the phone.

"Sharon, this is Teresa." … "Fine. Yourself?" … "Hey, I just read about the body in your log." … "Yeah, that's the one. We may have a tie-in over here. Any chance I can get that New York telephone number?" … "Great. Thanks, girl."

Teresa punched in the New York number and listened hard.

"Sorry. Wrong number," she said.

She ripped off the top page of her note pad, pushed back her chair, swiveled to the right, and got up in a continuous motion. She walked excitedly to Todd's office. The door was open. She stuck her head into the opening and knocked on the doorjamb.

"Hey, Terry. Got something?" asked Julia as she worked at her computer.

"Lieutenant, I think I've found something that ties to your chartreuse envelope case." Julia sat up straighter, making eye contact and motioned with her hands to give it to her.

"Our friends in the northeast precinct found a stiff named Cory Roberts. Records show an aka of *Sneak*. He had one gun shot to the brain, professional hit. Coroner estimated TOD between ten and eleven this morning. The maid found him when she went to clean the room. His room had been tossed and his pockets turned inside out. The only thing left was a wallet with credit cards. The killer was looking for something. But the crime scene guys, bless their hearts, discovered that he had a hide away heel on his shoe. They twist it off and out falls a piece of paper with a telephone number written on it."

"So?" said Julia.

"So, the telephone number has a New York area code" said Teresa.

"Get to the point, Ms. Johnson."

"Guess who answers the phone?"

"Terry!"

"Hello, Tornadic Growth Investments, may I help you?" said Teresa, with a Cheshire cat grin.

"I love you!" Julia said. "Now, get Tag and Marino in here, please. And, Terry? Great work. Thanks."

Julia shared the news with her two sergeants. "A guy called Sneak was found in the Bartlett area with a single shot to the brain. Turns out he also had the phone number of Tornadic Growth Investments in his shoe. Looks like the killer is still in town and is active. Marino, get the word to each of the protection teams that the killer is here, and has struck again. They need to stay sharp. Touch base with Teresa, she can give you the particulars and the contacts," Julia said. "Tag, Josh had a talk with Allison White. She knows Dorothy Osborne. Maybe it's time to talk to Ms. White. Josh and Allison have both been receiving emails from someone calling themselves Redstone. Have either of you heard that name before?" Both men shook their heads. "Okay. Looks like we've got another player."

CHAPTER 30

A BLAST FROM THE PAST

MAY *30 … One Can Only Deny Emotions For So Long.* Charleze strode into her office building. Her mind focused intensely as she considered Sneak and her full schedule for the day. The pressures of the market were beginning to wear on her. She hardly noticed a custodian who was emptying a trash can, and then it hit her, like an unseen charging bull. "What the …? That smell!" She was immediately overcome. That smell was triggering feelings and bodily responses she hadn't experienced in thirty years. She struggled to maintain her outward composure. She grabbed her stomach and put her other hand on the wall for support as the hall began to spin. She forced herself into the nearby ladies room, where she crashed into a stall door and dropped heavily onto the toilet seat.

"What's happening to me?"

Charleze fought to push her brain back in control, as it had always done for her. But, it was no use. She was seven years old again. *That smell. I haven't smelled that combination of cologne and sweat since those horrible nights when Mommy dragged me into her bedroom and left me with that awful man. That man who did terrible things to me. That man who wouldn't get off me for so long … and I couldn't breathe. That man who hurt me … That man who smiled at me and said he'd be back … That man who came back again and again.*

Charleze was experiencing the full fury of a trauma-related flashback, buried for so long, and triggered by that smell. Long ago she had sought refuge in her genius. She had willed herself to forget all those painful memories and feelings. She had successfully walled them off, and put them out of her conscious life—at the staggering cost of insulating herself from feeling much of anything again.

"Oh, my God!" Her body was convulsing, and tears were streaming down her face. "I can smell him ... I can feel him ... I ... I can ..."

It was ten, maybe fifteen minutes before the neuro-chemicals had begun to run their course, and her body was able to calm down. Charleze was sweaty, nauseous, exhausted, and her head was pounding. She willed herself to her feet, and after a few seconds convinced herself of her balance and leg strength. She cracked the door of the stall and peeked out. No one had come in. The contents of her purse were spread from the doorway to the stall, leaving a trail to the Prada handbag lying at her feet. On wobbly legs she made it to the row of sinks and mirrors. After her eyes focused, she saw someone who looked as bad as she felt. Her eye shadow and mascara had run down her cheeks and dripped onto her dress, adding to the sweat stains and wrinkles. Her hands were still trembling slightly as she splashed water on her face. With effort, she began to collect the items from her purse. When she picked up her BlackBerry she punched in the number seven for her driver. He answered on the second ring, as he had been instructed.

"Austin," she said in a weakened voice. "Pick me up at the side exit of the building."

"Yes, ma'am," said Austin. "I'm parked just down the street. I'll be waiting for you."

Charleze pulled some tissues from the dispenser and held them up to the left side of her face as she departed the Ladies room, hugging the wall leading to the side exit. The car was there before she was. Austin had opened the rear door and was waiting for her.

"Dr. Mitchell!" he said. "Are you alright, ma'am?"

"I'm fine," she snapped. "Just take me to the penthouse, the private entrance."

"Yes, ma'am." Austin closed her door and trotted around to the driver's door.

Charleze searched her purse for her new migraine prescription. She pulled the bottle out, grabbed a Perrier from the mini-fridge, and took a double dose. She pulled her BlackBerry, punched three for her secretary, and cancelled all appointments until further notice.

Austin opened the car door for her at the private entrance of her building.

"May I help you, ma'am?" he asked.

"No, I'm fine. I'll call when I need you," said Charleze, and she proceeded to her penthouse.

The pills were doing their thing. She shuffled to the bedroom, shedding shoes and clothes as she went. She fell into bed and, in a short time, was asleep.

CHAPTER 31

THE HIT MAN STRIKES AGAIN

MAY *30 … The Gray Buick LeSabre.* Driving an unmarked car, Julia parked in a lot across the street from R&O Industries, where she waited for Josh to come out. She reflected on the events of a long and emotion-filled day, beginning at three this morning. As usual, her mind was going in all directions at once. Hell, I can't remember having back to back days that were this heavy, let alone having all of this in one day … I could kick myself for breaking down at the Proctors, especially in front of everyone. At least I didn't do it in front of the kids. It's tough always having to be the one in charge, the logical one, the tough one. It's true, there were few people in this world I trust as much as Tonya. There was no one else I would dare to take off my *in-charge* mask in the presence of. She smiled. Poor Josh. Talk about the need to maintain an in-control image. He must be in worse shape than me. I've shared so much with this family that I'm starting to take this threat personally. I need to be able to step back, and put my in-charge mask back on so I can do my job. She took a cleansing breath, and with her cheeks full, blew it out loudly.

The sight of people leaving the building helped re-energize her. It didn't take long for the R&O parking lot to empty out, as a solid stream of employees headed home. Then she saw it, a gray Buick LeSabre with dark tinted windows. Julia sat up straight, gripping the steering wheel. The car was parked at the east end of the parking lot, on the opposite corner from the building exit. She couldn't see the license plate from her position, and decided to get a better look. She fired up the engine, dropped the gear shift into drive, and, keeping one eye on the LeSabre, began moving slowly passed the remaining parked cars on her way to the driveway.

She turned left on the cross street, temporarily losing sight of the LeSabre. After two hundred feet she turned right into the R&O parking lot, and re-established visual contact. It was then, out of her peripheral vision, she saw Josh coming down the walkway from the building. She turned to look. He was holding up his briefcase in his left hand and fiddling with his watch as he approached the blacktop of the parking area. He wasn't paying attention. "Wake up, Josh!" she urged from inside her car. But it was too late—the LeSabre was already moving toward him. She mashed her horn as she turned the wheel slightly to the left and accelerated.

Josh heard the horn, and looked up to see one, no, two cars speeding toward him. He spun around with his briefcase in hand, and took off at a dead sprint for the nearest squared brick column standing in front of the building entrance. He glanced back to see the gray car closing the gap. It was going to be close. He turned back to face the building, took one more step and tripped, taking a head-first dive on the concrete short of the brick pillar he had focused on. His briefcase opened as it hit the concrete, scooting almost to the sliding glass doors, spewing papers and journals all the way. The LeSabre was bearing down on him. Josh was dazed by the blow, and was puzzled as he watched the gray car getting larger and larger. As his brain made sense out of what was happening, he was overcome with fear and unable to move. My God! I'm going to die. He lay there wide-eyed. He could only watch.

Julia's concentration was intense, focused. She had one chance. She aimed her car in between the LeSabre and Josh. Everything seemed to happen in slow motion, but in reality the sequence occurred within tenths of a second. There were sounds of squealing tires, crunching and tearing metal. The LeSabre smashed into the right front fender of Julia's car, sending it into the same brick column that Josh had been trying to get behind. The impact slammed Julia against the driver side door, busting out the side window with her head. She was bounced back to an upright position, and thrown toward the steering wheel. Next she heard the loud BAM! of a gun shot, and she felt its force full in the face. Everything went black.

All movement stopped. Silence. The air filled with smoke and dust. Josh looked down to see his legs under Julia's car, just behind her left front tire. The quiet was pierced by the squealing of tires as the driver of the LeSabre threw his car into reverse and gunned it. The intense speed and spinning of the front tires was counter to the LeSabre's slow extraction from Julia's car. The car stopped, the driver jammed it into drive, and, with another squeal of rubber, leaped forward to the parking lot driveway.

Julia slumped forward with her face buried in the airbag. Somewhere in the distance her name was being called.

"Julia! Julia! Are you all right? Julia!"

"Wha ...?" she asked weakly as she sat up unable to stop her head from flopping backward against the head rest. The inside of Julia's head was a cloudy mush, like the middle of a moon pie.

"Oh, thank God. Julia, you saved my life," said Josh breathlessly. Josh could see her eyes were not focusing. "An ambulance is coming."

Julia's right hand came up and touched the back of her head. It dropped into her lap covered with blood. She moved her head ever so slightly from side to side.

"I think it'd be best if you didn't try to move," said Josh as he touched her shoulder. Then, as if filled with a geyser that could no longer be contained, he blurted out, "That car was going to run over me. You came out of nowhere and cut it off. The collision forced your car into the column. You saved my life. That's when I heard your air bag blast open. I could've been killed. You could've been killed. *We* could've been killed."

"Saved my life ..." echoed in the background. "... Could've been killed ..." Julia mumbled as she tried to make sense of the words she believed were coming from inside her head.

"Julia. Julia," he said. She looked toward the voice, then lost consciousness again. Josh looked around, desperate for the ambulance to be there. No sign. A handful of people were rushing towards them.

"Josh. Are you okay?" someone asked excitedly.

"You're bleeding," another said.

"I am?" said Josh. Looking down, he saw blood dropping. He rubbed his forehead with the back of his hand and found his hand covered in red. "I hadn't noticed," was all he could say.

Julia was coming around. This time she knew where she was, remembered how she got there. She found Josh, with his bloody face, looking down at her.

"You OK?" she asked him weakly.

"I think so."

"What about the other car?" she managed, shifting into her police role, and noticing the blood on her right hand.

"The driver gunned it in reverse, then squealed out, heading south. The car was smashed in. He left the glass of his headlight on the black top," answered Josh.

Julia reached for the two-way, but saw it lying out of reach on the floor next to the passenger door. She slowly rotated to the left and found the phone on her belt. She pulled it out and punched four.

"Union Station," answered Teresa.

"Tereza, thiz Todd," she said almost in a whisper. "I'm at the R&O in Mizipi. I've been in a wreck."

"A wreck! Are you hurt Lieutenant?" asked Teresa.

"Josh and me ... a little banged up. Ambulance on way. Need all-points ... gray LeSabre, major damage ... left front, last seen ... heading south." Julia continued in short, painful breaths. "... caution ... assume armed ... dangerous."

"I'll put out the bulletin, and send someone down there now," said Teresa.

Julia dropped the phone, and lay back in the seat. She thought she heard an ambulance siren. Everything went dark again.

***

The driver's door was undamaged and allowed ready access. Julia roused at the calling of her name. After checking her vitals, placing a cervical collar on her, and getting a verbal report as to where she was hurting, the paramedics determined the advisability of transporting. She requested Methodist Hospital in midtown Memphis, down the street from Union Station. They carefully guided Julia from her car and onto a stretcher. One of the paramedics looked at Josh and suggested that he join her in the ambulance. They didn't want to delay transporting Julia, but Josh clearly needed to be checked out. They would evaluate him while in route.

Now in the ambulance, his forehead bandaged, Josh followed Julia's direction and called the precinct to apprise Teresa of their destination. Teresa caught up with Marino and Tagger who were driving with flashers towards R&O. They did a quick U-turn. Marino gave Tonya a call.

"This is Sergeant Marino." ... "Your husband just called to say he's in an ambulance with Lieutenant Todd." ... "As far as we've learned, she was in a car wreck. We don't know how badly she's hurt." ... "At the R&O building." ... "I believe Josh has a few bumps and bruises as well." ... "Yes, he's in the same ambulance." ... "I'm sorry, we don't know anything else at this point." ... "We're going to meet them in the ER at Methodist Central." ... "Yes, ma'am. On Union." ... "I'm guessing twenty-five, thirty minutes." ... "We'll be looking for you."

Tonya called with the news. The plan was for Brandon to stay with the grandkids, while Tonya and Jennifer drove to the ER. The elder Proctors hurried over to their house, and Jennifer jumped in the waiting car with Tonya.

***

It was a typical Friday night in the emergency room, as injured, fragile, and frighteningly sick people were negotiating the metal detectors, washing their hands as required at the waterless soap dispenser, clarifying their insurance, taking a seat, and when their name was called, checking in with the triage nurse. Almost all were accompanied by someone who appeared either concerned and empathetic, or bored. Periodically an ambulance would pull up, and a person on a stretcher would be wheeled into the examination rooms ahead of all those in the waiting room. A few of those who had been waiting began to moan, or cough and wheeze loudly each time someone was judged more serious and taken ahead of them, hoping their plight would rise to the threshold resulting in their name being called. At the same time, others became convinced that their problems were not as serious as they had believed earlier, and they considered leaving.

When their ambulance pulled up, Josh and Julia were triaged and taken directly into evaluation rooms. Within minutes, Tonya and Jennifer joined Marino and Tagger in the waiting area, who by now had learned a little more of what had transpired. They assured the women that, although bandaged in several places, Josh had walked in under his own power, and Julia had waved at them from her stretcher.

Josh received treatment for scrapes and lacerations, given medication for pain, and was released with a prescription. Tonya and Jennifer both jumped up as he came through the wide wooden door. He looked as if he'd been mauled in a street fight. His face was swollen. There were bandages on his forehead and left cheek, and there was shiny medication covering the scrapes on his nose and chin. The white of bandages flashed through the tears in his pants legs and shirt.

"I'm okay. Really, I am."

"Oh, Josh." said Tonya as she put her arm around his back and led him to a chair.

"What happened, son," asked Jennifer.

"Julia saved my life."

"Saved your life?" said Tonya.

"I was fiddling with my watch as I walked to the parking lot. I heard a car horn, and looked up to see two cars coming toward me, one from the right and one from the left. I did an about face and started running back to the building." Josh's speech became louder and faster. "I saw the square brick pillars and thought I might be able to get behind one of them. I stupidly looked back at the gray car. I tripped and fell face first on the cement. I watched that gray car bearing down on me. I thought I was going to die." Tonya squeezed his arm. Jennifer gasped. "Then out of nowhere, Julia drove her car between the gray one and the pillar. There was a huge crash. She saved my life. She risked her own life to save me." His eyes were looking somewhere else. Tonya squeezed even more. Josh's focus returned to the Emergency Room, and to the four people staring at him. They moved him to a chair.

"How about Lieutenant Todd?" Tagger asked.

"She was unconscious when I got to her. Her window had been busted out and her face was buried in her air bag. She was bleeding badly from the back of her head. She came around when I called her name, and started asking police kinds of questions about the gray car. She's the one who called the station. Then she passed out again. The paramedics came shortly after that. They talked to her, and she came to. She's been conscious ever since. The paramedics said that they were pretty sure she had a concussion." Josh's medication seemed to be kicking in. He slumped back in his chair.

"I'm going for the car," said Tonya.

"We'll meet you outside," said Marino.

***

The doctors took longer with Julia. She endured several x-rays, and a CT scan for her head injury. Nothing was broken, but in addition to a concussion, she sustained heavy bruising on her left shoulder and arm, as well as her chest and face. It took seven stitches to close the gash in the back of her head. Julia was admitted overnight for observation. Marino arranged for a female officer to stand watch, and to accompany any person entering her room. Tagger sent officers to R&O to inspect Josh's car for any tampering of the brake line or for explosive devices.

***

Julia woke the next morning to see this monster of a Black man staring down at her. Her vision cleared.

"Mornin, Tag," she said. "You spend the night?"

"Nah. Marino arranged for Henderson and Tillers to take turns being here with you," said a concerned Tagger, as he motioned to the officer sitting in the corner.

Julia glanced over. "Hey, Sherry. Say, I don't snore or pass gas in my sleep, do I?"

"Mornin, Lieutenant. I never heard nothing. And even if I did, I wouldn't tell," smiled Tillers.

"How're you feeling?" asked Tagger.

"Julia stirred a little, becoming aware of her bruises, and then the headache. "Ouch! She winced, holding her head, and then her shoulder, and then her head again. "I feel like I've been hit by a truck."

"Correction. Hit by a Buick LeSabre," said Tagger. "They found it this morning, abandoned on a back road in Desoto County. Latest report was that there were no obvious prints and nothing left in the car. The driver's side air bag had been taken out. Looks like the driver fully intended to hit someone or something. They hauled it back to the lab for a more thorough look."

"And Josh?" she asked as she suddenly remembered him.

"He was banged up pretty good from falling on the concrete, but it was way better than getting hit by a car," said Tagger. "They treated him for some cuts and released him last night. His wife and mother took him home. He couldn't say enough about how you saved his life. Nice work, Lieutenant. That was quick thinking, and quick reacting." Julia managed a slight smile of acknowledgement. "We set up a 24/7, and we're restricting the family to the house. We went over his car for tampering. Everything looked clean, and one of the guys drove it back to the Proctor house."

"Yeah, but who's going to pay for my car?" Julia joked, and then winced again. "Anything else I should know about?"

"I drove over to Allison White's last night. She was a nervous wreck, and, after getting over the initial shock of seeing a hulking brother on her door step in the middle of the night, was happy I was there. She told me she and Josh were planning to meet in the morning to compare emails, and figure out what this Redstone person was trying to get them to do. I suggested that we go with them back to R&O so they could do just that. Marino and I'll pick each of them up this afternoon. Before I left, I arranged for Eva Rodriguez to stay in Allison's house over the weekend," said Tagger. "She's made arrangements for her mother to watch her kids. Rodriguez has some flexibility during her regular shift. She'll leave when Allison goes to work on Monday, then be there when she returns, for the night."

"She's up for sergeant isn't she?" asked Julia.

"Yah," he said. "She's an impressive officer. Dependable, gets along with even the hard asses."

"You do good work. I should get you on my investigative squad some day," Julia tried to joke. Again, wincing ... Her brain was getting back up to speed. "I know I sorta messed up your priorities, but any word on Dorothy or Durnst?"

"I haven't had a chance, I've been tied up with this pansy ass lieutenant," said Tagger.

"Sorry Tag. I really do appreciate you and Marino looking after me," said a more serious Julia.

She wasn't sure, but she thought Tagger was blushing.

CHAPTER 32

THE HUG BALL

MAY *31 ... The Power Of The Family.* Tonya had been watching Josh sleep since about 2:00 AM. She was too scared to sleep. She couldn't imagine life without her ultra logical Josh. It was horrifying to think that he was almost killed yesterday. Remind me to thank Julia, again, she thought prayerfully.

The sun had been sending light through the skylights of their bedroom for an hour or so, but Josh hadn't moved. He'd taken his prescribed meds at the hospital, and then again before going to bed. She was sure that was the reason he was sleeping so soundly. She heard hushed voices and looked up to see Ollie and Daniel easing the door open and peeking in. There hadn't been much time to talk last night as Tonya put Josh to bed immediately. She waved them in, put her finger to her mouth, and indicated they could sit on her side of the bed. Although a bit of a challenge, Tonya managed to hold them both, as the three of them watched silently while Josh slept.

Twenty minutes later Josh stirred. He opened his bruised and puffy eyes. Ah yes, the skylights, as he began to figure out where he was. Then without warning he was pounced upon.

"Daddy!" squealed Ollie. "You're awake!" Tonya tried to hold her back but Ollie had been too fast.

She reached for her. "Ollie, give Daddy a chance to breathe."

Now awake, Josh held Ollie. "She's just fine, hon."

Daniel being way more cool than Ollie got up and casually walked

191

around to Josh's side of the bed and looked at him. Josh held up his scraped hand and Daniel bent to hug his father. Tonya couldn't wait any longer, so she slid over into Josh and made it a four person *hug ball*. There were smiles of relief everywhere. Then came the questions that had been damned up for the last eight hours.

"What happened to you?" asked Ollie.

"Did someone really try to run you over with their car?" Daniel asked.

"How did you get away?"

"Did you fight with him?"

"Were you scared?"

"Where's he now?"

"Where does it hurt?"

"How come your eyes are so closed up?"

"How did you get this bruise?"

"Did the police catch him?"

"Did you know there's a police car in front of our house?"

"Is he gonna do it again?"

"Is he gonna come here?"

Josh did his best to describe the previous evening's events in some detail, putting the emphasis on Julia's protective actions. But he was at a loss to answer the questions about their fears. He didn't know who the bastard was, or maybe it was that woman from the Ford Explorer. He didn't know if he or she was going to try again. He didn't know if he or she was going to come to their home. He didn't know what he was going to do to keep them all safe. Tonya stepped in.

"We're going to do what Lieutenant Todd told us we've been doing so well. We're going to come up with a plan, and we are going to do what the police tell us to do. Now I want both of you to get dressed and while you're doing that, I want you to think of what you will do that can be part our family plan. Now, go." She and Josh made eye contact. Tears were forming in both of their eyes. Gone were the anger and hurt that seemed so petty now. They embraced for a long time. Then, Tonya inspected and kissed every one of Josh's cuts, bruises and aches.

Nana and grandpa had spent the night at their house. Jennifer rose early and baked a cinnamon swizzle pastry for breakfast. She cut a large piece, wrapped it in a sheet of paper towel, and took it and a mug of coffee outside to the officer sitting in the squad car. Josh and Tonya had not come downstairs yet. Ollie was talking excitedly about things that she was going to do. Brandon surmised correctly that she had been instructed to come up with a few things she could be doing to assist in this difficult situation.

"I'll practice my martial arts, so when that bad man comes here I will kung fu him," Ollie announced.

"You don't know any martial arts," Daniel said.

"I do so. I watch Power Rangers all the time," she said as she aimed a kick in his direction. To his credit, Daniel let it all drop.

Daniel sat up straight, looking adult like, and said, "I'm not going to play my iPod, so I can listen more carefully in case someone tries to break into the house. And, I'll keep this whistle in my pocket so when I see him I can make a lot of noise and bring help."

"Those sound like important things to me, I know your parents will be impressed," said Brandon. The kids seemed to be reassured they had something specific to do in the face of this even scarier situation.

CHAPTER 33

REDSTONE'S MESSAGE

M AY *31 ... There Once Was a Man From ...* By five Saturday evening, Josh and Allison were riding in the back seat of the police car, with Marino driving and Tagger in the passenger seat.

"Turn left here," Josh said. "This road will lead straight to the R&O parking lot. We usually have only a few people in the building on Saturdays," said Josh.

But as they got closer they could see several cars in the parking lot, and there were a few dozen people standing around the yellow taped site of the car crash. "Wow!" said Josh. "I guess I was wrong about that. Pull around left and see if we can sneak in the back way. Our key cards will open the back door as well."

People saw the police car driving around to the back of the building, but no one saw Allison or Josh ducked down in the back seat. They got out of the car. Josh was moving very slowly. He couldn't believe how much of him hurt. The others waited while he gingerly limped towards the door. Allison passed her key card over the reader and the doors clicked loudly.

"My office is on the second floor. We'll be meeting in Josh's office, down this corridor, on the end," said Allison. Tagger went with her.

Marino accompanied Josh. Watching his slow progress, Marino yelled over his shoulder, "If you get to Josh's office before we do, wait." Josh started to smile, but it hurt his lips.

***

196 JAMES C. PAAVOLA

Josh had his PC up and running by the time Allison and her newfound best friend Tagger came in. She pulled up a chair next to Josh, cleared a space and opened her laptop.

"Any changes since our discussion yesterday," she said.

"Yeah, I'm even more motivated," said Josh.

"I hear that," said Allison. "Let's start by pulling up all the emails from Carl over the past month." Tagger and Marino moved in closer.

Both scrolled down their saved incoming emails. It wasn't long before Allison yelled out, "I've got five."

Josh chimed in, "I have two from Carl."

They noted that they each had an email from Carl dated a week ago on Friday the 23rd. In fact, as they quickly discovered, the email had been sent to both of them. The subject line said *The Orient Express*. Each one clicked it open. The text consisted of only one line, "Attached is a schedule for the Orient Express. I hope we can ride it together one day."

"I remember this email," said Josh, "mostly because it seemed so strange. I never opened the attachment."

"Me neither," Allison said. "Why would he send us something about a train? Did he ever talk to you about taking the train?"

"No. It's a new one on me," said Josh.

"I wonder if he's talking about Hercule Poirot?" said Marino, a little more loudly than he had intended.

"What's a errcue parole?" asked Tagger.

"Poirot was the brilliant but eccentric Belgium detective in many of Agatha Christie's murder mysteries. And, *Murder on the Orient Express* was the name of one of her more famous books," answered Josh. Glancing at Marino, "That feels a bit far afield, Sergeant. But let's see what's in the attachment." He clicked on it. "Whoa! What's this?"

After a few seconds Allison said, "This makes no sense ... Is this ... a limerick?"

Josh studied it. "Yes, and it looks like some kind of riddle as well." Here, I'll print off hard copies for all of us. The printer whirred and spit out four copies. Josh distributed them. Marino and Tagger found a chair, and everyone began to study the text.

The background at this site is laid out.
The solution for entrance in doubt
Tell me what's his name
The one of great fame
The one who lived and did fly about

As for the key essential to rend
One must look to ones digital blend
Required for our job
Unique from the mob
You must sequence four each from the end

Allison encouraged them to talk out loud so everyone could benefit from the other's interpretations, associations, and guesses.

"Site—laid out ... a place ... X marks the spot ... treasure ... a cemetery?"

"His name ... who flies—Lindbergh ... Wright brothers ... Flash Gordon ... Batman ... Superman ... the President?"

"To rend means to tear apart ... to split ... to disturb?"

"Digital blend—Interlocked fingers ... folded hands ... a new type of computer?"

"The mob—mafia ... group ... mindless?"

They all stared. Nothing was coming.

Josh said, "I think we need some other eyes. How about if someone runs this by Mailene?

And I'll take it home and run it by Tonya and my parents."

"Sergeant, can we go to Mailene's? She's an old friend of mine," asked Allison.

"Sure, Ms. White. No problem," said Tagger.

"I'll make a few more copies," said Josh.

"Well, actually I think it'd be better if we didn't distribute this, because it may be the reason someone tried to kill you, Josh," Marino said. "They know you have this, and we might be putting more people in jeopardy." Allison flinched as she made the connection.

"Right. Would it be okay if we just showed it to the people we mentioned, but not give them a copy?" Josh asked.

"I think that'd work. The people you mentioned are not going to be talking to anyone else," said Marino.

CHAPTER 34

BRET THORNTON

MAY 30 ... *Hit Man Number Two.* Bret Thornton was driving fast. He didn't want to be anywhere in the area when the cops showed up. He was flying down a two lane paved Mississippi road with flat farm land on either side. The western sun made it difficult to see. All he needed was for some cow to waltz across the road. He knew he would be out in the open, but he had calculated no more than seven minutes. That calculation had not considered the effect of the sun. He was going fifteen miles an hour slower than planned. Regardless, he would soon be turning down a dirt road that was eventually shaded by rows of large magnolias. It was there he had hidden his black Ford F-150 pickup. He found the road, and with great restraint dropped his speed to ten miles an hour, keeping the dust cloud to a minimum. He could just barely see the trees. Fifteen minutes later he pulled off the road, and parked next to his F-150.

As he got out of the LeSabre he glanced at himself in the side view mirror of his truck. He had quite a gash, and it was still bleeding. Where the hell'd that broad come from? I had Proctor square in my sights, and then this Chevy comes out of nowhere and cuts me off. Was she just someone who was picking him up and didn't see me? Or did she actually mean to cut me off? Was she a cop? I hope she's dead whoever she is. He wiped off the blood and taped up his forehead the best he could. He collected cleaning compounds from his truck and, still wearing latex gloves, proceeded to clean his own blood off of the steering wheel and floor mat of the LeSabre. He drove off, leaving the banged up car behind. Well, it's on to plan B. He stopped at a Shell station's automatic car wash to get the Mississippi dust off his truck.

***

May 31 … One Down, Four To Go. Next morning, Thornton checked his gashed forehead in the mirror of his hotel room. He'd used super glue and a butterfly bandage to close the gap. It seemed to have worked, but he wasn't too excited about the black and blue goose egg developing underneath it. Damn Mac. "It has to look like an accident," he mimicked. Well, what could go wrong with that? I tried to tell him. I don't do accidents.

He shifted his gaze in the mirror and focused on the gray metal case lying on the bed. Next to it sat Sneak's brown spiral pocket notebook in which he had written information on Proctor, White, Osborne and Paul Chisholm. He turned from the mirror. He had four jobs to do. I need to get my ass in gear. No more accidents. I'm doing it the way I do it best. Now, for a little recon. He changed into his running clothes, laced up his New Balance shoes, and stuffed a fanny pack with a bottle of water, his license, a set of small binoculars, Sneak's brown pocket notebook, and a .38 pistol. He headed for his truck.

Thornton pulled into a picnic area of Overton Park. There were a few mothers with children, three men talking beside a parked car, and a half-dozen parked cars with no sign of their former occupants. He parked the pickup, got out and began a series of runner's stretches. He walked to the internal paved road bordering the picnic area, and began to jog northward. He found the path marked in Sneak's notes, and geared down to a walk as he stepped off the road to the right. The trees were thick here. The temperature dropped. He followed the foot-wide path until he saw snippets of color—passing cars on his left. Leaving the path, he walked through the trees and brush. After about twenty yards, he stopped and pulled the binoculars out of his fanny pack. He scanned the houses across North Parkway and, moving about five yards to his right, found a clear line of sight to the Proctors' house.

"I'll be damned—Sneak did something right."

He estimated the distance at about 325 yards. Close enough for an accurate shot, and far enough away for a clean escape. He smiled as he looked through a window on the south side of the house. Two kids, probably his wife, and yes, there's Proctor himself. Oh, tsk tsk, look at how banged up he is. This won't be anything like you're gonna look tonight, he thought.

He checked around for the best firing position, and found a smallish tree with a branch about five feet above the ground. The intersection of the trunk and the branch would make a good support for his rifle. He made mental notes as to how this little tree lined up with the street light to the left, the traffic light on the far right and the street light straight ahead. Taking small steps, he counted the number of paces back to the trail, and identified a large root sticking up in the path as a marker for coming off the trail. He counted his steps back to the road, and then the number of steps to a **NO PARKING** sign. Then he began a return jog to his truck.

He didn't see the brown Pontiac LeMans.

CHAPTER 35

LIMERICKS

MAY *31 … The Odds Are 129 Million To One.* Tagger stood on the porch as Mailene and Allison hugged each other in the doorway and cried.

"Ladies, let's move inside," he said as he gently guided them while glancing back at the street, and closing the door.

"I'm so sorry, Mailene," Allison said through her tears. "Your dad meant the world to me."

"Thank you," Mailene said, now fighting back more tears. "Daddy always talked about you. I think he wished I'd been more like you and followed in his footsteps."

"Nonsense. He never stopped talking about how proud he was of you," said Allison. "Have you heard what happened to Josh Proctor?"

"No." She froze. "He's not—"

"No, Josh is okay, but last night someone did try to run him down in our parking lot. Something very strange and very dangerous is going on. And as far as we can tell, your father was trying to warn Josh and me."

"You?" said Mailene. "Are you in danger, too?"

"I'm afraid I am. That's why Sergeant Tagger's with me. I don't know enough to be able to fill you in. But Josh and I received an email from your father on the day he disappeared. We're baffled. We thought maybe you could help us understand what he wrote." Allison pulled the printed copy from her purse, unfolded it and showed it to Mailene. "Does this have any meaning for you?"

Mailene took the paper and began to read. "Well, Daddy always loved to write limericks. Sometimes they were a little risqué, and almost always corny. He liked to mess with people's minds, so that words weren't used in exactly the manner one would expect. You know, like a pun or slang?" She looked at the limericks again. "I don't have a context, so I'm a little at a loss. Let's see … *site*, for example, could mean a place but it could also mean a website." Allison's eyes opened wider. "And *rend* could mean tear apart. But it could also be an abbreviation for render, to give."

"Oh, this is great, Mailene," said Allison. "Anything else jump out at you?"

"Nothing right now," said Mailene. "I'll try to think about it some more. If I come up with anything, I'll give you a call."

"Thank you, Ms. Huong," said Tagger. "You've been a great help." He turned to Allison and said, "We want to be back to your house before dark."

"Yes. Thank you so much, Mailene," Allison said as she hugged her good-bye.

***

It was late by the time Marino dropped Josh at home. Anticipating Josh's injured mouth, Tonya made a plate of mashed potatoes, bite-size pieces of chicken, and green peas. He was grateful for a soft-food dinner. After eating, Josh asked everyone to come to the table because he had something he needed help with.

"Ms. White and I received a limerick puzzle from Dr. Huong in our email. No one's been able to figure it out. We think this is a special clue to helping understand what's been going on. Everybody find a place where you can see it," he said as he set his copy on the table. Josh read it aloud.

The background at this site is laid out.

The solution for entrance in doubt

Tell me what's his name
The one of great fame
The one who lived and did fly about

As for the key essential to rend
One must look to ones digital blend
Required for our job
Unique from the mob
You must sequence four each from the end

No response. Nothing from Tonya, Jennifer, Daniel, Ollie or Brandon. Josh read it again, slower. No response.

"Nobody has any ideas?" Josh said.

Daniel wore a funny look on his face. It was as if he were thinking about something, but afraid it would be too stupid to say. Josh saw it. "Daniel? You look like you've picked up something."

"Well, this probably has nothing to do with what Dr. Huong was trying to say, but it looks like Harry Potter to me."

Josh's heart sank. Not Harry Potter again, thought Josh. Daniel had read all seven of J.K. Rowling's Harry Potter books, seen all the movies to date, and spent hours talking to his friends about Hogwarts. Daniel picked up on Josh's physical reaction and lowered his head as he stepped back.

Keying in, Tonya asked encouragingly. "What about the limerick makes you think of Harry Potter?" Daniel hesitated. "Yes, I really want to know. You seem to be the only person in the room that even has a single idea. Please tell us."

Daniel hesitated, then pointed at the first section of the limerick. "See this here?" he asked. "Well, Harry Potter was always known as *the boy who lived*. And not only that, he was one of the best at flying on his broom." More silence.

"Daniel, that's the best interpretation I've heard tonight," Tonya said. Daniel managed a smile. Never mind it was the only interpretation of the evening. "So, if you're correct, what might the *site* be?"

"Well, there are a ton of websites devoted to the Harry Potter books, games, clubs, and clothes 'n stuff," Daniel said.

"Could it be that easy?" Josh said. "Amazing."

The phone rang. Ollie answered. "Daddy, it's for you."

"Hello," said Josh ... "Oh, hey, Allison." ... "What'd she say?" ... "Yeah. Our son, Daniel also identified *site* as possibly a website." ... "Here, let me put you on the speaker phone. We're all gathered around the table, and my Mom and Dad are here as well."

"Hello everyone," said Allison.

A group *Hello* came back.

"Staying with the first limerick, if we assume it's a website, what would be the *name*?" asked Allison.

"Well, Daniel says the lines all support Harry Potter as the mystery name," said Josh, still skeptical.

"He what?" she said. "Oh, I see ... Yes. That does sound like it fits. Not only that, Carl was a Harry Potter fan. So it makes even more sense. Way to go, Daniel." Daniel broke into a grin.

"Okay, now for the second half of the limerick," said Josh.

"Mailene suggested that *rend* could be short for *render*, or *give*," said Allison.

"If we're talking about a website, could the *essential key* to give be a password?" asked Tonya.

"Absolutely," said Allison. "So what's the password?"

Jennifer tossed out, "Does *digital* refer to fingers, or numbers, or high-tech?"

"Hey, we didn't think about numbers. That would mean what blend of numbers is *required for our job*?" said Josh.

"Actually, it goes on to say the blend of numbers is *unique* from everyone else," said Jennifer. "Could it be a social security number?"

"Bingo!" shouted Allison. "Now, for the last line."

"Does *four from the end* mean the last four digits of a social security number?" Josh asked.

"That sounds good, but whose social security number?" asked Tonya. "Carl's?"

Silence. Then Allison's voice came over the speaker. "Josh, remember this email was sent to the two of us. Could *each* mean each of *us*? If so, the password would be comprised of the last four numbers of our social security numbers."

"I think you've got it. My last four numbers are 9-7-5-3," said Josh.

"Mine are 7-4-3-2," said Allison. "But which one goes first?"

"I don't see how we could know that, so why don't we just have two possible passwords. One that is 97537432, and one that is 74329753. First one doesn't work, we plug in the second," said Josh.

Daniel came back into the room. "I just googled *Harry Potter*, and got 129 million possible results," he said. "I tried *Harry Potter website*, and found 42 million possible results. Last, I tried *password protected Harry Potter website*, and only got 120,000 possible results."

"129 million!" Josh said in exasperation. "Maybe it's time for a break. We'll try again tomorrow."

CHAPTER 36

SCRAMBLING IN THE BIG APPLE

MAY *31 … Another Hit Man.* "This is Memphis, Tennessee. Not New York, not Detroit, not Los Angeles," Mac ranted. "I'm supposed to have one of the top hit men in the country, and he can't even knock off a hick nerd. On top of that, he makes a little hit 'n run accident look like a damned Dukes of Hazard crash scene. Now the police are involved, and *Billy Bob* Proctor will be on guard as well."

At its core, Mac's rage was stoked by fear. He could feel his plan unraveling, and he was at a loss for how to get back on track. He'd gambled when he brought others in to do his work. When it was just him, he never had to worry about a job being done right. He'd killed Tibett and Sturgeon with skill and planning. No one had been the wiser. He simply stuck the barrel of his nine millimeter in their mouth and when they said *ahh*, put a needle in the underside of their tongues. The poison, derived from snake venom, attacked their central nervous system until they could no longer breathe. The poison had metabolized by the time he put them behind the wheel of their respective cars and drove them off the road. After that, he turned it over to others to complete the plan.

That damn Sneak, Mac thought. He did everything I told him not to do. He shot Huong while he was still in his office. He used that tired old popgun of his, and it misfired, twice. And he never got rid of it like I told him. On top of that, he did a shit job of hiding the body and the car. And then Thornton botches a simple hit and run. I'm not going to lose millions of dollars because of their incompetence. I'm not going to jail because they screwed up. He pulled out his iPhone. Too many loose ends. I hate loose ends. It's time to hear the roar of the tiger.

CHAPTER 37

THE SHOT

M AY *31 … A Crack Shot.* Laid out on the bed was a set of black clothes—pants, shirt, wind-breaker, and baseball cap. On the floor, a pair of black hiking boots, black socks, and a gray metal gun case. Thornton was preparing to do some night work. After nightfall he put on his socks first, then pulled on his short sleeve black shirt, and black pants. He laced up his boots, and swung into his shoulder holster, holding his .38. He slipped into his wind breaker, grabbed the gun case, and put on his cap. Once outside, he double checked the lock on his motel room door, and walked to his F-150.

Thornton drove to the Overton Park picnic area, parked his pickup, and waited twenty minutes to allow his eyes to adjust to the dark. He turned off the internal cab light so no one would be able to see him when he opened the truck door. Grabbing the gray metal case, he got out, and quietly closed the door. His black outfit and the lack of moon light gave him good cover. He crossed from the parking area to the internal paved road and turned right. Walking in the dark, even on a paved surface, was challenging. The slightest dip resulted in a teeth rattling step. Thornton kept his knees slightly bent. He could make out the **NO PARKING** sign on the left, and knew it was forty-two more steps to the path. Forty-three, forty-four, forty-five, and then he spotted a slight break in the trees. He turned right from the road into the woods. He only vaguely was able to make out the path. It wasn't as straight as he remembered it earlier in the day. He shifted to baby steps and continued counting, his right hand held out in front at face level to protect his eyes. After sixty-two steps he slowed down feeling for the root with his toe. No root. He moved cautiously forward, finding it on the sixty-sixth step. He made a ninety-degree left turn from the path, and moved cautiously into the trees. It wasn't long before he could make out the traffic light and one of the street lights, peeking through the branches. He adjusted his direction accordingly. The farther he moved, the more the street lights negatively highlighted the leaves, the tree trunks, and the branches. The other street light blinked into view, and he made his final adjustment.

Using the street lights as background, he found the skinny tree with the perfectly located branch that would allow him to steady his rifle. He laid the case on the ground and opened it. A dismantled high-power sniper's rifle was still packed inside, along with a scope. Thornton pulled out the scope and looked for Proctor's house.

"Yes!" he hissed.

The blinds were still open and he had a clean line of sight through the window overlooking the driveway. The Proctors were moving to the den to watch TV. Josh chose the easy chair directly in front of the window, clearly visible.

Thornton smiled as he assembled the rifle. He snapped the scope into place and raised the rifle, placing it in the angle created by the tree branch. This is going to be easy money, he thought as he adjusted the scope for the 325-yard shot. No more accidents. He inserted a .30 caliber round and chambered it with the bolt. He pulled himself to the rifle in a standing position, snuggled the butt into his shoulder, and let his right eye get used to the light coming through the scope. He had an unimpeded shot, and Josh's bandaged head was centered in his cross hairs. Following technique, he brought his finger to touch the trigger. He took a deep breath, let half of it out so as to control the affect of his breathing on the trajectory of the bullet. He began to squeeze the trigger.

CRACK!

Special Agent Maria Louise Lopez watched the smoke drifting from the barrel of her 9-millimeter Glock. "Not tonight, you son of a bitch." The FBI personal reference letter was correct. Maria was a *crack shot.*

Directly but cautiously she walked the fifty or sixty feet to where the shooter lay on the ground. She kept the muzzle of her pistol touching his head while she checked his pulse. He was very dead, with the rifle lying on the ground just out of his reach. Maria's shot had slammed into his left temple, killing him instantly. With the pistol still at his head, she patted him down, and extracted the hand gun she found in a shoulder holster. She carefully pointed the rifle down as she ejected the round and slid it into her pocket. Only then did she pull her phone to apprise Masterson of the situation. She looked over at the house.

I didn't mess up this time, she thought.

CHAPTER 38

AFTER SHOCKS

MAY *31 … No One Is Immune.* Masterson advised Maria to get out of the woods and rendezvous with him at Molly's, a Mexican restaurant just south of the park. She didn't need to get herself killed by excited cops who found her in the dark with a gun. She made her way back to the brown Le Mans. Masterson gave Maria five minutes then called Julia's cell.

Maria parked in the rear parking lot and made her way inside the restaurant. Masterson was already waiting for her at a table not far from the bar. Music was playing in the background which helped to mask their whispers.

"You okay, Lopez?" asked Masterson, concern in his eyes. Maria nodded, but he could see that her cheeks were flush, her eyes were wider than usual, and she was a little jumpy. "Good work out there, Lopez. Real good work. Tell me what happened."

A waitress came by. They ordered nachos, the seven layer dip, and two frozen margaritas.

"I shot him," said Maria with a mixture of surprise and guilt. "I never shot a real person before. I've shot deer and rattle snakes, you know, but never a person."

The waitress returned with the standard appetizer of chips and salsa, along with the frozen margaritas, the likes of which Maria had not tasted since leaving Texas. She thought of home, her family.

"It jacks you up every time you have to shoot someone, but especially the first one," whispered Masterson looking at her intently. "Now you listen to me, Lopez. You had no choice. And if you hadn't shot him he would've killed Josh, or one of the other Proctors. You know that, don't you?"

Maria's eyes rolled up to look at him. She took a long breath, and looked into her drink, "Yeah, I know."

"Now tell me how it went down," said Masterson.

Maria sucked a mouthful of her drink, and slowly began swallowing. She looked up. "Well, this morning I saw this black F-150 driving past the Proctor's street. I can't tell you why, maybe it was his slow speed, but I decided to follow him. He turned into the park. I watched him get out in his running shorts and a bulging fanny pack. He started jogging. Seemed like a heavy load for a jogger. I kinda walked his way, saw him leave the paved road and go into the woods. I waited. A short time later he came out but he was walking funny—taking small, slow steps. It looked like he was pacing off the distance. But why small steps? My nighttime hunts in Texas flashed in my head. We took baby steps because we couldn't see in the dark."

"Brilliant," said Masterson, shaking his head.

"Of course, I didn't know which night he might come back, but I thought I couldn't afford to skip any night. After he left, I walked up the road and into the woods on the path I'd seen him take. It wasn't long before I could see the traffic on North Parkway, so I moved in that direction. I got chills all over when I could see the Proctor's house, and the blinds of the den window were open."

"What? Open?"

"Yeah. There was a clear view, and good cover. I called Marino and told him about the blinds being open. He said he'd take care of it. I left, got a burger, and came back just as the sun was setting. Then I waited."

"Why did you wait so long before you took action?"

"It was pitch dark. I heard something, maybe an animal. It wasn't until he passed in front of the street lights that I could see the outline of a man. But I didn't have a clear shot. I had to move to my left, as quietly as a cat. By the time I found an open line of sight, he was lining up his shot. I drew my Glock, got him in my sights as quickly as I could, and fired ... hit him in the temple," Maria paused, stared into her margarita. She recovered. "I checked him out, pulled his pistol, cleared the rifle and called you." Maria reached into her pocket and retrieved the unspent round. Keeping her fist closed with her knuckles down, she slid it across the table to Masterson.

"Lopez, I will never say anything demeaning about you again," said Masterson. "I'll even attest to your, *fun loving, outgoing, and enthusiastic nature.* But especially that you are a *crack shot.* Well done, Lopez. Well done."

Maria smiled, feeling embarrassed. But she was also feeling better about the shoot. And sneaking in there somewhere, she even was feeling just a little proud of herself. To hear it coming from Lawrence Masterson was all icing on the cake.

"Sir?" Maria asked for permission to speak.

"Yes."

"Thanks for not throwing me off the Mississippi Bridge after I messed up so badly tailing Proctor that first day," said Maria.

"It's okay. I didn't like that Le Mans anyway. And besides, the Explorer fits me better." He smiled. Maria smiled too. Then all that famous energy came rushing back, just as the waitress came with their nachos and seven layer dip. "Two more margaritas, please."

Maria felt better, but she knew she wouldn't be sleeping well tonight.

***

They heard the squawk of the two-way. "Johnson, it's Marino. I'm coming up the steps. Let me in," said Marino in abrupt phrases. Officer Johnson moved to the front door, checked the peep hole, threw the lock, and let an obviously agitated Sergeant Marino in. Without a word he strode over to the den where the family was watching television, and quickly closed the blinds on the large window. He crossed to Johnson and snapped in an angry but quiet voice, "What the hell are you doing? Why are these blinds open?"

"I went around and closed all the blinds and drapes hours ago, Sergeant," replied a puzzled and nervous Johnson.

"Well, they *were* open, wouldn't you say?" Marino said.

"I'll check all the others," said Johnson as he wheeled, and proceeded with a sense of urgency to inspect each window in the house, upstairs and down.

The tone of the room had changed, a negative edge was palpable. Each family member had stopped whatever they'd been doing. Everyone was looking at Marino, wanting an explanation, but at the same time not wanting to know. It had to be bad news. Officer Johnson returned, slightly out of breath.

"All the other blinds and drapes were closed, Sergeant."

Still glaring at Johnson, Marino directed in a much calmer tone. Motioning to the dining room table, "Could y'all come in here for a minute?" When everyone was settled around the table, Marino breathed and cleared his throat. "Something just happened that you need to know about." He looked to his left and saw Ollie with her eyes as big as saucers. He regrouped. "I'm sorry to have barged in like I did. I was very concerned about the blinds being open."

Ollie was becoming even more upset, as she slowly raised her hand. Marino saw her, but was not sure he understood. Tonya spoke up, "What is it, sweetie?"

Ollie couldn't take her eyes off of Marino. And in her bravest, but softest voice she said, "I did it." Marino was at a loss.

Tonya asked, "You did what, Ollie?"

Continuing her petrified gaze at Marino, she said, "I opened the blinds." Marino cocked his head, and he felt some of the outrage dissipate.

"I heard Sarah and Molly playing outside," she said. "I opened the blinds to see them."

It was perfectly quiet. All eyes were on Ollie and Marino. Marino reached out one of his big hands and patted Ollie's shoulder.

"That's okay. I understand now," Marino said calmly. Ollie relaxed a little, but did not look away from him.

Marino took a few seconds to recover his thoughts. He decided he needed to tone down his information, for the sake of the kids. "Just a little while ago we caught a man with a gun in the neighborhood. I wanted to be sure you were safe." He looked over at Ollie and gave her a slight smile. "We need to keep the blinds and curtains closed darling, at least for a little while longer." Ollie nodded. "Thanks for telling me."

"Is that all?" asked Josh.

"That's all for now," Marino said.

Tonya, hoping for more information, had followed Marino's actions carefully. "Please stay and have a piece of pie, Sergeant," she said.

"Thanks. That would be nice," said Marino, as if he and Tonya were on the same page.

Tonya went over to Ollie and gave her a long hug. "That was very brave of you sweetie. I am truly impressed that you told the truth, even when you were so scared." Ollie was still shaking a little, and welcomed being wrapped in the comforting physical and emotional arms of her mother.

Marino stood and walked past Johnson. "We need to talk," he said, as he walked into the living room. Marino was facing away from the dining room, but Johnson's face was clearly visible. Josh watched as Johnson's eyes lit up and he took a half-step back. Marino closed the gap. It was a one-sided conversation, with Johnson doing all of the listening, punctuated with an occasional "Yes, Sergeant." and "No, Sergeant." Daniel had already returned to his hand held video game, and Ollie had wandered over to watch television. Josh left the table and walked to the kitchen to find Tonya.

"I'm glad you got the sergeant to stay," said Josh. "There is definitely something else he didn't say because of Ollie. I hope he hangs around until the kids go to bed."

"That's what I'm hoping for as well," Tonya said.

Marino was clearly interested in staying until Ollie and Daniel had gone to bed. Tonya took a little extra time with Ollie to make sure she would be able to sleep. They gathered around the living room table again. Marino was much better prepared this time.

"I'm sorry about scaring the dickens out of Ollie," he began. "I wasn't thinking very clearly. Minutes before I came over, one of our agents discovered a man aiming a rifle into your den window." Both Tonya and Josh gasped. They had goose bumps and their hearts were racing. Marino continued, "The man was shot and killed by our agent, as he was about to pull the trigger. That's why I freaked out about the open blinds."

Josh's eyes darted from one set of windows to the next. "Wh ... Where was he?"

"Across North Parkway, in Overton Park," said Marino. He had a high-powered rifle and scope. We're still investigating, but I'm pretty sure we'll find that he did this sort of thing for a living. We don't know yet if he's the same person who tried to run you over. But we aren't taking any chances."

"Why's this happening?" Tonya blurted out. "What did Josh do to these people? What did Dr. S. and Carl do to deserve this? How many of them are there? When will this end?"

"There's so much we still don't know," Marino said. "I can tell you that so far, this looks like a very complicated scheme involving BP Technologies. Please believe me. We're working very hard on this."

"This makes *two* times you've saved my life," said Josh.

Tonya asked, "What can we do to make this nightmare go away?"

"Right now our best lead is Huong's website. We need to crack it," said Marino.

"Sergeant, who do I have to thank for saving my life tonight?" asked Josh.

"A little bitty gal from Texas, and she's one hell of a shot," smiled Marino. "Special Agent Maria Lopez. You'd like her."

"I already do," said Josh.

"I don't have anything else for you right now," said Marino. "I know Lieutenant Todd will be keeping in touch." He read the question in Josh's eyes. "Yes, she's okay. She was released this afternoon. Thanks for the pie. I may be back for another slice." He smiled, and excused himself.

Neither Josh nor Tonya slept well that night. Neither did Daniel, who had been listening to Sergeant Marino's explanation.

***

His thoughts tended to be more visual than analytic, and to manifest themselves like movie trailers, video games, or day dreams. The subject of the vignettes were inspired by internal drives—the need to be accepted by peers, the need to be competent, sex, and the need to be independent. The images were colored by emotions like happiness, guilt, anxiety, or depression. The director of these fanciful productions made sure they complied with the guidelines of adolescent invincibility, regardless of how they might be judged intellectually or realistically. Thus, the hero always won the day. And, if he were injured, he recovered quickly and miraculously. Even if the theme were about his own suicide, as the hero he would be present at his funeral to see how sorry everyone was that he was dead. And, just as magically, he would be together with them again the next day with the only change being that they were treating him with more respect.

So it was this night that Daniel lay on his bed thinking, or fantasizing, or daydreaming. He had special powers. He could sense imminent danger (kind of Spidermanish). He could be transported to appear at any place simply by concentrating on the place (kind of Harry Potterish). And, he had advanced Tai Kwon Do and gymnastic skills (kind of Jet Li-ish). He would know when his Dad was in danger, and would teleport himself to the site of the assassin, and vanquish him with a barrage of kicks, flips and karate punches. Such an elaborate sequence did not occur only in his mind's eye. His muscles tensed to act out every punch and kick he threw, and every defensive back flip he completed. Daniel returned from his action reveries with clenched fists and a sweaty shirt. He pushed his fears aside. I'm gonna get that guy. I'll save Dad. He'll see me as a hero.

But at fifteen, fantasy does not go unchallenged. The fears returned. What if he couldn't sense the danger? What if he couldn't get there in time? What if his skills weren't good enough? Dad would be dead. His emotions were getting all confused. He was bombarded with feelings of dread, loss, ineptness, and sadness. Then he thought of all the times he had been angry with his father, because he wouldn't let him go out with his friends, or when he made fun of him for liking Harry Potter. And he remembered the times he had dissed his father in front of his friends. The feelings morphed to ones of guilt. If he dies, it will be my fault, he thought.

***

"Name the countries of South America and each of their capital cities," directed Ms. Standish. All the other children began writing. I was watching the clock. Just forty minutes until the bell. I had to know. I had to see him. Ms. Standish scrunched together her eyebrows, and threw some mean looks at me. I began to work on the assignment. But no letters were showing up on the paper. No matter how hard I pressed—no letters. Only four minutes left till the bell. Ms. Standish told everyone to pass their paper to the front of our row. There was nothing on my paper. I raised my hand but she wouldn't call on me. Sandy was yelling at me. She snatched my blank paper and passed it to the front. The bell rang and everyone began to move. I tried to talk to Ms. Standish, but the class pushed me out the door and down the hall. Rene called for me to hurry. Her mother was waiting to drive us home. I didn't know what to do. Rene came back and pulled my arm until we climbed into the car. The car stopped at my house and I got out. I ran to the porch and my Daddy opened the door. He wouldn't look at me as he walked by. He seemed mad. He must be mad at me for opening the blinds. "Daddy, I'm sorry. Please come back. Daddy, don't you love me anymore? Please come back. I'm sorry. It was my fault. I won't open the blinds anymore." Still asleep, Ollie's tears dampened her pillow.

***

She was in one of those just-awakening periods. Her eyes were still closed as she lay mostly on her left side. She moved her legs slowly, stretching the bottom left leg, pulling the top right leg higher, returning them and doing it again. It was incredibly sensual, and stimulating. Her body felt alive, and even the touch of the sheet was exciting her. Tonya visualized Josh sleeping next to her. This would be the perfect morning for her to rouse him, arouse him still half asleep, and consume him. It would be a morning he would never forget. She considered all the delicious ways she could do it. She wriggled quietly out of the T-shirt she always wore to bed. Then out of her panties. Skin on skin. She could hardly contain her excitement. He was a side-sleeper too. She reached behind her head slowly, and not feeling his arm next to her pillow, guessed correctly, he was lying on his right side facing away from her. She pulled the sheet up and moved under it to him. She maneuvered herself into a spooning position, taking care to place her left arm over his top arm to protect her face in case he startled. He had not awakened. She moved in closer, feasting on the touch of his body from her knees, to her thighs, her stomach, her breasts. Her heart was racing and she felt the familiar tingling in her stomach, moving down to her thighs. She pulled herself ever so much closer, and nibbled on his shoulder. She was positively alive everywhere, all he would have to do would be to touch her. She'd absorb him until he was a part of her. She rolled him slightly, turning his head to her. She opened her eyes and SCREAMED! Josh had no eyes, no face. Instead, only a blood-splattered black hole.

Tonya snapped to a wide awake sitting position, her heart pounding, the fine hairs on her body standing at attention, her muscles taut, and sweat dripping from her hair line and arm pits. What the hell was *that*? she thought. It was so damn real? Was it a dream? She barely dared a glance to where Josh was lying, still not moving. She was terrified. He was lying on his right side just as in the dream. There were no breathing sounds. There were no movements. She was frozen. Surely, he could hear the pounding of her heart, the way she could as her blood crashed into her eardrums. Surely, the noise would wake him—if he were alive. My God, Josh *is* dead!

Then she heard it, a half-breath. Was that Josh? Or is there someone else in our bedroom? She listened as hard as she could. She concentrated, as her body tensed to focus all her senses to her hearing. She heard it again. Where did it come from? Please, God. Please, make it be Josh. She still had not dared to look. She forced herself. The sun had yet to rise, but she could make out the outline of his hip. It was not moving. She used all her strength and inched her hand toward his hip. She stopped and brought it back, closed her eyes and drew on courage she didn't believe she had. She tried again. Her hand hovered just over his left hip bone. She forced it to settle. Nothing. No movement. She pulled at him in the most tenuous manner possible, and he moved. She pulled a little harder, and he rocked back. She had to know, and she grabbed his hip and pulled it to her. Josh rolled towards her, and she saw his eyes. He had a face. She pounced on him, crying. Josh struggled to understand what was happening. Soon, he understood enough to know she needed to be held.

"What's the matter, hon?"

CHAPTER 39

INTROSPECTION

SUNDAY *morning, June 1 … Smelling The Roses.* Charleze hadn't been in the office since her overpowering flashback last Friday. This was the first weekend off she could remember since opening her own company. But curiously, she was not concerned. Although tired, it was more of a peaceful tired. She was feeling appreciably better, and her body was recovering. She sat at her breakfast table, with coffee and a bagel, looking out over Central Park. Unusual for Charleze, her brain was not in control at the moment, at least not the left hemisphere.

It had been the highly evolved verbal, logical side of her brain that had been her salvation all these years. It brought her academic and professional success, while affording her refuge from the pain of unconscionable abuse. Now, this morning, it felt foreign to explore the world through the lens of the right hemisphere. She allowed herself to feel relaxed, and though it was not easy, she was trying to use other senses to experience the world—the green of the park, the color of the flowers. *The coffee tastes especially good this morning,* she thought.

Her flashback had opened a stream of memories that seemed alien to her. *Was that really me?* she kept asking herself. The intensity of the flashback had one benefit. She had been so overwhelmed that her feeling sensors were exhausted. As a result, she could revisit and consider these memories without the gamut of horrific feelings and physiological responses associated with them. At least those weakened associations were cutting her some slack for the moment. She pulled back from the window and looked around her penthouse.

The home she grew up in could fit inside her apartment six times over. She was taking in the beauty of her original paintings and sculptures for the first time. Each room had been meticulously furnished. She had not noticed before with this sense of appreciation. For all these years she'd really only paid attention to her office area, with its dozen monitors hooked to stock, bond and commodities markets all over the world. But not today.

This was hundreds of miles from her hometown, and light years beyond how she grew up. Here, she was her own boss. Nobody ordered her around, nobody put her down, and nobody sold her body to the lowest bidder. No more living from trick to trick. No more squeezing enough money out of the drug funds to buy groceries and clothes.

But I haven't really gotten away, have I? she thought. There was nowhere I could have hidden because I've been carrying this with me all these years. My past exploded from its hiding place with a vengeance, and kicked the shit out of me. I guess I'm not as tough as I thought I was. I guess I'm not really in control. I haven't really changed. The only difference … now I've been selling my soul to the *highest* bidder.

She found herself struggling with a vaguely familiar feeling—guilt. But this time, maybe it was her fault. Charleze had another new feeling. She felt empty, and she longed to be close to someone. She pulled her BlackBerry and punched in the number for Susan Determan.

CHAPTER 40

IN THE LIGHT OF DAY

JUNE *1 … Sorting Things Out.* The seriousness of the last two days' events, warranted a Sunday mid-morning meeting, Julia insisted. The lack of hair on the back of her head highlighted her new stitches, and the early stages of two black eyes were evident. She was making no sudden moves. She brought the donuts and coffee cup up to her mouth, instead of the usual lowering of the head or leaning of the body. Her head and body turned from side to side as a unit. The men were uncharacteristically sensitive, as they tried to anticipate any need she might have. They moved her chair, got her coffee, a doughnut, a napkin, and refills. Julia didn't know whether to be embarrassed or bothered. She chose to be touched, and grateful.

Fortified with police-issue coffee and donuts, Julia, Marino and Tagger were listening intently as Masterson shared Maria's report of the previous night's shooting.

"That was cutting it way too close," observed Julia.

"Like someone else we know," said Tagger, looking at Julia.

"What a stakeout. Sixty feet in the dark? What a shot," said Marino.

"And she's just a rookie?" said Tagger. "How's she handling this?"

"Well, she looked okay last night," said Masterson. "I'll keep checking on her."

"Do we need to pull her from the rotation?" asked Julia.

"Definitely not," said Masterson. He hoped he hadn't spoken too soon. "I'll let you know if I see any red flags."

Julia was used to the MPD's mandatory post-shooting relief from duty with pay, pending an investigation and interview with one of the psychologists. She was convinced that Maria could use more help, especially as it was her first shoot. She made eye contact with Masterson and asked directly, "Would you mind if I looked in on her as well?"

Masterson was relieved. He knew something more needed to be done, and he was also aware he didn't know how to do that for Maria. "That would be great, Lieutenant. I took a shot last night, but I think she'd appreciate talking to a woman." Julia ignored the gender-related implication, and, thankful for his acquiescence, gave the smallest of nods.

Then it was Julia's turn to share what the MPD had collected.

"Brad Thornton is out of New York City. He's been suspected in no fewer than six assassinations internationally, but no proof. He's been arrested a handful of times, and except for juvenile court, has no convictions. Tracking down the information from the key in his pocket, we found the motel where he'd been staying. A search of his room led to the discovery of cleaning fluid and rags. We're hoping to find a match with samples found in the Buick LeSabre. We found seventy-four thousand dollars in cash. There was also a brown spiral notebook with comments and details on Josh, Allison, Dorothy, and a new buyer at BP Technologies, Paul Chisholm. It looks like Allison would have been next. Like us, he apparently had no idea where Dorothy has disappeared to. The slug that killed Sneak Roberts came from Thornton's .38. But it's not the slug that killed Huong."

Tagger was looking at his notes. "Roberts, Thornton and McMillan all served time together as thirteen and fourteen year olds in the Bronx. It's starting to look like a juvy reunion for the class of '75."

"Great class. Wonder if there are any other alums floating around the Bluff City," said Marino.

"So, Thornton kills Roberts, but who kills Huong?" asked Masterson. "What was Roberts doing down here? Did he do Huong, or is there another killer still in play?"

"I think we have to assume there's still another alum here," said

Julia. "So, instead of relaxing our guard, we need to continue our 24/7 on Josh and Allison. What is it that these two know? Where is Dorothy Osborne? And let's find Paul Chisholm."

***

Mac had not heard from Thornton. "What's that dildo doin? He's gonna screw around and have my ass in a sling." The phone buzzed.

"Yeah!" Mac yelled into the phone … "What?" … "Who shot him?" … "That sorry sack a shit." … "You sit tight." … "I still have a backup plan." … "No, damn it. I told you. Sit tight." … "You keep doin your thing." … "Just chill." … "That's right. I'll be in touch."

CHAPTER 41

DO BLONDES REALLY HAVE MORE FUN?

JUNE1 ... *Chocolate Helps*. I need to find one of those T-shirts with *Shit Happens* written on it, and maybe a similarly inscribed wall hanging as well. It's the story of my life. I exceeded in math, and adolescent male classmates were freaked out, and shit happened. I was reasonably good looking, and my adolescent female classmates were freaked out, and shit happened. I got a great graduate education and work with great people, and shit happens. I mind my own business, and shit happens. I just can't catch a break. Allison White ruminated, feeling sorry for herself. It was a chocolate kind of night. "I need some more Rocky Road ice cream."

Psychologically speaking, Allison had good reasons to feel sorry for herself. Shit really has happened to her, and all around her, since she was twelve. A good looking blonde who was also very intelligent. No, that's not an oxymoron, but it was a formula for disaster for this adolescent. She caught nothing but shit from her peers. She was the poster girl for blonde jokes. Her lack of positive peer interactions sabotaged the normal development of her social skills, assuring an anxious and shy demeanor, a perfect target for non-retaliated ridicule. Getting up every morning and going to school was excruciating. After high school, she chose to stay with her mathematical talents and went head to head with the overwhelming number of male students in her college math and science classes. Some of the young men she met in college were not threatened by her intelligence, but rather were drawn to her beauty. Allison gratefully and thirstily welcomed their affirming attention, only to be blindsided by their primary focus on sex. When she finally acquiesced, she discovered her name had been added to the list of *easy* coeds being emailed about campus. Where was the fairness?

Things were different in The University of Memphis graduate engineering program. The herd had been thinned considerably, as most of the immature, mean spirited, and disrespectful male students simply didn't make it to graduate school, or had actually matured. At last, this was an environment she felt comfortable in. What wonderful experiences. As an added bonus she secured a field placement with Carl at BP Tech. It was so stimulating, and he was the perfect supervisor, allowing her to develop at her own speed. She'd learned so much. And for the first time in her life, everything matched with her mathematical and science skills. After graduation, he tried to employ her, but budget problems forced a freeze on hiring. With the help of his glowing letter of recommendation, she was offered a job at R&O Industries, and took it. R&O has been a great place to work. But just when things were coming together so well for her, shit happens again. Carl has been killed. Someone has tried to kill Josh, twice. And now her life may be in danger.

Here I sit with my third bowl of ice cream and a police officer living in my house, sulked Allison. What's wrong with this picture?

CHAPTER 42

THE MINI DEBRIEFING

JUNE 2 ... *Befriending and Tending.* Maria did not sleep well. Her emotions were frayed, and her brain wouldn't stop firing. She played and replayed the events in Overton Park, challenging each of her actions. Is there such a thing as a good shoot? I killed a man. Could I have handled it differently? Was it really like Masterson said? I didn't have any choice? Maybe I shouldn't have let it get that far. Maybe if I'd called for back-up. But, it was just a hunch. I didn't know for sure if he was after Josh, or if he was even going to show up last night.

The battle waged in her head, in her stomach. Of course, the late night refried beans and spices weren't helping. She felt physically ill. She suffered through cold sweats, and threw up twice. And, her right hand would start shaking, all by itself. Occasionally, she allowed herself to hear Masterson's words, *Good work out there, Lopez. Real good work.* That meant so much to her. She hoped she deserved his praise. She hoped her brother would agree with him.

The next morning, Maria was spent. It was getting late, and she was still tossing and turning in her bed. She didn't think she'd be able to report to her assigned protection rotation of Proctor. She didn't want to put him in danger due to her inability to concentrate, and to make the right decisions quickly enough. She decided to suck it up, put one foot in front of the other, and make it through this day. She'd see how she felt as she got closer to her afternoon shift. She'd tell Masterson if she wasn't able to get on top of this. He'd understand.

Maria took a long hot shower, letting the water's curative powers wash over her. She toweled off, blow dried and combed her hair, put on a touch of make-up, got dressed and went into the kitchen to get something to eat. Only toast and tea. She wasn't sure she could keep anything else down.

Maria was cleaning up the breakfast table when she heard a knock at the door. She automatically reached for the Glock on her hip, but she'd forgotten to put it in its holster. She started to panic as her eyes darted around the kitchen looking for it. The knock came again, louder. Maria moved quickly to the living room where she found the dismantled pistol she had cleaned last night. Amazed at her own dexterity, she reassembled the Glock in seconds, loaded a clip, chambered a round, and moved towards the front door of the condo. There was a third knock, this time the person shouted,

"Maria. It's Julia Todd. You up yet?"

Maria blew out a big breath and, after checking the peep hole, cleared her weapon, holstered it, unlocked the door, and said as nonchalantly as she could, "Hi, Lieutenant. What brings you out here?"

"I wanted to check on you. I thought maybe you could use some company this morning," said Julia with a smile and carrying a to-go tray of McDonald's coffees. "May I come in?"

"Of course. Yes, please, come in," said a somewhat befuddled Maria. She showed her to the kitchen and they sat at the table. I heard all about how you drove your car into the killer's car to save Josh. That was so brave, and so smart of you to come up with that action at the last second. Julia took off her sun glasses, and Maria saw the bruises under her eyes. "How are you doing?"

Julia passed one of the coffees to Maria, and opened one for herself. "Thanks. I'm comin along, still trying to shake the cobwebs out." She pulled the lid off her coffee cup. "Looks like the man you shot was the same man who drove the LeSabre. He was a professional hit man named Brad Thornton. I think we have some kind of sisterhood going here. Maybe it should be *the sisterhood of the last second?*"

Maria smiled. "Whatever it's called, I'm proud to be in it with you, Lieutenant." They toasted with their recyclable coffee cups.

"Masterson filled us in on the details of what happened last night," said Julia. "You're one very impressive officer. We're so glad you followed your hunch, and that you stopped Thornton from killing Josh. And, I'm pretty sure Josh is, too." She waited to see Maria's reaction.

Maria watched the steam rise from her coffee cup, forcing a smile. "It's very nice of you to say that, Lieutenant. Thank you for coming out to see me."

"How're you doing? I mean how are you *really* doing?" Julia asked.

"I've never killed a person before, and I'm kinda torn up about it," Maria replied slowly, almost apologetically, thinking that her comment didn't sound tough enough to be worthy of a real cop.

"You look like I did the other night when I didn't get much sleep," smiled Julia.

"Oh, I was hoping that it didn't show so much," Maria blushed as she pushed her hair around randomly. "Yeah, last night was tough."

"Thank God. I'd be concerned if you hadn't had a rough night. What you went through is one of the more difficult acts we deal with in our line of work. And the fact that it bothered you means your humanity is still in tact. I'm very glad to hear that," said Julia.

"Really? You mean what I've been going through is a … normal?" said Maria.

Julia smiled again. "Absolutely, Maria. It is *so* normal." She took a sip of coffee. "Do you mind talking about what you've been going through?" Maria shook her head. "Why don't you start by telling me the details as you remember them?"

"I've never even met Joshua Proctor, but I remember being pissed off that someone had tried to kill him, and that they'd hurt you. I was going to make it my business to see that it wouldn't happen again," said Maria.

"So, one of the things you remember is that you were angry before the shooting?"

"It had never crossed my mind until right this second, but I guess so," said Maria.

"Why do you think that is?" asked Julia, wishing Tonya was here to help her sort this out. She had teamed with Tonya on eight or ten critical incident stress debriefings. But Tonya had always taken the lead with questions about feelings.

"This sounds crazy ... I think this may be why I'm feeling so guilty about killing him. I mean, maybe if I'd been more professional, and less angry, I would have done things differently. Maybe I could have stopped him without having to kill him."

Julia felt sure it was important she affirm Maria's feelings, and that she not simply gloss over her statement just because it didn't make any sense to her. She was scrambling. Think, damn it. What would Tonya say? Then, an idea. "Have you ever had a situation in which being angry helped you do your job better?" she asked, hoping Tonya would approve.

Maria was a little taken aback, but she thought about it. "Well, actually, now that you say it that way, getting angry has often helped me get beyond being afraid to try things. And, being pissed off helped me get myself together and become the best in my hand-to-hand self-defense class. And, it helped me prove that I could be just as good as any man in my graduate program."

"So getting angry has in fact helped you do a better job?" she threw out for

clarification, frantically searching her memory for the next question Tonya might ask.

Maria nodded, still trying to understand what was going on.

"Would you say that sometimes getting angry has helped you be more competent, to make quick decisions, and to take decisive actions?" asked Julia.

Maria nodded again, and her eyes opened, revealing a sense of hopefulness. "So, you think I shouldn't feel guilty?"

"I think that's a question for you to answer. If I've understood, first it seemed like you identified being angry as a possible reason for mistakenly shooting Thornton." Julia scrambled to find the most helpful things to say. "Then, just now, it sounded like you associated being angry with doing a better job, which led you to make a more professional decision as to how to save Josh's life. Am I in the ballpark?"

"Yes, I think you are. It makes sense. I have to say that I still feel guilty, but not as much," said Maria.

"Okay. Now walk me through last night," said Julia. This was the part of the debriefings that she felt the most comfortable doing— details and procedures. She asked focused questions, but, hopefully in a nonthreatening manner. She listened closely and worked hard to be supportive. Maria talked, and cried, and smiled, and relaxed.

"What should I do now, Lieutenant?"

"Well, I'd like you to do what all our officers do in situations like this. I'd like you to talk to one of our psychologists who's been helping us through experiences like this for years. I already checked his schedule, and he has a one-thirty open this afternoon. Here's his card. Just call and confirm that you'll be there. Then, I think you and I should do what ever he advises. If he says he wants you to take some time, then that's what we do. If he says you're ready to return to work, that's what we do. Agreed?"

"Agreed," said Maria. She stood up wanting to hug Julia, thought better of it, and shook her hand.

"I'll clear this with Masterson. I'm sure he'll want to hold your weapon for you until you're on the job again. I hope to see you back in the rotation by next week. We need you," Julia said, as she set what she thought was a realistic expectation of down time. She returned to her car, poured herself in, and collapsed. Her head hurt, and she winced at the sunlight. She was exhausted. How do psychologists *do* this all day long?

CHAPTER 43

HEDGING HER BETS

JUNE 2 ... *Getting Her House In Order.* She opened the embossed envelope to find a statement showing a balance of $73,397,231.83 U.S. She exhaled slowly. She opened the Bank of Switzerland account years ago in the name Renee Washington. Her adult life had been focused on getting as much money as possible. There never seemed to be enough money for her to believe she wouldn't ever have to return to being Charleze Renee Washington. It's difficult to imagine a person dreading to have to live on *only* seventy-three million dollars, but Charleze Mitchell did. She tried to convince herself that she could live on it if she had to. And, she'd have to, if everything else went belly up. The market was getting worse overall. Within the past four months Bear Stearns, one of the largest investment banks on the Street, had collapsed, three commercial banks had failed, and the large IndyMac Bank was on the verge of going under. Tornadic Growth Investments was not immune. And to make things worse, Mac's part of the plan seemed to be unraveling, and that could translate into some serious jail time. It was Monday morning. She couldn't take any more time away from the office. She called Austin.

***

Charleze hesitated before entering her building. Her body and spirit were still recuperating from the shock of three days ago. Would it happen again? She urged herself on. Come on girl. You don't have a choice. You can do this. Charleze opened the door, inched inside. So far, so good. She pushed forward, her steps uncharacteristically measured. The custodian was nowhere in sight. Charleze breathed for the first time. She passed the ladies room where she had found refuge. Still okay. Ten steps more and she was comforted by the return of her posture, and then her signature walk. She prepared herself to face the financial storm clouds of the day.

Her secretary stood as Charleze entered the outer office. She handed her a stack of phone messages and, walking beside her, began summarizing the priority issues of the morning. Everyone, it seemed, wanted their money—creditors and investors. Fourteen of her staff had submitted their resignations, anticipating a major collapse.

It was looking as if she had miscalculated the timeline. Even if BPTX made their announcement tonight about the production of their new artificial hip, she might not be able to hold off the investors and creditors long enough to short the stock. She needed a backup plan, maybe two. Charleze Mitchell would land on her feet by doing what she had learned to do so well, by hedging her bets. She found the first telephone number online, but decided the call needed to come from a non-traceable cell, which she would buy later that evening. Reaching under the middle drawer of her desk, she retrieved the mini-disc. Attached was a business card. She punched in the numbers.

"Mr. Millerman's office," came the standard greeting.

CHAPTER 44

ALL THAT TRAINING PAYS OFF

JUNE 3 ... *Not In My House.* Her mind always seemed to be going in four or five directions at once. It worked even into the night, sometimes keeping her from going to sleep, sometimes waking her early. This morning her mind was busying itself asking and answering challenging questions about her career choice, and her competence as a cop. The chartreuse envelope case has been so frustrating. *Why have I been so slow to put the pieces together? This case went beyond the city limits of Memphis, and all of a sudden I'm in over my head. I really am just a southern hick cop. Yes, we've been able to save Josh's life, but each time it's been at the last possible second. What about the next time? What happens when the realities of statistical probability catch up with me? Next time I will be one second too late. And, Josh, or maybe Allison will be dead. I don't know if I'm up to this.*

Julia was about finished with her morning run. A good weather day for Memphis, not too hot, not too humid. Her neck was still sore, but otherwise she felt strong for the first time since the car crash. She decided to throw in some twenty-second sprints for the last mile, before arriving at the Inside Out Gym, and hitting the heavy bag. She had a good workout, and an easy run home.

The shower felt great. She loved lathering up when her muscles were taut, and especially those times, like now, when her tummy was flat. It gave her a palpable sense of physical competence. It was within this context of positive feelings that she revisited some of the questions her brain had bombarded her with earlier. *This has been one of the most complex cases I've worked. It's been slow going, but I've been able to establish a surveillance regimen that saved Josh twice, and put away at least one of the bad guys. Now, how do I stay ahead of this thing?*

She toweled off, gave her face the minimum of beauty enhancements, and did the doggy shake of her head, letting her hair fall into place with the help of a few rakes of her fingers. She pulled on her clothes and holstered her weapon, and made her way to the coffee shop and some pre-work transition time.

Julia sat at a table in the Deliberate Literate, skimming *The Commercial Appeal* and savoring her coffee. The bell on the front door jingled. Glancing over the top of her newspaper, she watched as two young men entered the shop, their eyes intense, their gait purposeful. The second one through the door had his right hand in his jacket pocket, on this warm June day. The first man walked to the counter, the second trailed. Julia scanned the location of the customers and made her decision.

In a seamless motion she unhooked her holster strap, lowered the paper, quietly slid back her chair, and stood. Carrying her coffee cup, she moved as a typical customer looking for a refill. She followed a path that brought her just behind the second man, approaching from his right. Now within five feet, she could see the outline of something other than the man's hand in his pocket. She grabbed the pistol grip of her still holstered weapon, positioning herself just off and behind his right shoulder. From that position she could see a bulge in the back waistband under the shirt of the first man. The man nearest her moved. She saw the grip of a pistol coming from his jacket pocket, as he yelled "This is a—"

Julia drew her weapon and hammered his hand with her Glock just as the gun cleared his pocket, knocking it to the floor. He yelled. Without taking her eyes off the man at the counter, she rammed a stomping kick into the outside of his knee, bringing a string of cuss words as he grabbed his leg and collapsed in pain. The remaining man reached for his gun as he pivoted to see his companion on the floor. Julia threw her coffee in his face. In that second of disorientation, she took a step toward him, grabbed his shirt, and powered a sharp knee into his groin, doubling him over. She drove her elbow into the back of his head, dropping him to the floor beside his buddy.

With her weapon trained on them, Julia snatched up the first man's pistol, and pulled the pistol from the waistband of the second man. She cuffed them together at their wrists, and called for assistance on her two-way. Her work day had begun a little sooner than she'd anticipated.

Her intense focus was interrupted by loud clapping and cheering from the patrons and workers, who were all on their feet. She grinned sheepishly at the accolades of the customers and wait staff, as in another compartment of her brain she envisioned the paperwork she would have to complete.

Police arrived in minutes, and transported the would-be holdup men. The shop manager brought Julia a replacement cup of coffee and a biscotti. She could not have been more appreciated. It was a good morning to be a cop. After shaking everyone's hand, she finished her coffee and biscotti. Julia tried to calm her heart rate. She walked slowly to her car, slid in, took a few deep breaths, then drove down the street to the Union Station. She walked in to another round of applause and cheers from her fellow officers. Maybe the paperwork won't be too bad, she thought.

CHAPTER 45

AND THAT MAKES THREE

JUNE 3 ... *The Tiger.* His weapon of choice was his bare hands and feet. He was proficient in the martial arts, and had honed his skills as a mercenary, fighting in Serbia and Africa. He was also skilled with weapons, but shooting *marks* took the thrill out of it. He relished the extra excitement of killing people face to face, barehanded. Fritz Wilhelm, aka *the tiger*, was in his late thirties, with blond hair that hung past his shoulders. He was well built, but not in a muscle bound sense. He stood about five-ten and weighed about 170 pounds. There were calluses on his knuckles from repeatedly breaking boards and bricks. He treated his body like a temple—a strict vegan, exercised daily, and neither drank alcohol nor smoked. Wilhelm was not unattractive. But he had a distant judgmental look, with just a hint of a sneer, as if he could read a person's thoughts, and didn't like what he'd read. The nickname, the tiger, came from his fellow mercenaries who marveled at his ability to stalk, quietly sneak up on, and kill his targets even when they were much larger than he was.

The tiger had been staying in a hotel room for three days in Bartlett, a city located adjacent to the northeast section of Memphis. There were pictures of marks, and related information to be studied. This was his second favorite part—the stalking. He would soon be doing his favorite part—the killing. Thornton had been on his list, but the cops took care of that for him. He was looking forward to taking out Proctor because it would prove how much better the tiger was than Thornton. But he would do him later, saving Paul Chisholm for last. Allison White was first. While Thornton had been trying to knock off Proctor, the tiger had been stalking Allison. He knew her daily routine, as well as the routine of the patrol cars that monitored her neighborhood. She was not long for this world.

Killing women gave the tiger a sensual pleasure. The more attractive the woman, the more intense the rush. He would enjoy watching her eyes just before he broke her rib cage and stopped her heart with his bare hand.

His plan was almost complete. When the call finally came from Mac giving him the go ahead, he felt as if he had been freed. He didn't know what she had done to deserve killing, but that decision was up to someone else. What he did know was that he would take great pleasure in being the instrument of her death.

Finding her house had not been hard. Allison lived in a section of Memphis called Cordova, on the east side of the city. Hers was a high ceilinged, single story house, with tall windows dropping almost to the floor. The middle class subdivision, probably built twenty-five or thirty years ago, was well maintained. Cars only rarely parked in the streets. The lots were larger than most, dotted with young trees, shrubs, and an occasional mature oak or sweet gum. The houses tended to be elevated above street level and sat well back from the curb, with long climbing driveways. The only sidewalks were the ones extending from the individual driveways to the front porches. Allison's house was the second from the cross street, a light red brick with pale yellow trim.

The tiger had scouted her neighborhood thoroughly, driving the area every two to three hours for a day and a half. It wasn't long before he was able to predict when a cop car would pass by her house. In just two days, he was able to identify the characteristics of the route each of the six rotating cops drove. He learned that the early evening cop, whose watch began at six and ended at ten, tended to return to the house every fifteen minutes.

The tiger expanded his scouting of Allison's neighborhood in concentric circles until he found gang graffiti, which in this case he recognized as marking the territory of the Vice Lords gang. In the early morning hours he drove this area until he found groups of youngsters wearing the gang's traditional red colors. The tiger approached the gang bangers with five thousand dollars cash, a specific time table, an exact street crossing, and a unique idea.

Knocking heads with the cops and getting arrested was always good for a primo gang initiation. In the youth gang culture, special recognition was given to those members who had an arrest record, even better if he or she had done jail time. The younger the offender, the less jail time they did, and the sooner they'd earn their stripes and be back on the streets.

The tiger knew a police car would enter an intersection six blocks from Allison's house at 8:50 P.M. His plan involved having a prospective female gang member steal a car, run the stop sign at that intersection, and plow into the squad car's front wheel. It would be enough to put the cruiser out of commission, giving him all the time he would need. He promised the gang leader another ten thousand dollars upon successful completion of the job.

On Tuesday evening the tiger turned on to Allison's street at 8:47 P.M., as the patrol car pulled away. He stopped his car across the street, a few houses down. Consistent with the previous two days, he observed the same lone car parked in the driveway. The curtains were drawn but he could still make out two distinct shadows in the house. One had to be White. The other could be a cop. He decided the biggest thrill would come from simply going through the front door, and seeing how fast the other person was, cop or not. He eased his car into the driveway, got out and confidently crossed in front of his car onto the sidewalk, and up the three steps of the front porch. The tiger rang the door bell. A rather gruff female voice from inside.

"Who are you and what do you want?" Rodruquez demanded.

He smiled. Must be a cop. He looked down at his right hand which was cradling a security key card for R&O Industries with Allison White's name on it. He'd found it in Allison's office when he broke in earlier this evening.

"I have Ms. White's key card to the office building. She must have dropped it," the tiger said.

"Leave it in the mailbox," Rodriguez said. She looked at Allison for confirmation.

Allison grabbed her purse, and quickly searched through it. "My key card isn't in my purse. Maybe I did lose it," she whispered.

"I don't mean to cause any trouble, but I promised the security guard that I'd put it in Ms. White's hand personally," the tiger said.

"Are you sure?" Rodriguez whispered.

Allison nodded.

Rodriguez gestured for Allison to move across the room. She unhooked the strap on her weapon.

Almost a minute passed before he heard the clicks of separate door locks. He looked in as the door opened. A female cop. He could see Allison standing quite a distance away, behind the officer, on her right. The officer had her right hand on her still holstered weapon, and was standing in a defensive position with her left foot forward, and her shoulders turned slightly to the right, in tandem with her feet. The tiger held up the card and smiled broadly.

Rodriguez relaxed for a half second, as she reached for the card. The tiger saw the change. He burst through the door and moved toward her. She maintained her stance and drew her weapon. He quickly blocked her gun hand with his left hand and sent a deadly, straight open-handed blow to her throat with his right—crushing her wind pipe and breaking her neck. Rodriguez stood, a surprised look in her eyes, then dropped straight to the floor in a heap. Her Glock discharged as it hit the floor, shattering the television screen. The tiger took a second to lock into his memory the end result of his latest kill.

Allison screamed, spun, took two quick strides to the side door. The tiger looked up. She turned the lock with her left hand, and wrenched the door open quickly with her right. She bolted through it, jumped over the steps to the driveway, and turned left running toward the street. Her heart was pounding against her ribs. She felt as if her legs were made of lead and she was running in slow motion. She chanced a glance over her shoulder. He was coming through the door. She returned her gaze to the front and thought she saw a shadow as she passed her car, heading for the street. The tiger was right on her heals. He was pumped with the thrill of a fresh face-to-face kill. He was almost high, and was smiling as he gained on Allison. He exuded confidence. He envisioned the move he would make to take her quickly to the ground, and then the killing blow he'd use as she stared up at him. He calculated that he'd have her in six more steps. CRASH!

There was a massive collision as the tiger ran squarely into Lawrence Masterson. Masterson didn't budge. The tiger took the full brunt of the body blow. He was stunned, lying on his back. At first he thought he'd run into the side of the house. He opened his eyes to see this huge Black man. He pulled his knees up to his chin and, with his hands palms down on the cement beside his head, executed a gymnastic-like kip, bringing him immediately to his feet. Masterson had yet to pull his weapon. The tiger unleashed a series of rapid spinning kicks and punches that bounced off Masterson's stomach, chest and head without fazing him. The tiger had never seen anything like it—a mountain of a man. He decided retreat was the better option. He pivoted to get away and ran immediately into Tagger. He was on his back again. He only saw a blur as Tagger fell on top of him knees first, breaking his ribs and immobilizing him. He continued in a fluid move to turn the tiger over and slap cuffs on him. He looked up at Masterson, who was fuming, and wanting another piece of him. Masterson stepped back and growled, "He should know better than to mess with two of the baddest brothers in town."

Masterson heard Allison gasp, turned and found her cowering by the rear fender of

his car. He held up his badge.

"I'm Special Agent Lawrence Masterson, ma'am. Are you hurt?"

Allison stood slowly and shakily. "I'm okay, but I'm afraid Officer Rodriguez is dead." She pointed to the front door.

Hearing that, Tagger drove a knee into Wilhelm's back, breaking something else.

"You son of a bitch," Tagger seethed.

He left the tiger at the feet of Masterson moaning and squirming in pain, as he ran to Rodriguez. He pulled open the front storm door and found her. His stomach dropped. He knew as soon as he saw the position of her head—she was already dead. He checked for a pulse anyway, but there was none. "She has two kids!" He yelled to nobody in particular. He pulled his two-way and called the station.

"I have an officer down."

"No, it's too late for an ambulance."

"I need a car to transport the asshole who killed her. On second thought, he might be needing an ambulance."

Within minutes, eight police cars converged on the site. The officers were there to confirm for themselves that one of their own was dead, and to get the bastard who did it. Julia also made the scene. She did not order the incoming officers back to their assigned areas. She understood their need to be there in support of their fallen comrade. She quietly got the word out for the extra officers to help keep the neighbors back from the house, and to allow access for the ambulance and crime scene investigators.

She found Tagger and Masterson. "Are y'all okay?"

"It'd probably be a good idea to have the paramedics take a look at Masterson," said Tagger. "He took a lot of heavy-duty karate kicks."

"Bullshit," said Masterson. "If anyone needs looking after, it's Tagger. I'll bet he has that asshole's bone fragments stuck in his knees."

Julia looked from one to the other impatiently. "Both of you! Forward, march!" she ordered loudly, pointing in the direction of the ambulance. They grumbled all the way.

Julia searched for Allison. She found her sitting alone on the steps of her side porch, just outside of the prying rays of the street light. She was shaking and appeared to be cold, despite the eighty degree temperature. Julia approached and sat down beside her.

"A hell of a night," she said as she put an arm around her. Trusting Julia's embrace, Allison allowed herself to go limp, and began to sob.

Tagger was right. Masterson did take some major league shots. His ribs were seriously bruised and his face was swelling.

"I'm gonna grab some extra strength Tylenol and a few bags of ice on the way home," said Masterson, holding his ribs. He was starting to feel every one of the tiger's expertly delivered kicks and punches, as the adrenaline wore off.

"That sounds like a plan. You did good out there tonight," said Tagger.

"Correction. *We* did good out there tonight," said Masterson, as he turned and made his way to the Explorer.

"I expect to see video of the dude bouncing off you in the NFL highlight films this week," Tagger yelled after him.

***

Officer Johnson let Marino in. Tonya and Josh met him in the foyer. "It's been another tough night. Sergeant Tagger caught a man trying to attack Allison tonight. She was not hurt, but of course, she's not doing real well emotionally. One of our officers was killed."

"What? Allison attacked? An officer killed? What the hell's going on?" said Josh, wide-eyed.

Tonya found herself in synch with Josh. "How many more of these assassins are out there? When is this ever going to stop?" She needed Josh, but he'd stormed off. She went to find him.

"This is all my fault. Keeping everyone in danger is my fault. I need to get away from here so you'll be safe," said Josh.

"The hell you do!" said Tonya. "You're staying right here where you belong—with us." Making sure she had eye contact, she said sternly, "None of us is doing well in this craziness, and I'm trying to keep a lid on for the kids. But I can't do this all by myself. Hell, I can't even do it just for me."

Only on rare occasions had Josh heard Tonya go off like this. His mind was trying to make sense of her words, and as it did, even that little cognitive exercise gave him a slight opening from the overwhelming fear he had been experiencing.

"I'm just so scared," he said.

"Damn it, we're all scared. Someone's trying to kill you."

Silence.

Tonya held out her arms. Josh moved to her. They held each other, for a long time.

"We probably need to get back to Sergeant Marino," Josh said.

Marino and Johnson were talking as they returned to the living room. They looked up.

"Sorry I freaked out, Sergeant," said Josh.

"Nothing to be sorry about. I'd be acting a whole lot worse if it were me," said Marino. "Getting back to Allison ... I hate to put something else on you, but she's not doing so well, and we were wondering if it'd be okay if she spent the night here with y'all."

"Of course Allison can stay here. Do we need to pick her up?" said Tonya.

"No. Sergeant Tagger will bring her here. I'll give him a call now. Thanks. I know how helpful this will be," said Marino.

***

He was feeling panicky. How do I get out? On each side were twelve-foot hedges, neatly trimmed and thick. He couldn't see through them. He was half running and half speed walking on a three-foot wide path that intersected at ninety degree angles with other paths, and sometimes would dead end into other hedges. I have to get out, he told himself. He shifted to running exclusively. The choice points came more quickly. Left? Right? Or straight? The longer he ran, the more turns he made, the more desperate he became, and the more his panic mounted. I've been here before, haven't I? Yes, and the last time, I turned left. This time I'll turn right, as he dashed off in search of a way out of this puzzle. I *have* to get out. Something flickered just ahead of him on his right, about chest high. It was a red spot, which seemed to be saying *chase me*. Then, when he turned left, it disappeared only to reappear on the hedge to his left. He caught up to it for a second before it bounced back on the hedge. In that second he felt a pull on his right sleeve at the forearm, and saw a leaf flip up underneath the red dot. He glanced down at his sleeve as he continued to run. His sleeve was torn, and there was an area of red surrounding the tear. His mind struggled to understand. He touched the torn area of his shirt sleeve. When he pulled his left hand back he could see that the red had transferred to his fingers. It was wet. "Blood!" he gasped. "I've been shot. Someone is trying to kill me."

He glanced over quickly to the hedge and found the red dot just behind him, and understood there was a laser sight trained on him. The panic was overwhelming. He tried to run faster, but the harder he tried the slower he moved. He felt as if he were running in two feet of mud, sucking each foot back as he struggled to lift it for the next step. The red dot was moving closer to him. He couldn't get out of the way. He twisted left and twisted right, but he couldn't free himself from the mud. Any second the red dot would touch him. I can't get out of the way. I can't move … I'm gonna get—

"Josh. Josh. Honey. Josh, wake up," Tonya said softly as she stood beside the bed and set her hands beside his biceps, being careful to avoid his punches and kicks. "It's just a dream, Josh." He opened his eyes wide with terror. He wasn't seeing. He was still feeling. He grabbed Tonya. She jerked away. "Josh! You're hurting me," Tonya yelped. "Wake up!" She flicked on the nearby table lamp. He winced, and his eyes ached to focus. As his flailing subsided, Tonya dared to touch him. She continued talking to him. He oriented slowly.

Office Johnson heard the noise and came up the stairs, his hand on his weapon and his heart pounding. Everything was dark, until light shot out from under the bedroom door. He listened intently.

"You've had a bad dream," Tonya assured him.

"A d … dream?" he managed. He was breathing heavily, his muscles burned, and he was blurry eyed as if he'd hit the *wall* in a marathon. He recognized Tonya, but was still unsure of his surroundings. She sat on the edge of the bed and reached to hold him. The assassin had struck again. Neither Josh nor Tonya dared to sleep again that night.

Officer Johnson breathed easier, took his hand off his weapon and quietly retraced his steps.

CHAPTER 46

IS ANYBODY HOME?

JUNE *3 ... Backup Plans.* Mac couldn't understand it. Nobody was answering their phone, or returning his calls. What the hell was happening? He went to the websites for *The Commercial Appeal* newspaper, and the two largest Memphis TV stations.

Nothing in the paper, he thought. Let's see, WMC has a preliminary report of a man arrested after killing a female police officer with a karate punch. Oh, shit! That has to be the tiger. He's always working on the edge, but karate chopping a cop?

Everything was clicking along just fine, he thought. All of a sudden the cops are all over this. These hick Memphis cops can't be that good. Someone's been tipping them off. Could it be Charleze? No, that wouldn't make any sense. She has just as much to lose as I do, maybe more. Chisholm? Why haven't I heard from Chisholm? No, I think he's just hiding from me, which is smart.

A later check of Memphis news reports confirmed that Wilhelm had been arrested for killing a police officer. The reports were sketchy, but he could find nothing about Proctor, White, Osborne, or Chisholm.

He ran it all through his head one more time. Chisholm had called to say the switch had been made on the surgical screws. At least that part had gone through. Wilhelm had been held prisoner several times all around the world. No way he'd talk to the Memphis cops. So, no one knows anything, but those three nerds may have been able to crack Huong's crazy poem. No way I can know what information Huong had, but I need to know what they know. Neither Sneak nor Thornton had been able to find Osborne. So that leaves White and Proctor.

CHAPTER 47

REGROUPING

JUNE 4 ... *Scrambling To Stay Ahead.* "Mornin, Lieutenant," said Marino as he and Tagger walked into the squad room, carrying their coffee.

"Morning, fellas," answered Julia. Thanks again for all your work on this, and for watching out for me in the hospital, and for covering Josh and Allison. I really do appreciate it." Adding emphasis, "We know they do."

"What's a team for?" smiled Tagger. And Marino gave a "cheers" salute with his coffee mug.

"What's up with Agent Lopez?" asked Marino.

"She's taking a few days leave. This was her first shoot. You know, it takes a while. In the meantime she's being seen by one of the psychologists. I'm hoping to have her back in the rotation by Sunday or Monday." Turning to Tagger, Julia asked, "How are you feeling, Tag?"

"None the worse for wear," said Tagger, rubbing his knees. "But I'm guessing Masterson is nursing some pretty sore ribs this morning."

"I understand that Wilhelm thought he had been in a pinball machine, and he was the pinball between Masterson and you," Julia said. He smiled. "Allison is still alive. You did good."

"What can I say. Wilhelm's a pretty small dude, really," said Tagger. "I have an appreciation for our new FBI friend. He don't take no prisoners."

"Yeah, and his little Texas sidekick doesn't hold anything back either," said Marino. Then, looking at Julia. "Without you and her, Josh would be dead for sure."

Tagger said, "I just heard on the way in that there'll be a burial ceremony on Saturday, with a full honor guard." The other two nodded. The tone turned serious and reflective as they thought about Eva Rodriguez, and her children.

"Well, we still have work to do," said Julia, snapping everyone's thoughts back into the room. "From what Masterson tells me, we need to be worrying about this McMillan character coming to Memphis. Either of you have any ideas as to who his target might be if he comes?"

Marino jumped in. "It seems to me it'd be Josh, Allison, and Dorothy because they might still break Huong's code. He may have put together enough to clearly point the finger at Mitchell and McMillan. Or at least McMillan is worried that he did."

"And that he's passed that information on to Josh, Allison and Dorothy," Tagger said.

"I agree," said Julia. "See what you can do about having the Airport Authority keep a watch on the incoming passenger manifests professor. And there's Dr. *Red Leather Chairs* Durnst."

"I can't imagine that candy ass being dangerous, but he might still be involved in the overall plan," said Tagger.

"As for the code," said Marino, "there were a whole slew of folks working on that thing yesterday, and they seemed to have gotten very close. I think we should do anything we can to help Josh and Allison find that solution."

"Let's not forget Dorothy Osborne," added Julia. "She's been staying under the radar, and that's good, but, maybe she has the information they need to break the code. Tag?"

"Still nothing," said Tagger. "Same goes for Paul Chisholm. I went out to BP Tech to talk to him. They haven't seen nor heard from him since last Friday. I went to his apartment, and it looks like he skipped. All his clothes and his car are gone. The neighbors haven't seen him since Sunday. The place has been scrubbed meticulously. The crime scene guys could dust for any print that he may have left, but I'm not sure it's worth pursuing. Your call, Lieutenant."

"Let's do it," said Julia.

✳✳✳

"Dr. Mitchell," came the secretary's voice over the intercom. "There are two gentlemen to see you."

"Send them in," said Charleze.

CHAPTER 48

THE WEBSITE

JUNE *4 ... Huong's Message.* Looking around the dining room table was demoralizing. Brandon was having a senior citizen flashback. He hadn't seen this many dark-circled bloodshot eyes, pillow hair, and facial skin imprinted with the embossed patterns of sofa pillows since his fraternity days. Not a fleck of make-up, and no motivation to find any. Everyone was staring. It was pretty clear that no one had a decent night's sleep. It would be a challenging day. Officer Johnson had made a pot of coffee. It was police station strength. But then, it needed to be.

They were fortunate to have two very good therapists in the room. Good therapists who were struggling with their own fears, but were not going to let anyone get away with keeping to themselves and not participating in the discussion.

"Thanks for inviting me over last night," said Allison, sipping on her coffee. "I don't think I could have stood it at my house."

"I couldn't imagine staying there after having gone through what you did," said Tonya. "You're more than welcome to continue to stay with us."

"We're obviously in this together," added Josh. He turned introspective. "I know we should be happy to be alive, but why am I so scared and jumpy and pissed off?"

"Because, my dear," said Jennifer, "that's how people normally respond to having somebody try to run them over, shoot them, and kung fu them, not to mention watching someone get killed right in front of them." She looked at Allison, who managed the smallest of un-smiling grins. "It's not unlike what our troops have been experiencing in Iraq and Afghanistan. It's not over yet, and, heck, it's not just you. Your father and I are having similar feelings as well. One way or another, we're all affected, and the last thing we should do is avoid talking about it."

"It sure doesn't seem normal to me," said Allison. "I'm just feeling so out of control. I don't think I'll ever get my life back again."

"Oh, Allison," said Tonya, "You're alive today precisely because you were in charge of your life. You were together enough to get away from that murderer. I know it doesn't feel like it, but you were sensational. We're all so relieved that you had the courage to do what you did."

"Sure didn't feel like courage. I was scared to death, and still am," said Allison.

"Just think about the definition of a hero as being a person who takes action in the face of great danger and great fear," encouraged Jennifer. Looking at Josh, she added, "And the same goes for you, buster."

"Hey, what about me? I need one of those *warm fuzzy* things too," said Brandon, again flashing on the sixties—perhaps seeking a more comforting time in his life.

"Come here, big guy." invited Jennifer, smiling as she recalled the forty-year old term for *positive strokes* in the pop psychology of the day. "I'll be your warm fuzzy."

"The same goes for you sweetie," Josh said as he grabbed Ollie to him.

"Stop, Daddy! You didn't shave and your beard hurts. That's not fuzzy, that's scratchy. I'm going to get one of those fuzzy things from Mommy," said Ollie as she squirmed to free herself from Josh's grasp and climbed into Tonya's lap to snuggle.

Daniel was last to come downstairs and was making his way into the dinning room where they all were. In understandable fashion he had bundled the fearful emotions he'd struggled with all night, and funneled them into something he felt more comfortable with—anger. Currently, that anger was being focused outward. "Is that all there is—coffee?" he complained.

Jennifer rose to walk him to the kitchen, linking her arm in his, and responding to the fear emotions hidden beneath the angry facade. "Now, my dear sir, what would you like for breakfast this morning?"

Josh called after him, "Daniel, after you get something to eat, we could really use your help breaking this code."

Still working hard on his fifteen year old cool, as well as on his anger, Daniel didn't acknowledge either his Nana's touch, or his father's request. But he didn't pull away from Jennifer, and he was thankful to be included. *Maybe I'll be the one to break the code, and maybe get everything back to normal,* he thought, as the stage lights went up on another hero vignette.

***

Fortified with food and caffeine, they gathered around the computer, intent on cracking the code. Josh, Allison, Daniel and Tonya took turns at the keyboard as everyone shouted out different words and combinations that might be part of the website address. They began with blends of *hip*, *Harry Potter*, and *BPTX*.

"Harrypotter'ship" ... "Harryship" ... "Hipharry" ... "Harryandthehippogrif" ... "Potter'ship" ... "HarrypotteratBPTX" ... "aBPTXhipforHarry" ... "BionicHarry" ...

"BionicPotter" ... "Bionicharrypotter" ... and on and on and on.

They broke for lunch, briefly. Later in the day Marino joined them. He took a turn at the keyboard. They must have typed in a thousand versions, probably in actuality only one hundred separate potential passwords, ten times each. No luck. They were getting punchy. Allison vented her frustration.

"I *hate* Huong's Harry Potter."

Daniel was at the keyboard, and just naturally typed in, "huong'sharrypotter." The PC began to whir. All eyes were staring at a black screen with yellow writing, "Welcome to Dr. Carl Huong's Website." There was a flashing white rectangle, the word *password* typed below it. No one moved for an hour's worth of fifteen seconds.

"Did I say that?" asked Allison

"You did, indeed," said Josh. "Great job, Daniel," he said, patting him on the back.

"What's the password?" hollered Daniel.

"Start with the last four numbers of my social security number," said Josh. "9-7-5-3"

"And add mine," said Allison. "7-4-3-2"

Daniel did as directed and clicked on ENTER—*Invalid Password. Try Again.*

"Daniel type mine first," said Allison. "7-4-3-2, and your Dad's next, 9-7-5-3."

The page yielded. Marino pulled out his cell and called Julia and Tagger.

I, Carl Huong, Ph.D., hereby submit the facts as I know them for your consideration:

A.   In early May of this year, I overheard one side of a telephone conversation involving Paul Chisholm, a new lead buyer for BP Technologies, in which he was saying, "We can't do that. Forest Brothers is a horrible shop." I did not think much of it at the time. I shared this with my boss, Dr. Haverford Sturgeon.

B.   A week or so later, Paul Chisholm approached Dr. Sturgeon and me on separate dates attempting to get us to agree to sign off on a purchase order to buy surgical screws from Forest Brothers Industries. We each told him under no circumstances would we allow Forest Brothers screws to be placed in our prototype artificial hip.

C.   On May 10th I was working late, and Chisholm came to see me. He said he was worried about Dr. Sturgeon, and maybe I could calm him down a little. He was vague, yet scary. I quickly scratched out a note for Dr. S. I used a hideous chartreuse colored envelope because I knew it would stand out. I left it on his desk. The next evening he died in an auto crash. The police said it was an accident.

D. On May 11th I received a tip from a friend in New York. There was a rumor that brokerage houses were being contacted by a Charleze Mitchell, manager of the Tornadic Growth Investments hedge fund, about the prospects of borrowing unusually large numbers of shares of BPTX stock, in preparation for shorting it. I began to check out their website, as well as that of the Securities and Exchange Commission.

E. On May 12th of this year, I was within hearing distance when the same buyer, Paul Chisholm, was having lunch with a man I had never seen before. The man was Caucasian, looked to be in his mid-forties, over six feet tall, good build, well groomed, very stylishly dressed. They talked about a man whose name I couldn't catch (it sounded like "speak").

F. On May 17th I discovered that someone had hacked into my computer. As best I can determine, all my incoming and outgoing emails over the past six weeks were downloaded. Most of those emails concerned our prototype replacement hip, and involved Dr. S, my student Dorothy R. Osborne, Allison White, and Josh Proctor. Other things may have been downloaded, but I have no way of knowing what they might have been.

G. On May 18th I called the SEC, and was referred to Special Agent Lawrence Masterson of the FBI, which I learned was what Dr. S had done a few weeks earlier. I told my story. He said he needed something more concrete. He confirmed he was looking into the hedge fund run by Mitchell.

H. On May 19th I went to see Chisholm at the end of the work day to talk to him about Forest Brothers Industries. He was not in his office. I checked the warehouse. Upon entering,

I observed him placing surgical screws in boxes marked Archer's Toilet Tissue, and storing them against the wall. Afterwards, he made a phone call. I heard him say he had a shipment of recalled Forest Brothers screws, and he would switch them for the T&O screws when the production line for the new hip was ready to run. He then said, "I don't see any reason to bump him off." I returned to the warehouse the next night and replaced the recalled Forest Brothers screws in the Archer's Toilet Tissue boxes with the far superior T&O surgical screws. So, if he does make a switch, it will not involve Forest Brothers parts, and the prototype hips will be fine.

I.   For the past few days I've had the feeling that I was being followed, and I've heard clicks on my office phone at the conclusion of calls. I realize that I sound paranoid, but I can only say what has happened.

J.   I decided to alert my graduate placement student Dorothy R. Osborne (who goes by her middle name of Ruby), and two colleagues, Allison White and Josh Proctor. These three people know more about our project than anyone else. I'm just not sure what I'm alerting them to.

K.   On May 23rd just now, after work hours, Chisholm came to my office saying he was taking a great risk, but he had to warn me that my life was in danger and I needed to leave immediately. He reminded me that he had warned me about Dr. S, and that I was next. I am just taking time to put this on my website before I leave.

"My God," said Allison. "He knew he was going to be killed."

"There's the motivation for murdering Sturgeon. And here's the tie to Forest Brothers and the hedge fund. We were close, but Huong had the missing pieces," said Julia. "This information would have put us on the right track to McMillan and Mitchell."

"Any chance the dude at lunch is McMillan, and the man being talked about was Sneak?" asked Marino.

"This all works with the telephone number in Sneak's shoe, tying him to Tornadic Growth Investments," reminded Tagger.

Isn't a ruby a *red* stone? thought Josh.

"Dr. Huong must have been killed right after he sent the email," said Allison.

"Who are these people?" Tonya was fuming. "Who could stoop so low as to swap bad parts for good ones in a person's hip replacement? How cruel. Not to mention killing Hav and Carl. And, this is why they've been trying to kill Josh and Allison? These people are sick!"

"We didn't know anything about this," Allison said. "I still don't understand why they've been trying to kill us too."

"They must've hacked into Huong's computer again and discovered that he'd written the limerick email. They figured y'all'd be able to break the code and get this information to us," said Julia. "They didn't know how much Huong knew, or that we were close to putting the pieces together ourselves. But, they couldn't take a chance. And, in fact, they still may be trying to silence you two."

"What! Why can't you just tell them you already have the information, and then they wouldn't have any reason to kill us," Allison said.

"Done," said Julia. "I'll get a press release together for the six o'clock news."

No one had noticed the reactions of Daniel and Ollie. This *game* of breaking the code had been fun. The enthusiasm of the grownups had been therapeutic. But the tone of the conversation had shifted. It was tense, angry, fearful. Feeling abandoned and vulnerable, Ollie retreated to a corner chair. Daniel eased out.

CHAPTER 49

AND YET ANOTHER ONE

JUNE *4 … Darrell Shanks.* The plane landed at Nashville International. An elderly white-haired man with a neatly trimmed beard was being pushed in a wheelchair by an airport personal service assistant. He was wearing a gray business suit and matching brimmed hat. He held a cane across his lap. The assistant wheeled him to the baggage claim, and retrieved a large brown leather suitcase. He pulled the rolling suitcase while pushing the man to the Avis car rental desk, and happily took the twenty dollar tip.

"Yes, I can drive. It's my left leg that's the problem," he said, as he signed for a gray Chevy Silverado. "And it's easier for me to get in and out of a pickup."

Pulling his suitcase and walking with the assistance of his cane, he made his way slowly to the Avis lot. He found the pickup, climbed in, adjusted the mirrors, and cranked the engine. Following the exit signs, he took I-40 west toward Memphis. He pulled into the first rest area. A steady stream of travelers moved in and out of the restrooms, none dressed as he was. He waited for a lull in the pedestrian traffic. Moving quickly, he carried a small black athletic duffle bag, but not his cane. Five minutes later, a scruffy looking man in his forties walked out of the restroom wearing faded jeans, a black t-shirt with a large face of Johnny Cash, old Nikes, a well-worn blue baseball cap with a tractor trailer rig sewn on the front, and dark sunglasses. He carried a small black duffle bag.

About an hour later, the Silverado pulled into a nondescript motel, with what appeared to be several former motel names still visible in the various shades of washed out paint on the outside wall. Opening the truck door, he was hit in the face by the heat and humidity, taking his breath away. Sweat formed almost immediately. He reached across the seat, grabbed a battered black suitcase, and walked toward the motel entrance. Inside he found a threadbare, brown patterned carpet, and the reek of mildew. The dull gray walls had been papered years before, as evidenced by the many edges curling away from the walls. The lighting was fluorescent and low. An elderly woman with stained teeth stood behind the counter. Her uniform was clean and pressed, but was clearly too small for her. She greeted him with a smile.

"Y'all have a reservation, hon?" she sang out, with a southern accent so thick it took an extra two seconds for him to figure out what it was that she probably said.

"Yeah, Darrell Shanks," he said with a slight southern drawl. He dabbed the sweat from his eyes.

"Hotenuffoya?" she said as she leafed through the index cards in the box. "Ah, here it is. You'll be staying with us for two weeks, Mr. Shanks?" she said.

"Yes, ma'am," he answered. "I have a new job, and I'll be looking for a place to stay permanent."

"Hope it all works out for you. The reservation was made with a MasterCard. Do you want to use the same card to pay for the room and any charges, hon?" she asked.

"Yeah," he said, handing her his card. She put it in the manual reader and pulled the bar across it to make an imprint. Taking back his card, he said, "Any chance there's a package for me?"

She'd never been asked that question before. "I don't rightly know. Let me check back in the office." Within minutes she reappeared with a loose leaf notebook-size package, wrapped in brown paper and stamped by UPS. Across the top in large red and white block letters was written, DYNASTY MEDICAL: YOUR DIABETES HEADQUARTERS.

"Here you are, Mr. Shanks," she said as she handed it to him. "And here's your key. Room 127, down this here hallway a might. Enjoy your stay, hear?"

Shanks put the package under his arm and carried his bag to room 127. The room was heavy with humidity. Everything felt wet. He switched on the air conditioner that stood under the window. The window looked over the parking lot. He noted the nearest light pole where he would park his pickup, and be able to keep an eye on it. He closed the curtain, pulling the hanging white plastic rod. A TV blared from one of the adjoining rooms. His was not working. He checked the bathroom. There was a white strip across the toilet seat, but the toilet clearly hadn't been cleaned. The towels were paper thin and small. There were two paper wrapped plastic drinking cups, and one very small bar of wrapped soap. Stains were visible on the comforter. He pulled it off the bed, and with a melodramatic flair, dropped it on the floor.

"Welcome to Tennessee," he grumbled aloud.

He pulled a map from his bag. Tucked inside the map were directions he'd copied from the R&O Industries website. Looks like the long way around is the best, he thought. All these expressway changes could be tricky, but I better follow them. So, I get off at Hacks Cross and head into Mississippi for a few miles to Olive Branch. I'll leave early enough to give me plenty of time. He'd passed a Stuckey's and a Waffle House on his drive in. After flipping a coin, he walked across the road to Stuckey's for lunch.

At four that afternoon, he drove out of the motel parking lot. The traffic was heavy as he approached the Memphis area. He followed the traffic, taking the flyover, to I-240. He exited onto Highway 385, following it to the Hacks Cross exit. Then it was a straight shot south across the Tennessee state line. His calculations had been good, and he breathed a sigh of relief when he rounded the corner and found the R&O Industries complex in front of him. Cars were pulling out of the lot. He parked his pickup and made his way to the security desk inside the front doors of the main building.

"Darrell Shanks," he said to the guard at the desk. "I'm here to start my new job with the cleaning crew."

The guard pulled up the duty roster on his PC. "Yup. Here's the notice. 'Darrell Shanks, employment begins 6-5-08.' Come with me, and we'll get you fixed up with an ID badge and a set of keys. It's good you came in a little early. I'm pretty sure we'll have you up and running in time to meet with your new boss. He'll give you a tour of the place, and get you some coveralls, and gloves and such."

The directory on the wall in the lobby indicated that Allison White's office was on the second floor, room 208, and Joshua Proctor's office was on the first floor, room 102. By 6:45 PM Shanks was running a buffer on the second floor. Only a handful of employees were still in their offices. He turned off his buffer and listened. He heard no one in his immediate area. He noted the security camera in the hallway. He would move quickly, and have an excuse ready if he was challenged. Using his new master key, he unlocked Allison's office door and stepped inside. He left the door open to make use of the hall lights.

Her office was nothing to write home about. It was of moderate size, with a fabric covered couch, two matching chairs, four sets of tall bookshelves, three horizontally stacked metal file cabinets, and a big wooden desk facing the wall opposite the couch. Wide vertical blinds covered a large window through which he could see the rear parking lot. A laptop computer sat on a small work table that, along with four chairs, took up the middle of the room. The bookshelves were packed with books and journals, and held a sprinkling of photos. Her desk was clear, except for what appeared to be one or maybe two days' worth of mail, arranged in a neat stack of letters sitting atop a magazine, a professional journal, and two books still in their individual mailing boxes. Next to the mail were telephone messages. The oldest was timed and dated this morning. Maybe the tiger did get to her after all, he thought. He heard voices, moved quickly from her office, closed the door and began buffing the floor.

After the 10:30 PM meal break, he set up his equipment to buff the first floor. Just after midnight he'd worked his way to Josh's office. Again, he checked his surroundings, unlocked the door, and stepped inside. He saw pretty much the same arrangement as in White's office, except that

Proctor had a PC, and what appeared to be family photos everywhere. He retreated to the hallway and finished his custodial assignment. It was apparent to him that White and Proctor had not been in their offices today. Both of them out? he thought. What's that about? When would they be back?

The next day Shanks arrived early again. He made a point of walking the halls to see if he could pick up on anyone talking about White or Proctor. No luck. He identified the special areas designated for secretarial staff, and took note of the security guards and their overlapping schedules. Once the employees had left for the day, he began his custodial duties, which this night involved sweeping the halls with an oversized broom and a flaky green cleaning compound. He checked the desks of the secretaries as he made his circuit. He was looking for telephone cheat sheets that were often kept close to the telephones for ready access, or taped on the pullout shelves just above the top of the side drawers. He reasoned that White's and Proctor's names and numbers would be kept by those secretaries in the same departments. And, later in the evening, he found one. He opened the appointment calendar looking for any indication of when White or Proctor might be coming back. Nothing.

Friday, Shanks continued his routine of coming in early and nosing around. During his duties, he spent more time in Allison's and Josh's offices, searching their files. He brought drop cloths to Josh's office, and used one to cover the bottom of the door, and one to cover his head and the PC monitor, so as to keep the glow from lighting up the window and washing under his door into the hallway. He reviewed every entry, email, and log of website hits he could find. He found Dr Huong's email with the crazy poem attachment. But there was no indication that he had figured out the poem. He decided to continue through Tuesday or Wednesday in hopes Allison and Josh would show up.

CHAPTER 50

RECOVERY: FIRST STEPS

JUNE 4 ... *Gaining Strength From Others.* After Ollie and Daniel were tucked in bed, the five adults sat around the dining room table, not wanting to be there, not wanting to leave.

"That was some limerick, and some website name," said Allison with a nervous laugh. All agreed, nodding and smiling, yet silent.

"I owe Daniel big time for not believing Harry Potter could be the name of the mystery person," said Josh. Another silence. This one was longer. People were avoiding eye contact. Jennifer broke the silence, and everyone looked up, gratefully.

"I've been trying to think what would be the most helpful for Daniel and Ollie?" she said, drawing everyone's focus away from themselves. "It's my understanding the police want us to stay confined to the house for several days." There were nods of agreement. "So, what can we do for them?"

"They seemed to be doing just fine," Josh said.

"Yes, they really dug in and worked hard while we had a project. Daniel especially," said Tonya. "But this project was mostly over Ollie's head. I think she seemed better because all of the adults were feeling good about having something specific to work on. You know, the kids' adjustment is heavily determined by what they read in us. If we seem focused and less anxious, then so are they. Now that we won't have a project to work on, we're all likely to revisit our own anxieties about this. Then, we'll see the kids' emotions change along with ours."

"So, we're supposed to act normal so the kids will act normal?" asked Josh mockingly.

"Exactly," said Jennifer. Surprised by the zip in her comment, Josh shrunk as if he were six years old again. "And," she added, "some of us are going to have a more difficult time acting *normal*."

"Boys and girls, boys and girls," Tonya said while clapping her hands like an elementary school principal. Josh and Jennifer both looked away, embarrassed as they became aware of how they had been acting in front of the others. Allison caught a laugh halfway out as she covered her mouth with her hand. Her eyes were still smiling.

"I'm sorry, dear," Jennifer said to Tonya, but not to Josh.

"Yeah, me too," said Josh as he avoided looking at his mother.

"This has been a very tough ten days or so, and Josh and Allison have had some harrowing experiences," said Tonya. "The rest of us have only dealt with those experiences vicariously. But that can be every bit as traumatizing, especially for children."

"And the fat lady hasn't sung yet," said Josh.

"Quite right, son," said Jennifer, and they looked at one another for the first time since their little joust. "That's what could make it impossible to act normal. But on the other hand, we're probably not going to feel any safer than we will in the next few days with all the officers here."

"Okay. So what are we supposed to do?" asked Josh.

"I think we have to take advantage of our adult time together to share our own reactions to these events. It's not helpful when we try to handle our fears by avoiding them, or by just toughing it out," said Tonya.

"I'm not sure I understand," said Allison. "Are you saying we have to talk about what we just went through? I don't think I can do that."

Jennifer stepped in. "I know it sounds backwards, because talking about a horrific event can be quite painful. But what we've found is this kind of pain tends to be short-lived. Then, after talking about it, the trauma loses some of its grip, and the person begins to heal. Whereas, when people bottle up their feelings, their pain can go on for years, oozing out and affecting everyone around them, and eating them up from the inside. This talking approach has worked well with first responders, traumatized children and adolescents, and with our returning combat vets. Of course, it's easier for some than others."

Jennifer and Tonya helped everyone talk through the events of the past few weeks. Each one had a slightly different perspective, and sometimes the facts were distorted. It was helpful when everyone had an accurate picture of the events. Jennifer and Tonya encouraged everyone talk about how these events affected them. They learned each had their own personal reactions. One result of these discussions was that the adults felt a strong bond among them, and they relaxed over the next few days. As predicted, when the adults were less anxious, so too were Daniel and Ollie. The fact the school year had come to an end didn't hurt.

***

"Lopez!" Masterson shouted as Maria showed up at his office door. "How're you doing? Are you just visiting or are you ready to get back to work?"

Maria smiled. "The doc said I was doing well, and he cleared me to get back in the saddle. Got an extra Glock in your desk drawer?"

Masterson couldn't help himself. He had an ear to ear smile. "It just so happens that I do." He leaned over, and then winced as his ribs were still quite sore.

"Here, sir. Let me get it," said Maria as she walked around to his side of the desk and finished pulling the drawer that Masterson had begun to open. She was still smiling as she reached in and picked up her weapon, an old lost friend. She checked to be sure it had been cleared, taking a few seconds to hold it in her right hand. She pulled the clip from the drawer and locked it into the pistol grip, then slid it into its holster and secured it with the strap. The weight on her hip was reassuring. "That's better," she said. Masterson was holding his side, but still smiling.

"I'll have to give you some lessons in how to block karate kicks, sir. When you're up to it."

"It's good to have you back, Lopez."

"Tell me, sir. What happened at White's house?"

"Sounds like you already have intell on that."

"I have some," said Maria. "I know the hit man was a guy with extensive training in the marshal arts known as the tiger, and I know that you and Sergeant Tagger made the scene. But that's about it."

"Well, let's see …" Masterson began. "Officer Rodriguez was assigned to Ms. White, staying in the house with her. Six of us were taking turns driving the neighborhood. Tagger and I met nearby for a late dinner before my ten o'clock rotation. We'd just started our Bloomin Onion when Tagger got a call saying the roving officer had been involved in a traffic accident and was no longer able to continue his patrol. We hightailed it out of there.

Rounding the corner on Allison's street I saw two cars in her driveway, one I didn't recognize. I pulled in behind. Tagger parked in the street. I'd just closed my car door when both the inside light and White shot out of the side door. I crossed in front of my car when I saw Wilhelm come out of the house in a full sprint, a wild ass grin on his face. I simply stepped in front of him. I don't think he saw me.

Bam! He's on his back trying to figure out what day of the week it is. Then he does this Bruce Lee shit. Springs to his feet and starts spinning and kicking. I just stood there. After about five, six kicks he looks at me and decides he's had enough. That's when he turned and ran smack into Tagger, who'd circled around behind him. Bam! He was on his back again. You should have seen Tagger. Before Wilhelm can bounce up again, Tagger drops all two hundred fifty pounds, knees first, into his ribs and makes a pussy cat rug out of the tiger. Flips 'im over and cuffs 'im."

"Whoa! That was a close call," said Maria.

"Yup. About as close as you and Thornton," Masterson observed, as if this were the first time that comparison had occurred to him.

"Great work, sir," congratulated Maria. "So, how are you doing?"

"I'm good. The swelling on my face has gone down, but, as you saw, my ribs are still a little sore," said Masterson as he absent mindedly moved his left hand over the paw prints the tiger had left. "Nothing was broken." Then his voice dropped. "Officer Rodriquez wasn't so lucky. That son of a bitch crushed her windpipe."

"I'm so sorry," said Maria with a pause. "What happened to the roving patrol car?"

"As far as the cops have pieced things together, Wilhelm paid the local garden club of the Vice Lords to have one of their female wannabes smash into the patrol car as a part of a gang initiation. He even told them exactly what time and at what corner to expect it. I wish I'd fallen on the bastard."

Maria waited until Masterson had calmed. "So, what now? Are we done with these bad asses?"

"I'm not so sure," said Masterson. "No one has seen McMillan since early this week. I wonder if he's on the run. On the other hand, he's mean and arrogant, and believes that he's indestructible. He just might be coming here. I told Lieutenant Todd I wouldn't put it past him."

"Did the police put a watch on the Memphis International passenger list?"

"Yeah. But that'd be too easy. Mac is smarter than that," said Masterson.

"I just don't know the area well enough," said Maria. "What are the next closest towns with an airport big enough to take a plane from JFK?"

"Good point, Lopez. I'm thinking St Louis, Nashville, Little Rock, Jackson. They're all around two hundred miles, give or take," he said. "I've asked the home office to have McMillan loaded into the face recognition program in place at the larger airports and train stations."

"In the meantime, I'll get back on Proctor," said Maria.

"I'm sure he'll be happy that you have his back, again. I'm still on White. She's staying in the Proctor house. As long as they're together, I'll concentrate on north and west of the house, you can have south and east. Just stay out of the woods," he teased.

CHAPTER 51

FRESH AIR

JUNE *10 ... It's Over.* Everyone sat tight at the Proctors' for a week. There was a police presence in the house, at least one officer with them, at all times. In addition, there was always a car with a police officer outside, and the blinds and curtains were always closed. Also watching were their guardian angels, Todd, Tagger, Marino, Masterson and Lopez. As far as anyone knew, they were just floating around somewhere out there. However, after the seventh day everyone in the Proctor house was going stir crazy. The team believed the previous week's news release had convinced Mac that Josh and Allison were no longer threats to him. Julia agreed to cut them some slack, with a modified police presence for a few days more—just to be sure.

Tuesday morning Josh and Allison drove to the R&O complex, and Tonya went to the clinic. Nana and grandpa stayed home with Ollie and Daniel, and were allowed to be out in the backyard.

Julia followed Tonya to work, and stationed herself outside the clinic. Due to last minute scheduling, Tonya had only three morning appointments, and two in the late afternoon. She was grateful to be back at work. Yet, part of her was distracted and anxious. This nightmare might not be over. She missed Josh. This was their first time to be apart in a week, and after all, someone had tried to kill him, twice.

Allison rode with Josh to R&O. Tagger led the way in his car, and Marino followed. Josh and Allison limited their conversation to mundane topics, the weather, the traffic, the colorful trees and flowers.

Nervous, they laughed a little too easily, and sported smiles longer than usual. This was their first trip out of a guarded house in over a week. As much as they needed to get out of the house, there was a part in each of them that was not convinced of their safety.

But, once inside the building, their anxieties slipped to a lower level of consciousness, as their boss and friends made them feel glad to be back. Allison and Josh headed for their respective offices. A week's worth of telephone messages, letters, journals, and queued emails awaited their attention. Allison responded to her calls, and was going through her emails. Three were from Redstone. The two oldest were repeats of the earlier ones. The most recent email said,

Congratulations. Channel 5 News said you solved the puzzle.

I'm so relieved for all of us. Ruby

Allison smiled, picked up the phone and called Josh to make sure he saw her latest email.

Masterson and Maria arrived at the R&O complex in separate cars for their assigned afternoon rotations, relieving Tagger and Marino at two. Masterson had pulled into the rear parking area, while Maria parked in the front. Coordinating with the security guards, they established a cross pattern of surveillance, walking the first and second floors, monitoring the surveillance cameras along side of the security guards, and returning to their cars. Each circuit took an hour.

Josh enjoyed getting back into the routine of work, and was surprised to see it was already 5:30. He stretched. His waste basket was half filled, and a third of his email had been answered. He would get the rest tomorrow. He caught movement in his peripheral vision, and turned to see the uniform of a security guard passing the opened office door. Time to leave, he thought. He was shutting down his computer when he saw a vague reflection in the chrome that framed the monitor, and the glint of something shiny. Josh flinched, pulling back from the monitor.

"Ow!"

Something slammed into the top of his right shoulder, near his neck. A syringe hung inches in front of his chest, along with the fist that held it.

"What the …?"

Josh grabbed the wrist with both hands, and pulled hard. The syringe moved away from him, and he felt his assailant's face smash into the back of his head. The assailant's free hand grabbed Josh around the throat. Josh tightened his grip, brought his elbows into his body, pulled his knees up, and dropped from the chair. As he approached the floor in that balled up position, the assailant had no choice but to follow Josh's body with his own. The back of the chair caught the assailant at his waist and, acting like a fulcrum, flipped him up. He heard the assailant's head hit the desk with a resounding crack! Stunned, he let go of Josh, and dropped the syringe. Josh grabbed the syringe and rolled away from the chair. He struggled to a standing position, and held the syringe in front of him, waist high, as if it were a knife. The assailant turned, holding his head. He squared up on Josh.

"What you think you're going to do with that, you little shit?" said Shanks.

"Who are you? What the hell do you want?" yelled Josh.

"Your worst nightmare," said Shanks. And I want you dead." His face was hard. He leaned forward and started to step toward Josh. Josh faked a step to his right, then pulled back. Shanks lunged where he thought Josh would be. As he came by, Josh drove the syringe into Shanks' stomach with everything he had, then stumbled back. He was horrified to see Shanks still on his feet. Shanks rose to his full height. He looked down at the syringe. The plunger was still out. He laughed, and looked at Josh.

"That all you got, punk? he asked as he reached to pull out the syringe.

My, God, thought Josh. He's not even hurt, and he's going to use that syringe on me. I've got one shot at this. Instead of retreating, he stepped quickly toward Shanks and jumped, bringing his right leg up. Still in the air, Josh kicked, jamming his foot into the syringe, shoving the plunger all the way down, and driving the needle into Shanks' spine. Josh fell away, smashing his shoulder on the floor.

Shanks let out a scream. His legs collapsed instantly, and he crashed to the floor—his face inches from Josh's. Josh froze. Shanks' eyes filled with terror, then closed.

Josh heard running. First Masterson and then Maria charged into his office, guns drawn. They caught themselves, stopping at the security guard's body.

"You all right?" yelled Masterson, sucking air.

"Guess so," said Josh, holding his shoulder. He was breathing heavily, eyes wide, muscles taut.

Maria bent down to check on Shanks. "He's dead, sir," she said. "My God! He's got a syringe buried in his belly."

"I saw that SOB coming out of the warehouse," said Masterson, breathless, as he absentmindedly rubbed his bruised ribs. "I knew he looked familiar, but it took me a few minutes before I realized it was McMillan in that guard uniform. I buzzed Lopez, and we tried to get to you guys. Lopez was heading for your office. I was on my way to White's when I heard the commotion. I ran back here."

Josh turned to Masterson. "McMillan? You mean the guy y'all've been talking about?" Maria helped him into a stuffed chair.

"This is the guy," said Masterson. "What happened, Josh?"

"I'm not sure … I was shutting down my computer, and I saw a reflection in the frame of the PC—something shiny. I jerked back a little. All of a sudden, I was hit on my collarbone with an arm, and this needle was right there." Josh made a cup with his hands in front of him, to the right of his head. Continuing to use his hands, he recreated the struggle. "I just kicked him as hard as I could, right on top of the syringe. He collapsed … that's when you two came in."

"Amazing. You are one very lucky man, Joshua Proctor," said Masterson.

"Damn!" said Maria. She pulled her phone and punched in the numbers.

"Lieutenant Todd! This is Maria."

"Whatsup, Maria," said Julia.

"McMillan is dead," said Maria.

"McMillan? The McMillan we've been looking for?"

"Yes, ma'am. Right here at R&O," said Maria.

"What about Josh? Allison?"

"They're OK."

"Details, Maria. I need details."

"McMillan was wearing a security uniform. Agent Masterson recognized him as he entered the R&O building, and we came in after him. But it was all over by the time we got here," Maria said.

"What was all over?"

"Well, we're still trying to put the pieces together. It looks as though Josh caught McMillan sneaking up on him in his office, and was able to block his attempt to stab him with a syringe."

"A syringe!"

"Yes, ma'am. There was a struggle. Josh got the syringe, and drove that baby right through him."

"And Josh is OK, and McMillan is dead?"

"Yes ma'am. Josh is a little shaken up, but he's fine. And McMillan won't be bothering anyone ever again."

"Tell Josh I'll be bringing Tonya down there ASAP."

"I'll tell him, ma'am." Maria clicked off.

"Josh. Lieutenant Todd said she's picking up your wife and bringing her here right now," said Maria.

Even though this crime scene was in Mississippi, Julia took charge, and called the Memphis crime scene investigators and the coroner's office. She contacted the officer sitting in front of the Proctor house, bringing him up to speed. She directed him to pass the information along to Josh's parents, making sure that they understood he was okay. Then she went inside the clinic and had the secretary call Tonya out of her therapy session. Wide, fearful eyes were the first thing Julia saw when Tonya opened her office door.

"Josh is okay, but he's been attacked again." Julia attempted to reassure an anxious and visibly shaking Tonya. Making quick apologies and hurriedly deferring to the secretary to handle things, they ran out of the building and climbed into Julia's car. They drove to R&O with siren and flashers.

"How do you know for sure Josh is okay?" Tonya challenged.

"Agent Lopez called to tell me that McMillan was dead. He'd attacked Josh with a syringe, and Josh was able to defend himself. He stabbed McMillan with his own syringe. I could hear Josh talking in the background."

"A syringe! Was he stuck with it? What was in it? How did he sound?"

"No, he wasn't stuck with the needle. He sounded a little out of breath." Julia was aware that for today at least, she was the psychologist, as her purposefully calm answers were in dramatic contrast to Tonya's highly anxious questions.

"What else did she say?"

"That was pretty much it. They were still trying to sort out the details from Josh. I told her to let Josh know I was bringing you down there."

"Why is this still happening? Will it ever stop?" demanded Tonya.

"McMillan was the mastermind of this part of their scheme. Now, he's dead. It's over."

The rest of the ride was quiet, as each woman kept their thoughts and fears to herself.

***

Allison walked casually down the hall to pick up Josh for their ride home. As she came closer to Josh's room she heard several voices. Maria heard her, and moved to the doorway to stop her from coming in and seeing the body. She was too late. Allison's eyes opened wide and she screamed when she saw enough to know that someone was lying on the floor motionless.

Maria took her hands and said, "That's *not* Josh. Josh is fine. But there was another attempt on his life. This time it was the man behind this whole thing—McMillan. He's dead."

Allison went pale, her knees buckled. The much shorter Maria held on and guided her to a lying position on the floor. She quickly gathered an armful of books from Josh's office, stacked them under Allison's feet to elevate her legs, and sat on the floor beside her until she recovered.

***

Within an hour the crime scene investigators and coroner were on site. The others had gathered in the lobby. Dried tears showed on Tonya's cheeks as she held Josh, on one of the sofas. Josh was still on full alert. Eyes wide, face red, tense. Allison was sitting in one of the nearby stuffed chairs, slowly rubbing her hands, staring into space. The law enforcement contingent gathered on the opposite side of the entrance area.

"We won't know what was in the syringe till the lab techs analyze it," Julia said. "But the fact McMillan didn't use a gun would imply he was more interested is finding out what Josh knew than in killing him, at least immediately. If that's the case, then we might be talking about some type of truth serum. Looks like either Mac didn't hear the news report that Huong's information had been found, or he didn't believe it."

An Officer approached the group. "Lieutenant!" Julia looked up. "We found the body of a security guard in the men's room of the warehouse. He's wearing only his boxers, a watch, socks, and shoes. He's about the same size as the dead suspect, ma'am. Looks like he was killed for his uniform. The head of security identified the suspect as a new member of the cleaning crew, using the name Darrell Shanks."

"And the body count keeps growing," said Julia. "Keep up the search of the premises, top to bottom. I want to be sure there are no more bodies."

"I can't believe Josh was able to take out Mac," Maria said for about the fourth time. "This guy must be part cat, and he still has six more lives to go."

"I'm worried about Allison," Tagger said. "I thought she came through her attack okay, but this thing happening to Josh, almost in front of her, may have put her over the edge."

"Tonya's in no shape to help right now. We'll have one of our other volunteer psychologists see her—tonight if possible," said Julia. "I'll make the call now." She pulled out her phone as she walked away from the group, and from Allison.

"I could kick myself for not recognizing Mac sooner," said Masterson.

"Don't beat yourself up, man," said Marino.

"Say, Masterson," said Tagger. "Do you think this is finally it? Do we have to worry about any more of these high paid goons? And what about Chisholm?"

"No. I really think this is it for any more attempted murders," answered Masterson. "Mac would have been the last one to come to Memphis, and he only came because he thought it needed to be cleaned up. I'm sure he still believed the screws had been switched, but he didn't know how much Huong had figured out as to who was behind this wild ass scheme. As for Chisholm, he's strictly a con man. Murder's not part of his thing. That's why he tried to warn Sturgeon and Huong. My guess is that he split as soon as he could, just to get away from McMillan."

Julia walked back to the group. "Tag would you drive Allison over to Dr. Notting's office in Germantown? He can see her in thirty minutes."

"No problem," said Tagger. "I know the way." He walked over to Allison, knelt beside her chair on one knee, and talked calmly to her. She looked up and nodded. Tonya was watching, and held out her free hand. Allison got up slowly, crossed to the sofa, bent over and embraced Tonya, and then Josh, who was showing signs of recovery.

"Thanks for killing that son of a bitch." Allison kissed him on the cheek. Then she said through clenched teeth, "That God awful son of a bitch." She stood and turned to Tagger, who walked her to his car.

Tonya sat up and took Josh's face in her hands, pulling his gaze to hers. "I love you, Joshua Proctor." Josh managed a smile, and kissed her.

CHAPTER 52

THE PLAN COMES TOGETHER

JUNE *11 … At Last.* He painstakingly took the six copies of the signed patent application apart, taking care not to leave any staple marks on the pages. He laid the copies in front of him on the clean desk. Then he took six copies of pages 2, 6, 9, 14, 17, and 21, and slipped them in place of the original pages in each of the six sets of signed copies. The old pages had the name of BP Technologies as owners. The new pages listed Charleze R. Mitchell as the owner of the new patent.

Charleze was in her car when the phone buzzed.

"Hello," she said … "Give me the good news first." … "You're certain. All the pages were swapped?" … "Good. We will be the proud owners of the patent on the best artificial hip joint in history." … "It takes that long?" … "Well, we can wait it out. What about the next piece of good news?" … "Production on the new hip begins this week—finally! Mac told me the screws had been switched." … "Good. We'll just sit tight while everyone bids the price up, then we'll go short, big time. This will be a real score. OK. What about the bad news?" … "No! Mac is dead? What happened?" … "I don't believe it. Killed by one of the engineers? Jesus." … "Keep me posted."

Charleze punched in another phone number.

"Hello yourself," said Charleze … "Yeah, I just heard. What's your read on everything?" … "Are the cops clued in?" … "I hadn't thought of that. But Mac did us a favor by trying to off one of the engineers in the R&O building. It takes the heat off BP Tech as the focus of their investigation." … "Don't worry about Parsons. We don't need him anymore." … "Yes, I'd recommend that you put your own money into shorting BPTX." … "Keep me posted. I want to know the second he makes the announcement."

***

A late afternoon press conference was held on the lawn of BP Technologies, CEO Frederick Durnst announced the research and development findings of their groundbreaking artificial hip joint. He embellished the importance of the findings, although not by much, and artfully omitted any references to Sturgeon and Huong. He hyped his forecast for record sales in the near term, as well as for five years going forward. BPTX stock jumped twenty-three percent in after-hours trading, and continued to climb following the next morning's opening bell.

***

This pop is even better than I expected, Charleze thought as she monitored the market in general, and BPTX in particular. I'll give it another day before the market starts to reel the price back in. That means I should be ready to move on shorting the stock at the end of trading this afternoon. She checked her investment plan for the umpteenth time. She could feel it. This was going to be big. If she could hold off the creditors, this was going to put her back on top.

CHAPTER 53

ALL THE QUEEN'S HORSES AND ALL THE QUEEN'S MEN

JUNE *12 ... The Final Dominos Fall.* Six of them sat around the table, Julia, Marino, Tagger, Masterson, Maria, and Assistant Attorney General Taylor.

Taylor began, "I've read your reports and the ones from the lab. I've spoken with Lieutenant Todd to clarify a few areas. I have to admit to being a little confused about how Tornadic Growth Investments was going to make money by switching the surgical screws. But, I am quite anxious to get my southern fried fingers around the throat of one Charleze Mitchell. Towards that end I also compared notes with the SEC Inspector General in Washington D.C. He's pledged his full cooperation. He'll help pave the way in New York. What are we looking for? *Who* are we looking for?"

Masterson spoke up, "From my previous investigations of Mitchell, I would say that she is just as deceitful as McMillan, only she's a heck of a lot smarter. She would be less likely to be directly involved in murder, but she would not be above agreeing to it. She would be more likely to express absolute surprise as any of this scheme comes to light. She loves to wear *Teflon* dresses, so nothing sticks to her."

"I get it, Agent Masterson," Taylor said. "She's going to be tough to catch. There anyone else that might be involved in this scheme?"

"There's Paul Chisholm, who's disappeared," said Julia. "Masterson

291

thinks he knows who he is, but we haven't secured a photo from BP Technologies' HR division yet.

"And who do you think *he* is?" asked Taylor, looking at Masterson.

"Knowing some of the friends McMillan used to hang with, I'm guessing he's an exceptionally good con man named Frank Parsons," Masterson said.

"Would you be able to recognize him from a photo?" Taylor asked.

"Unless he was wearing an extensive disguise as Paul Chisholm, yes."

"There's also the CEO Durnst," offered Julia. "He just oozes creepy, but every report we have says he's clean."

"Sorry Lieutenant," said Taylor. As you know, *creepy* is insufficient criteria to cross the probable cause threshold."

"Is there enough to be able to check Mitchell's phones?" asked Masterson.

"Now, that's already in the works," said Taylor. "I really want to see who she's been talking to, especially down here in Memphis." The meeting broke up.

***

Shortly after Julia's return to the Union Station, Teresa buzzed in.

"Lieutenant, I think I found something. Can you come look at this?"

Julia left her office and moved in close to look over Teresa's shoulder at her monitor. "Whatchagot?"

"Isn't Maureen Lister the name of the secretary for Dr. Durnst?" asked Teresa.

"Yeah, I think that's her name. How'd you remember that?" asked Julia.

"I saw it in one of yours or Tagger's reports. I remember thinking it was a strange name," answered Teresa. "Now look at this Person of Interest Bulletin that came in this morning. Does she look like this picture?"

"I'll be darned," said Julia. "She wears a whole lot more make-up now, and her hair is long and blonde, but that's her. And check out those other M. L. aliases—Marlene Liter, Martene Liser, and Marilene Lissor. None of which seem to go with her God given name, Tracy Alexander. Who's looking for her?"

"NYPD. Seems there was some kind of stock market scheme," said Teresa.

"You've done it again, Terry. Good job," smiled Julia as she returned to her office.

"Send a copy to Tag and the professor."

"Yes, I've done it again." A big smile grew on Teresa as her chest inflated.

Julia picked up the phone and called Taylor. "I think we found at least one of our moles at BP Technologies. Durnst's secretary. NYPD wants her as a person of interest in a stock market scheme. But I'd sure like to get a look at her phone calls, and her belongings before we send her up north. What do you think?"

Four hours later Marino and Tagger were serving search warrants for Tracy Alexander's personal affects, her phones, her house, and her office. Another team whisked her back to the midtown station for questioning. They would let NYPD know they found their person of interest, and they could have her as soon as Memphis was through with her. Though she put on a tough front at the office, when she was charged for her role in five homicides, she sang like the proverbial canary. She turned over on Charleze, and Attorney Stanford. She also had a good understanding of the two-phase plan, involving the artificial hip sabotage and the patent application. Phone records confirm frequent conversations with Mitchell. Apparently her job was to be Charleze's contact in Memphis. And just for the record, she too thought Durnst was an anal-retentive jerk, and way too full of himself to be doing BPTX or its shareholders any good.

NYPD agreed to arrest Mitchell and hold her until someone could get up there and transport her back to Memphis to stand trial for the murders of Michael Tibett, Haverford Sturgeon, Carl Huong, Officer Eva Rodriquez, and security guard Clarence Torrey, as well as the attempted murders of Joshua Proctor and Allison White. As an aside, BPTX stock continued to climb, placing extreme fiscal demands on Charleze, and bankrupting Tornadic Growth Investments.

CHAPTER 54

THE HEALING PROCESS

JUNE *19 ... Even The Experts Can Use A Little Help.* "You look so tired. Tell me what's going on," said Jennifer.

Tears rolled down Tonya's cheeks. "I can't do it anymore."

"Can't do what, dear?"

"Josh is having nightmares most nights, which makes him avoid going to bed. He's exhausted from lack of sleep, irritable, and generally non-communicative. Of course, Ollie takes this personally. Daniel on the other hand seems to be so caught up in doing his anger thing, that I'm not sure he's even noticed a difference in Josh." Then Tonya let go a burst of one-liners, as if they had been sitting on a tightly wound spring waiting to explode.

"I can't do *anything* right. I can't handle it. I've always been able to juggle family and career, and still have time for myself. But I'm not able to it anymore. I don't have the energy. I no longer have the skills. I don't have the desire. I don't have a life. God. I feel so guilty. Like it's my fault." Jennifer moved closer and held both her hands, but sat quietly while Tonya composed herself.

"I can't give my clients the attention they deserve. I come home and it's like being in the middle of a nightmare family therapy session that I can't control. No one's satisfied. No one's taking responsibility. No one's picking up after themselves. They all have attitudes. And, there's no way to please Josh, Daniel and Ollie. Each one is doing their own thing, and each one wants something different at dinner. There's not enough of me to go around. We aren't a family anymore. For the life of me I can't understand why it should be my fault. I'm almost 39 years old with a PhD in psychology, but I still feel guilty, as if I were a little kid."

"I'm exhausted just listening to you," said Jennifer. "It sounds as if it feels like everyone is expecting you to fix this by yourself." Tonya nodded slowly, but didn't look up. "I'm guessing that there's a part of you that resents being put in that position." Tonya raised her eyes to meet Jennifer's. "And if that's true, the resentment makes you less committed to fixing the problem, which makes you feel even more guilty." Tonya's mouth dropped open. "Yes, dear, you know how that works. That's the way those emotional dominos always seem to fall."

Tonya squeezed Jennifer's hands, forcing a grimacing smile.

"Tonya, just because you're a psychotherapist, doesn't mean you can handle all of this by yourself," said Jennifer. "And from what you've told me you're in no condition to do it. It's like when the airline attendant tells you to put on your own oxygen mask before trying to assist others. That's because if you don't take care of yourself first, you won't be around to take care of anyone else." Jennifer paused, "That applies to your family *and* to your clients."

Tonya knew she was right on both counts. But hearing another mental health professional verbalize it only made her feel more guilty.

Jennifer pushed further. "Of course, you know better than most that the debilitating impact of trauma is only strengthened when you avoid facing it." Tonya gave the weakest of a nod. "Have you given any thought to contacting a therapist who specializes in treating clients who've been exposed to trauma?"

"I don't know Mom," Tonya said. "I guess I'd feel embarrassed. You know, it's what I've been trained to do. I shouldn't need help."

Jennifer smiled. "You really didn't say that did you?"

Tonya tensed. Then relaxed. "I'm afraid I did. But, it really sounded stupid when you played it back to me. I do need help. And my family needs help. And we need it now."

"Thanks to you, everyone had really handled this whole series of horrible events exceptionally well." Jennifer said. "And then this last attempt on Josh's life was like the straw that dropped the camel to his knees. It sapped everyone's energy, and with it the will to continue to confront the fears. You've already laid the foundation for a rapid recovery. With the right kind of help, you'll all get your lives back, and sooner than later."

CHAPTER 55

SAY WHAT?

JUNE *20 ... The Hedge.* Two female officers escorted Charleze Mitchell into the Union Station. Walking for Charleze seemed to be more of a well rehearsed production, exuding poise and confidence. She was dressed simply, wearing slacks and a blouse, with a wide lavender belt that crossed and hung down in the front. Her stylish shoes with a three inch heel matched her belt. Accessories were various versions of hoops in yellow gold, necklace, earrings, rings, and watch. She wore her hair short and relaxed, pixie style. Her eye shadow and eyelashes made her large brown eyes pop. She carried a brightly colored silk jacket across her handcuffed wrists. Teresa glanced down at her comfortable shoes and swore under her breath.

"Talk about a *brick shit house*. The plans must have been destroyed after she was built," said Tagger, mouth hanging open.

"Be careful, my friend," said Masterson. "She's much smarter than she is stunning, and she's even deadlier."

"We can still look can't we?" asked Marino.

"Only from a safe distance," said Masterson.

Julia motioned for the officers to seat Mitchell at the table, opposite the door. She took her seat and smiled at Julia. Attorney Tucker C. Millerman, III, was already seated on that side. By the looks of him he shopped in the men's aisle of the same high dollar store. Julia had her notes in front of her. She had just begun with a list of the charges when she was interrupted by two men in working blue suits who'd invited themselves into the room.

"Who the hell are you?" demanded Julia.

"We're agents Cornell and Sterling. Homeland Security," said the man nearest her as they each opened a billfold credential with their likeness on it. "May we speak to you in private, Lieutenant?"

It seemed like a long time before Julia responded. She was trying to sort out the meaning of this interruption. She decided that she needed to hear what they had to say. She stood and motioned for them to follow her back to her office. She glanced back to see Charleze with a larger smile.

Inside her office Julia closed the door and gestured for them to take a seat. She remained standing. "Now, what's going on here?" she demanded.

Agent Cornell spoke. "We're here to escort Dr. Mitchell back to DC. I believe you'll find our director has already spoken with your Director of Police and with your Attorney General." He paused. "What I'm about to tell you *will* remain in strictest confidence."

Julia did not acknowledge his order, but she had the horrible anticipatory feeling that someone was about to rain heavily on her parade. She picked up the phone and called the Director of Police.

"Yes, sir," said Julia … "But, sir—" … "It doesn't make any—" … "Certainly, sir, but you'd expect her—" … "No, sir." … "Yes, sir. I heard what you said." She hung up the phone and turned back to the agents.

"Mitchell will be invaluable to the United States government in our dealings with middle eastern and Asian concerns who are planning to undermine the financial security of this country through their dealings with the stock market, commodities, and bond market." Cornell continued, "She's received a clemency judgment for her involvement in this latest criminal scheme involving BPTX."

"There is no clemency for murder," Julia said, hoping it were true.

"First of all, there is indeed such an order," said Agent Cornell. "And second, she didn't really kill anyone. We both know that was McMillan's doing. Furthermore, I think you would have found that Attorney

Millerman has already prepared a very potent defense that would have taken any murder charges off the table before this ever went to trial. In fact, with the audio recordings she has, she probably wouldn't have done any jail time at all. There is some consolation in knowing that Mitchell lost everything when she shorted BPTX." Julia sat on her desk, not feeling consoled.

"Look, Lieutenant," said Agent Cornell in an understanding tone. "Everything I've seen shows what an outstanding job you and your team did to uncover this scheme and to protect the lives of your Memphis citizens. You are the buzz in Washington. I know you have to be so pissed that we are pulling the queen bee from your case. I'm sorry about that. But, at the same time, please believe me when I tell you Mitchell is uniquely qualified to make a major contribution to defending our country."

Julia still said nothing.

"Now, if you don't mind, we have a plane to catch," he said as he and Agent Sterling stood. She led them back to the interrogation room.

Julia directed the officers to uncuff Mitchell. "You're free to go with these gentlemen."

Charleze gave her hands to one of the officers, who took off her handcuffs. She then stood, draped her jacket over her left forearm and proceeded to glide to the door swinging her free arm, and her hips. She stopped, and turned to Julia.

"Mac had no idea what an impressive woman he was up against, Lieutenant. I do hope we meet again." Charleze reverse-choreographed her steps out of the station, followed by the two agents and Millerman.

The silence in the room lasted only as long as the guys could see Charleze. Then, an explosion of questions, and bursts of anger. Julia let it go on for a few minutes.

"There's nothing you can say that I haven't already said to the agents from Homeland Security, to the Director of Police, and to myself. The only thing you don't know that I do is Mitchell would never have done any jail time. She made enough selective tapes of her discussions with McMillan to make it clear that she had nothing to do with the killings and the attempted switch of the Forest Brothers surgical screws. Obviously she only kept the recordings advantageous to her. And since Mac is no longer around, who's to say different … What I'd like to say is that I couldn't be more proud of the way you handled yourselves on this case. And I truly appreciate the assistance from Agents Masterson and Lopez."

The room was silent. Everyone understood what had just happened, and they understood their Lieutenant had been put in her place by the command office and by Washington D.C. They were proud of her for standing up for them.

"I'll buy the first round," Julia said.

CHAPTER 56

THE EXTENDED FAMILY

JULY *30 ... Working Through It.* It was a rare summer when the Proctor family missed having at least one super barbecue—slow cooked pork ribs. 2008 would be no exception. The cooking responsibilities fell to the men, first Brandon, then Josh. This year Daniel was being baptized into the ritual. He and Josh prepped the ribs, and prepared the special Proctor sauce. They were up at 5:00 A.M. to light the coals, beginning an eight-hour effort. The fire would have to be monitored. New coals added, and, in the last half-hour, the ribs would be basted with the sauce. Brandon arrived at nine to prepare baked beans and coleslaw. Drinks were iced. Jennifer and Tonya organized the supporting essentials—snacks, plates, napkins, forks, and dessert. Ollie harassed the men, challenging their exclusion of females.

"How're you doing?" asked Jennifer.

"Oh, so much better," said Tonya. ""It hasn't been a cake walk, but, I think we've all recovered from last May and June. You were right, you know, on both counts. We needed a trauma-trained therapist, and we did have the strength to work through it. I don't know what we would have done without the therapy. Of course, we all still have our moments, and our unique anxiety triggers."

"Like the color chartreuse," said Jennifer.

"Sure. Even walking to the mailbox on a sunny day can trigger a boatload of feelings. But the feelings are not as intense, and we all bounce back more quickly each time."

"How about the upside?"

"That's easy," Tonya said. "Josh and the kids have been very good at making sure we all share responsibility for how the family functions, how it gets along. That was such a big issue for me."

"It takes my breath away," said Jennifer, looking out the kitchen window. "I haven't seen Josh laugh like this ... well, in a long time. And look at Daniel wrestling with his Dad. Here comes Ollie, jumping right on top of them."

"I love Ollie's squeals," said Tonya.

They watched, listened, enjoyed.

"Everyone aught to be here soon," said Tonya.

"I'm anxious to see Allison," said Jennifer. "Haven't seen her since we spent that week in the house, under police protection."

"You never met Ruby, did you?"

"Is that Dorothy? The woman no one could find?"

"That's her," said Tonya. "You'll like her. I think she and Allison have had the most difficult time. Both had seen someone killed. Both were threatened, and both felt powerless. They've worked hard, and made great progress with their therapist. They've become good friends in the process."

"I'm sure that friendship has been helpful." said Jennifer. "Ruby is a graduate student at U of M, right?"

"She just graduated," said Tonya. "And BP Tech will be hiring her, August one."

"I'm looking forward to seeing our guardian angels from the police department."

"They all said they'd be here—Julia, and Sergeants Marino and Tagger."

"I'm glad they were recognized for their efforts by their national organization—especially Julia. She was a Godsend."

"I haven't seen her since she received her award in DC. That was so awesome."

"And so well deserved."